ANNA JACOBS is the author of over sixty novels and is addicted to storytelling. She grew up in Lancashire, emigrated to Australia in the 1970s and writes stories set in both countries. She loves to return to England regularly to visit her family and soak up the history. She has two grown-up daughters and a grandson, and lives with her husband in a spacious waterfront home. Often as she writes, dolphins frolic outside the window of her study. Inside, the house is crammed with thousands of books.

www.annajacobs.com

By Anna Jacobs

THE GREYLADIES TRILOGY

Heir to Greyladies
Mistress of Greyladies

THE WILTSHIRE TRILOGY

Cherry Tree Lane
Elm Tree Road
Yew Tree Gardens

Heir to Greyladies

ANNA JACOBS

Allison & Busby Limited
12 Fitzroy Mews
London W1T 6DW
www.allisonandbusby.com

First published in Great Britain by Allison & Busby in 2013.
This paperback edition published by Allison & Busby in 2014.

Copyright © 2013 by ANNA JACOBS

A CIP catalogue record for this book is available from
the British Library.

10 9 8 7 6 5 4 3 2 1

ISBN 978-0-7490-1399-8

Typeset in 10/14.25 pt Sabon by
Allison & Busby Ltd.

The paper used for this Allison & Busby publication
has been produced from trees that have been legally sourced
from well-managed and credibly certified forests.

Printed and bound by

CPI Group (UK) Ltd, Croydon, CR0 4YY

This book is dedicated to Bridget (June 1947–July 2012), an inspirational wife, mother, grandmother, sister, sister-in-law and aunt. She began life in a farmer's cottage in the south of Ireland, without running water or electricity, and perhaps those early experiences helped develop her unshakeable optimism and positive approach to life, which gave strength and confidence to all around her.

Chapter One

Hampshire, Spring 1900

Harriet Benson hurried home from school to the neat terraced house, eager to share her news with her dad. Her street was one of the better ones, with the men all in work and families living decently, trying to help one another.

Until last year she'd been very happy here. Then her mother had died and her dad remarried.

Today she'd stayed at school late to help the teacher, as she often did, but her dad was due home around this time, so it was safe to go back now.

But she'd miscalculated and arrived a few minutes early, so the only one in the house was Norris, her stepbrother. He was washing his hands at the scullery sink, but stopped to stare at her when she came in.

As soon as she saw him, she started to back towards the kitchen door. She'd begun to get her woman's curves now and didn't like to be alone in the house with her stepbrother. The horrible, leering way he looked at her chest made her feel uncomfortable and more than once he'd touched her in a way he shouldn't. Only she hadn't dared complain, because her stepmother always took Norris's side.

He was across the room and had hold of her arm before she realised what he was doing. She tried to pull away and get to the front door, but he dragged her back from the hall into the kitchen. 'Don't go. We can have a nice little chat, you an' me. It's not often I get you to myself.'

'My friend's waiting for me outside.'

He let out a loud, jeering laugh. 'No, she isn't. You don't bring your friends home any more because my mum won't have nosy parkers coming here to check up on her. Which means you're lying.' He shook her hard. 'You . . . shouldn't . . . lie . . . to . . . me. I don't like it.' Raising his free hand, still damp and soapy, he grabbed her breast and tweaked it hard, hurting her.

It wasn't the first time he'd done that, but she'd been too embarrassed to mention it to her father, let alone her stepmother.

She cried out with the pain and tried again to get away from him, but he was much bigger and stronger than she was. However hard she struggled, his hands were all over her and he began breathing hard.

Then he yelled and let her go so suddenly she staggered back against the wall. As he crashed sideways to the ground, his flailing arms sent a chair flying across the room.

Harriet moaned in relief at the sight of her dad. He

usually smiled a lot, but today his face was dark red with anger and he was gazing down at his stepson with fists clenched, as if ready to hit him again.

'You young devil! If you ever lay one finger on my daughter again, I'll beat you senseless then throw you out of my house for good. I'd throw you out now, if it weren't for your mother.'

Norris got to his feet, backing away, scowling at them both. 'Harriet goes with other fellows. Why not me?'

She opened her mouth to protest at this lie, but her dad seemed to swell with fury. 'My daughter would never—'

Then his voice cut off and he raised one hand to his chest, groaning. The groan ended abruptly and he crumpled slowly to the ground, to lie there quite still.

'Dad! What's the matter?' Harriet knelt beside him. '*Dad!*'

But he didn't stir.

She heard footsteps and looked down the hallway. The front door banged back on its hinges and Norris ran out of the house as if the devil himself was chasing him.

She looked back at her dad, but he hadn't moved. He looked limp, not like himself. She knelt beside him, searching for a pulse, unable to find one, unable to believe . . . it couldn't be.

Sobbing, she ran to the front door, just as Norris turned the corner of the street and vanished from sight.

When she screamed loudly for help, neighbours came running at once.

She managed to tell them what had happened before she began sobbing.

Mrs Leigh from next door immediately put an arm round her. 'Where's your stepmother, dear?'

'She visits her friend Miss Dodson on Tuesdays. Town Close.'

Someone shouted that they'd fetch Mrs Benson.

Mrs Leigh called sharply, 'Stand back. Let the midwife through. She'll know what to do.'

A few people followed them into the house, standing quietly, waiting to see if they could help as they watched the midwife bend over James Benson, then look across at Harriet and shake her head.

'I'm sorry, dear. He's gone. If it's any comfort, he'd not have felt a thing.'

Harriet had guessed her dad was dead because she'd seen her mother lying in her coffin. Her dad had that same look to him, like a wax model of the real man. But she hadn't wanted to believe such a dreadful thing could happen.

Her dad had died protecting her from her stepbrother, so this was all Norris's fault. She'd never forgive him for that, never.

'How did it happen, dear?' Mrs Leigh asked.

She began to tell them what Norris had done, but her stepmother arrived just as she started and pushed across the room to slap her face. 'Shut up, you silly girl! You're hysterical. Don't know what you're saying. My Norris isn't even here, is he?'

The neighbours exchanged glances and muttered to one another, but didn't challenge this statement. Like Harriet, they were well aware that the second Mrs Benson would never hear a word against her son from her previous marriage.

But Norris Harding was a bad 'un, even though he wasn't yet twenty. Everyone knew that, too, just as they knew that neither he nor his mother were the sort of people who usually lived in a respectable street like this one.

Harriet clutched her burning cheek, too upset even to weep. Her dad was dead. What did Norris matter? What did anything matter now?

Then she had a dreadful thought: she'd be left in her stepmother's care. There'd be no one to take her side or protect her against Norris now.

After her gentle little mother died, her dad had remarried within three months, to his daughter's shock and horror. She knew a man needed a wife to look after his house and prepare his meals, but Harriet had been doing that, with a little help from the neighbours, and she'd been coping well, too. He hadn't *needed* to marry again.

She'd taken her worries to Mrs Leigh next door, who had sat her down and explained the facts of life. That accounted for the noises Harriet had heard in the night from her father's room.

'Men need their bed play, dear, some more than others.'

'But why did he have to choose someone like Winifred Harding. She isn't—'

'Your stepmother's a good-looking woman, for her age. You have to give her that. She caught him at a weak moment and now he's lumbered with her. The best of men can be fooled by a woman like that, even a man as nice as your father. Some men keep their brains in their trousers when they're near a woman who eggs them on.'

She patted her young friend's hand. 'You're old enough to understand that now. You'll just have to make the best of it, I'm afraid, dear. It's only for a few years, till you get married yourself.'

A few years! A few weeks would be more than enough of Winifred and her son without her father there. Who would take her side now? she thought again.

Harriet had watched the newly-weds carefully after that talk. At first her dad seemed happy with his new wife, but after the first few months she saw him start to look irritated, especially when Winifred spoilt her son or spoke too sharply to her stepdaughter.

James complained that Winifred was letting the house get untidy. She tried to blame it on Harriet, but he cut her short and told her he had eyes in his head and, anyway, the house was her responsibility, not his daughter's. Harriet had her schooling to do, though she would help with the chores in the evenings, of course.

Harriet couldn't help wondering what her stepmother would do to her now. Life would get much worse, she was sure.

She didn't even need to ask about one thing. There'd be no taking the special scholarship to the private girls' grammar school now, the one for girls who were 'exceptional' and suitable to be trained as teachers. The scholarships were much sought after because every year they gave two 'special' girls two years of extra education to equip them better for their future duties.

And Harriet had been offered one. She had a letter to give to her dad about it.

It saddened her that he'd died before he'd even heard the news. He'd have been proud of her and so would her mother.

Her stepmother had been against letting Harriet stay on at school, saying she should be out working by now, bringing in money, paying her parents back for all they'd done for her. That had caused quite a few rows but her father had held firm and Harriet had kept going to school.

There'd be no chance of any more education now.

Three days later, Harriet stood by her dad's grave, wearing a black armband and her best frock, which was getting too short and was embarrassingly tight round the chest. As she watched the solemn-faced men lower the coffin into the grave, tears rolled down her cheeks. She wanted to beg the men to wait a few more moments before they removed her father's body from her world.

As if that would bring him back!

Her stepmother sobbed once or twice, dabbing artistically at her eyes. But Winifred's handkerchief was dry, Harriet was sure.

She'd been disgusted by the gloating look on the woman's face as they waited in the front room for two old aunts and a distant cousin of Harriet's father to arrive for the funeral. No members of her mother's family had bothered to come. They'd not approved of the marriage and had stayed away completely after he remarried.

Mine, that look said as Winifred ran her fingers along the edges of the highly polished furniture, *all mine*.

Most of the pieces had come from Harriet's mother's side: the furniture and the delicate ornaments. Winifred would get everything now. It wasn't fair.

Her father's lovely horse brasses and her parents' books would no doubt be sold, because Winifred wasn't the sentimental sort. She'd often complained about having to polish the brasses, and she didn't read books, only women's magazines like *Home Chat*.

What Winifred loved best was her son and money, and her stepdaughter wasn't sure which of the two was more important to her.

When the funeral was over, the mourners walked back to the house, led by Winifred on her son's arm, flourishing her black-edged handkerchief. Her face was shaded by a new black straw hat topped with big puffs of ribbon and two black feathers, with a small net veil across her face.

Harriet followed with the neighbours, because she certainly wouldn't be welcome to walk next to her stepmother and stepbrother, even if she wanted to.

Norris was all attention towards his mother. Winifred's friends whispered how lovely it was to see him behaving so well. A son should be a comfort to his mother. Such a fine, strong young man.

The neighbours didn't say anything about him, nor did Harriet. She hated him and he was still eyeing her *that way* when his mother wasn't looking.

Once they got back to the house, Winifred sent her stepdaughter to the kitchen to make a big pot of tea, while she sat in the front room sipping a glass of port wine 'for my nerves' and queening it over the relatives and friends who'd been invited back. No neighbours had been invited. Winifred said they were a nosy, snooty lot.

Her father's relatives didn't stay for long, but Harriet found time to get his cousin on her own and ask if she could go and live with them.

'We've no room, dear. And it's no use asking the aunties because they're too old. I know it's all very upsetting, but at least you have a roof over your head and a stepmother to look after you. You should be grateful for that.'

Her stepmother's friends and relatives stayed on and it soon turned into a party. Winifred got out another bottle of the sickly sweet port wine and soon they were all laughing and talking.

What Harriet overheard them saying made her feel angry all over again.

'You've done well for yourself this time, Winifred.'

'You'll be really well set up here, my girl, what with the insurance money and all this nice furniture. Good thing you took out that policy, eh?'

'Don't forget, you've still got your friends. You'll not need to be lonely.'

The women clinked glasses with Winifred.

No one mentioned Harriet in the list of comforts. No one even said thank you when she refilled the big teapot and brought them clean teacups or glasses for the port.

But Norris looked at her every time she came into the front room, looked and smiled in that horrible way. He didn't offer to help with the heavy trays, just hovered near his mother, 'comforting' her and refilling her wine glass regularly.

At one stage his mother sent him out to buy two more bottles of port. Her voice was shrill and her face flushed now. She looked as if she was thoroughly enjoying herself.

She raised her glass to her son when he got back

and he clinked his own against it. 'Here's to the man of the house.' But she laughed when she said that and there was no doubt in anyone's mind that she would be the one in charge.

As Harriet was going back to the kitchen, she heard her name mentioned and paused in the hall to listen.

'What about the girl, Winifred?'

'What about her? She can get a job and bring me in a bit of money. Pay me back for all the care I've given her. I have to keep *my* money safe for my old age now that I don't have a breadwinner, so I can't afford to keep her in school any more. James was daft about that. I ask you, what use is all that schooling to a girl? She'll only get married and have children, like we all do.'

'It'll do her good to go out to work like the rest of us,' Norris said. 'It's a hard world out there and the sooner she realises which side her bread's buttered on, the better.'

It was a hard world in here, too, Harriet thought. She'd been run ragged since Dad died, treated like a skivvy and ordered around. It was what her life would be from now on, she was sure. Winifred was too lazy to do the housework if she could get someone else to do it for her.

And what sort of job would her stepmother find for her? Please, not the laundry or the meat works, Harriet prayed. She couldn't face the noise and steam of one, and the disgusting sights and smells of the other.

But you didn't get much choice when you were only fifteen. She'd be sixteen in June, nearly grown up, but she'd still have no money and nowhere else to go.

The next morning Winifred said abruptly over their first cup of tea, 'Today you'll have to go and tell that teacher of yours that you're leaving school straight away.'

Harriet had to try. 'I got a scholarship, Winifred. It's a real honour. It's to that posh grammar school and it pays all my fees. I could get a really good job if I went there. I'd earn a lot more money in the long run.'

'Only till you marry. Then the extra education would all be wasted. And what good would it do *me* for you to go there? It'd be years before you got a fancy job. Years I'd have to keep you. No, I've got you a job at the bakery in Compton Street and you start on Monday. I'll get the benefit of your wages straight away.'

She waited and added, 'Well? Aren't you going to thank me?'

Harriet looked at her pleadingly.

Winifred leant forward and poked her hard in the chest. 'Let's get one thing straight, my girl: I'd not have let your father send you to that fancy grammar school, even if he was still alive. Do you think I'll put up with you making posh friends and looking down your nose at me, like some of your snooty neighbours do?'

Her eyes narrowed. 'And you're under age, so you

have to do what I say. Don't you ever forget that. You're mine till you're twenty-one.'

Harriet held back her tears. She knew she could do nothing till she was older, and even then it'd be hard to get away without any money. From the sounds of it, Winifred was planning to take all her wages for the next five years. It wasn't fair.

Unless she married. And she didn't want to do that. Boys were so rough. And look how Norris behaved. Ugh.

No, she'd have to find another way to escape.

'Since you don't start work till Monday, when you come back from school this morning – and make sure you don't linger! – you can give the house a really good spring clean. From top to bottom. About time you did more around here.'

The following Monday Harriet started work at the bakery. She had to get there at four o'clock in the morning and work till four in the afternoon.

Winifred presented her with a battered alarm clock. 'Use this. We don't want them docking your wages for being late.'

It felt strange getting ready in the dark house, trying not to make a noise, but at least Norris wasn't around to bother her at that hour.

On the first day, she had to wait till the other employees had started work at the bakery before the foreman had time to tell her what to do. She felt a fool, sitting on a bench near the entrance with everyone staring at her.

He stared too, studying her clothes and grimacing. 'You've nearly grown out of that blouse, girl. Women who work here dress decently.' He looked at her breasts, but without the leer that Norris had, then turned to the woman next to him. 'Find out what else she's got to wear, Vera. If she hasn't any better things than these, we'll have to look for someone else for the job.'

'Her mother will get her whatever's necessary, Rodney. I know Winifred. She wouldn't have understood what was needed, that's all.'

'Well, make certain she does understand now. I only gave the girl a job as a favour to you. We run an immaculate place here and my girls have to keep themselves nice. We bake for the gentry as well as for others, and they don't want to see scruffy folk touching the food they eat.'

He turned away without speaking to Harriet again.

Vera smiled at her. 'Come on. I'll find you an overall. Tell Winifred to get you some new clothes before next week. Sturdy ones, because they'll need a lot of washing to get the flour dust out.'

It didn't take Harriet more than a minute's thought to say, 'She won't do it unless *you* tell her. She never listens to me.'

'No wonder, if you're so lazy. Well, you'll not be lazy here, or you'll be out on your ear.'

Harriet gaped at her. What had Winifred been saying about her now?

All day she worked hard, scrubbing floors, tables, walls, helping keep everything as clean as possible, doing things even before they asked her because it was obvious what was needed.

At the end of the day, Vera said in her abrupt way, 'I'll walk home with you and tell Winifred.'

'Thank you.'

Vera frowned at her as if puzzled. 'You worked well today.'

'I'm not lazy.' She met the older woman's eyes without flinching. 'And I never have been.'

'Hmm.'

Winifred grumbled but took Harriet along to the market on Saturday afternoon and bought her some plain, practical clothes. She didn't give the girl any choice about colour or style, just bought the cheapest and most hard-wearing garments she could find.

From then on, the only difficult thing about working at the bakery was going home on the afternoons Winifred went out to see her friends.

Three weeks after her father died, Norris caught her on her own again. He was hiding in the scullery and didn't come out till she'd checked that he wasn't in the kitchen and closed the front door.

Her heart began to hammer and she backed away from him.

'Your father's not here to protect you now. *I'm* the

man of the house and what I say goes.' He grabbed her arm and pulled her against his body. She could feel his man's part pressing against her and froze in terror. Mrs Leigh had explained only too clearly what that meant.

Her stillness must have fooled him into thinking she would do as he said, and with a laugh he let go of her to fumble with his trousers.

She kicked him in the shin as hard as she could, knocking him off balance, then fled down the hall and out into the street. Further along she bumped into old Mr Prentice and gasped, glancing over her shoulder at Norris, who was now standing at the front door, scowling.

The old man stared from her to her stepbrother, eyes narrowed. 'Giving you trouble, is he?'

'Yes.'

'Them Hardings are a randy lot, always have been. You can shelter in my house till his mother gets back.'

'Thanks.'

'And if you ever need shelter when I'm out, use my shed. I'll show you where I keep the key and there's a bolt to lock it from the inside as well. You're young enough to climb over the wall into the backyard.'

'Thank you, Mr Prentice. I'd better go in the back way now. I don't want Norris to see me going into your house or he'll know where I hide.'

'You do that. You're a nice lass and don't deserve such disrespect.' He scowled along the street at Norris, who was still watching them. 'We don't usually have that sort living in our street. His mother's a floozy, and looks it too, however fine she dresses. It's in the eyes. You can't mistake it. And he's a lout, a real rough head.'

She walked round to the alley at the back and got over Mr Prentice's back wall easily. The kind old man was waiting for her at the kitchen door and at once led the way into his house. 'Cup of tea?'

'Yes, please. But I'll have to watch out for *her* coming home. An' I don't want her to see me coming out of your house, either. She doesn't like me even talking to the neighbours.'

'You can slip out through the back again. We'll take our tea into the front room, so you'll see her coming past. I often sit there and watch what's going on. I don't miss much.'

The following week, however, Winifred was late coming back from her friend's and Harriet didn't dare delay going home any longer, because she had strict orders to get the tea ready.

Her heart sank when she found Norris sitting in the kitchen. She paused near the door, not sure whether to run away.

'I'm hungry,' he said. 'Hurry up with that food. Mum will soon be back.'

She started to get things out, filling the washing-up bowl with water to peel the potatoes. The way he sat there, watching, smiling as if he knew something she didn't, made her nervous. She tried not to go too close to him, but she had to get things out of the cupboard.

When she'd passed him safely a couple of times, she relaxed a bit.

That was when he put out his foot and tripped her.

As she lay sprawled on the floor, he got down to join her. She rolled away, screaming for help, suddenly more afraid of him than she'd ever been before.

He was too strong for her and dragged her away from the broken crockery onto the hearth rug. She kicked and screamed but he just laughed.

'It's no use calling out for help. That's one thing about posh neighbours. They don't come in without an invitation. So you might as well give in and do as I tell you.'

'Your mother will be back soon.' She tried to fend him off. 'She won't want you to do this.'

'She's going to be late today, won't be back for over an hour yet. And even if you tell her, she won't believe I forced you, so it'll be no good complaining to her. Anyway, it'll be too late by then. I'll have had you and no one else will want you after that.'

He was panting now, trying to get her clothes off, hurting her, laughing at her efforts to escape.

'We'll be doing this quite often from now on,' he said, pulling down her knickers. 'You'll soon get used to it.'

Nothing she did stopped him. Once she managed to bite his hand, but he slapped her so hard she felt dizzy for a minute or two.

By that time he had her knickers right off and was groping at her private parts, his rough fingers hurting her tender skin.

She didn't stop screaming or struggling, but he laughed and started to undo his trousers.

Then they both jumped in shock as dirty water and potatoes cascaded down on them.

'*What the hell do you think you're doing, Norris Harding?*' Winifred screeched.

'She was asking for it,' Norris said at once. 'Rubbing herself against me. I'm only human.'

Harriet scrabbled away from him, burning with shame, unable to stop sobbing.

'You must think I'm a fool.' Winifred raised her late husband's walking stick. It whistled through the air and caught Norris across the face. Again and again his mother beat him about the head and shoulders. He made no attempt to do anything but protect his face with his hands.

'You'll not do that again in my house,' Winifred said. 'Whether the girl is willing or not.'

By this time he was cowering in a corner, begging her to stop, blood oozing from the weals on his neck and hands from where the stick had slashed him.

The beating ended as abruptly as it had begun. Winifred stood staring at her son, panting with the effort, the walking stick quivering in her raised hand.

He made a movement as if to get away and the stick was levelled with his chin. He froze, staring at her.

'Go to your bedroom and stay there till I tell you to come out.' She stepped back.

He got to his feet and ran from the room, speeded on his way with a final slash to his backside that had him yelling in pain.

Then Winifred turned to Harriet, who had scrambled into her knickers and was standing in the scullery doorway, tears rolling down her cheeks and dripping off her chin.

The silence went on for so long that Harriet wondered if she should run out of the house while she could and take refuge with Mr Prentice. Winifred was studying her as if she'd never seen her before.

What she did say was quite unexpected. 'You're going to be quite pretty when you've grown into your body, young lady, and my Norris is like his father. I hadn't taken that into account. They want a woman more often than most, them Hardings do. Randy devils, all of them. Your father was a bit like that, too.'

Harriet dared say, 'I didn't encourage Norris, Winifred. I'd never, ever do that.'

'I believe you, because I saw with my own eyes how hard you were fighting. Go for the eyes next time someone attacks you. Try to scratch them out.'

Silence again. More assessing looks, then Winifred gestured to the scullery. 'Go an' wash your face, then come and sit down. I need to have a think.'

When Harriet came back, Winifred said, 'Brew us a pot of tea.'

She did as she was asked, then waited, filled with dread, her stomach lurching every time Winifred moved.

'Well, sit down. An' get yourself a cup.'

But the teapot wobbled when Harriet tried to pick it up.

'Give me that.' Winifred poured them both some tea, then sipped hers thoughtfully. 'I'm not giving up your wages,' she said at last.

'But I can't—'

'Quiet. I'll do the talking.'

She drank, frowning in thought, then poured herself another cup of tea, tipping some into the saucer to cool it quickly, then leant back, studying her stepdaughter as if she'd never seen her before. 'You talk more posh than I do.'

Harriet didn't know what to make of that remark.

'An' you know a lot of useless stuff too, like the gentry. Book learning and such. James said your mother's family were a bit fancy, didn't want her to marry him.'

The silence was broken only by the ticking of the clock till Winifred set down her empty cup. 'Ah. That was good. Nothing like tea for helping you think. Go an' pack your clothes. You can take your mother's suitcase off the top of my wardrobe. Pack every single thing you've got into it.'

'My books too?'

Winifred looked at her in exasperation. 'You and your damned books. All right. Take them. They're not worth much. Take everything you want. You'll not be coming back. I'm going to be renting your room out.'

'But where am I—?'

'Just do as you're told.' She went to the foot of the stairs and yelled, 'Norris! Down here.'

He came running down, scowling at Harriet, who moved along the hall and waited for him to pass before she went upstairs.

She got the suitcase down and began to pack, terrified of what would happen to her now. Where was she going? Surely Winifred wasn't going to put her in the workhouse?

She hid her mother's locket and brooch among her spare knickers and vests. Winifred didn't know she had the jewellery because her father had told her to keep the pieces out of sight.

After some hesitation, she went downstairs and knocked on the closed kitchen door.

Winifred came to answer her knock. 'I've not finished with Norris. Stay upstairs till I call you.'

'I just wanted to know if it was all right to take my mother's family Bible.' She gestured towards the front room.

'Books! That's all you think of. Yes. Take the damned thing. It's so old the leather's crumbling, so it can't be worth much. Take any of the books you fancy.

You'll want something to remember your parents by.'

Harriet managed to cram two of her favourite books into the suitcase as well as the Bible, but that was all it would hold and she had to sit on it to make it close. She didn't want to leave the others. Perhaps she could tie them up with string and make a handle of it to carry them. But she couldn't get the ball of string till Winifred had finished in the kitchen.

She brushed her hair and tied it back as neatly as she could, then sat on the bed waiting to be called down, feeling exhausted. She could do nothing about the bruises and scratches on her face. She couldn't do much about anything, it seemed. Other people were ordering her life now.

But one day she'd manage to do things for herself. Whatever it took, she would find a way. Her teacher had said she was clever. Now she had to prove it.

Winifred looked at her bruised and battered son. 'Sorry I hurt you so much. I got a bit carried away. I was angry with you.'

'She encouraged me.'

'I wasn't born yesterday. She damned well didn't. Look, Norris, if you can't control yourself, you'll get nowhere in this life.'

She let that sink in, then continued, 'I've got some ideas for making money. A lot of money. And I want you in it with me. But it'll be no good if you can't control yourself. Not just this, but your temper. We want to come out of it respectable. Before I'm through, I want a big house, servants, all sorts of things. And I'm going to get them, too. Are you in with me or are you going to carry on being lazy and getting into fights?'

'Money?'

'A lot of money.'

'Harriet's . . . a temptation.'

'I'm sending her away. You'll get your women quietly after this and treat them well. I don't want you spoiling my plans by having a reputation for roughing them up.'

He leant back. 'You never talked about this before.'

'I had James. He'd not have listened to my ideas. Now, I've a mind to do what I want.'

Norris nodded slowly. 'All right. You're on.'

'Good lad.'

She went to the foot of the stairs and yelled, 'Harriet! Come down here and bring your suitcase.'

When Harriet brought the suitcase down, she said, 'Just a minute.' She ran back upstairs and brought down the books. 'I need to tie these together with string.'

Winifred sighed. 'All right. Though what you want with them, I don't know. Books don't bring you money.'

Chapter Two

Doris Miller limped slowly across to the china cabinet and took out her best teapot, stroking it lovingly. Royal Doulton, it was. The tea set had been a leaving present from her last mistress. She only used it when she needed cheering up or felt lonely, and for some reason it usually did the trick.

She took a tray into the front parlour and poured herself a cup of best lapsang souchong. Not many people liked the smoky tea, which she drank without milk or sugar, but she loved it. It was such a beautiful dark colour, almost red, glowing against the blue and white of the willow pattern.

As she was pouring a second cup, the door knocker sounded. She smiled as she went to answer it. Not often someone came to see her in the evening. You'd swear that tea could work magic.

Her niece was on the doorstep. Winifred wasn't Doris's favourite relative, but she was family, and family had to stick together, so she held the door wider. 'Come in.'

It wasn't till Winifred moved forward that Doris saw the girl standing behind her, a tall, thin lass with lovely hair, red but of a soft russet colour, definitely not ginger. The girl had obviously been in trouble, because she had bruises on her face and her eyes were swollen with crying. 'Who are you, then?' Doris asked her gently.

Winifred turned round. 'Oh, sorry. You haven't met, have you? This is Harriet, James's daughter. Harriet, this is Mrs Miller, my aunt.'

The old woman nodded, then led the way inside. 'I was sorry to hear about your husband. I'd have come to the funeral but I had a bad cold.'

'At least he went quickly, but he didn't make old bones, did he?' Winifred said. 'Not many are lucky to live as long as you, Auntie.'

Which bit of flattery meant her niece wanted something. Hmm. Doris said nothing, watching in amusement as Winifred stopped to stare into the front room, studying its contents as if assessing them. If Winifred thought she was going to inherit all this, she could think again.

'It isn't all pleasure being seventy-two years old, I promise you.'

'You have enough money to live on comfortably, Auntie. You've done well.'

'Not many folk are as careful with their money as I've been. And not all employers pay you a pension like the Daltons do.' Doris turned back to the girl who was still standing in the hallway. 'Come into the kitchen, Harriet. You can leave your suitcase in the hall.'

'Yes, Mrs Miller.'

'It's "Miss", really. They called me "Mrs" when I was a housekeeper, and I've got used to it now. I was never stupid enough to marry or I'd probably be in the workhouse now.'

She led the way into the back room. She didn't allow many people into her front room, didn't want them knocking over her little tables or breaking her ornaments.

When they were all seated, Doris waited, but unusually for her Winifred didn't speak until prompted, just sat chewing her lip and frowning.

'What can I do for you, then? You'd not come here at this hour of the night if you didn't need my help.'

Winifred nodded towards the girl. 'It's my stepdaughter. Norris is after her. She doesn't encourage him, I'll grant her that, but I can't trust him to leave her alone if we keep living in the same house. He's as bad as his father.'

'Is that how she got the bruises?'

'Yes.'

'He's rough with it, then.'

She shrugged. 'He's a Harding. But he's got my blood in him too, so I'm hoping to teach him some self-control.'

'Hmm. Why did you bring her to me?'

'I can't keep her at home but I can't just turn her

out on the street. I thought . . . I *hoped* you might help her get a place in service. She's done well at school, won a scholarship to St Mary's, but of course *I* can't afford to send her there.'

'Oh? I'd heard you were left comfortably off.'

'And I'll need that money for my old age, won't I? You're not the only one who thinks ahead. I'm definitely not getting married again. That's two good providers who've died on me now.' She waited. 'Well? Will you do it, Auntie Doris? Find her a place in service?'

The old woman turned to Harriet. 'What have *you* got to say about this, girl?'

'I don't know what to say. It's the first I've heard about it.'

Doris let out a spurt of rusty laughter. 'That's our Winifred. Good at organising other folk, whether they want it or not.'

Harriet took a sudden decision. 'I think she's right about one thing, though. I can't stay there. Norris will find a way to trap me if I do, whatever she tells him.'

'Are you a hard worker?'

'Yes, I am.'

'Pity about the scholarship, but there you are. Life doesn't let you have everything you want.' She kept them waiting a minute or two longer, then said, 'All right. But she'll need an outfit if you want her to get a better sort of job, Winifred. A job that pays more money.'

Winifred scowled at her. 'You've told me about maids' outfits before. All those clothes! Who needs that many? No, it'll cost too much. Just find her a job as a general maid.'

Doris folded her arms. 'I don't deal with that sort of family. If I take her off your hands, it'll be a big country house she works in. Besides, she'll soon make up the cost of an outfit. She'll earn double what she'd make as a general skivvy to some backstreet grocer.'

Winifred looked at her uncertainly. 'Double?'

'Yes. And it'll put those snooty neighbours on your side if they see you treating her well.' Doris hid a smile. She knew how it galled Winifred that her late husband's neighbours would hardly give her the time of day. You'd almost think they knew about Winifred's mother, but the family had been very careful to keep that disgrace secret.

'Do you really think it'll soften them up?'

'I'm certain of it.'

'Might be worth it, then, because I'm not moving house. James bought it with the insurance money from his wife dying so sudden.' Another pause, then, 'You're *sure* she'll earn more?'

'Certain. Double. One other thing. If I do this, I get her first quarter's wages.' She looked challengingly at Winifred as she said that.

'Trust you to demand a share. You always were on the lookout for money.'

'Takes one to recognise one.'

'And after the first quarter, all her wages come to me?'

'Yes.'

'Very well, then.' She turned to Harriet. 'I'll want you to write to that nosy parker next door and tell her how well you're set up, thanks to me. I'll have your promise on that before we go any further.'

'But I won't be well set up if I don't get paid any money at all,' Harriet said indignantly.

Winifred glared at her.

Doris intervened. 'You'll escape from Norris once and for all, young lady. And you'll be well trained, able to earn a good living. Be grateful for that. They feed you really well in the big houses and there's always company. Your turn to get the money you earn will come later. Give Winifred your promise or you can go home this minute.'

Harriet gave in because the thought of living with Norris again made her feel sick. 'I promise I'll write to Mrs Leigh.'

Winifred stood up. 'Right, then. I'll be getting back.'

Doris held up her hand 'Just a minute. What about her keep while she's with me?'

Winifred breathed deeply but stayed where she was. 'How much?'

'A shilling a day for training and feeding her. Paid weekly, in advance.'

She fumbled in her purse and slapped two half-crown pieces and a florin down on the kitchen table. 'There. Seven shillings for this week.'

'More to come next Friday or I bring her straight back to you.'

Sighing loudly, Winifred nodded.

Doris escorted her great niece to the door, where they muttered for a moment or two, then she came back to the kitchen, where Harriet was sitting in her chair, her whole body drooping. 'You've had your first lesson today, my girl.'

'I don't understand what you mean.'

'Make sure you get some benefit when you do someone a favour. I retired from being housekeeper at Dalton House. The family give you a small pension if you work for them for over twenty years, but I had enough money saved as well to see me out in comfort. And why did I have that money behind me? Because I made sure I was paid for everything extra I did. Because I *saved* my money, didn't waste a penny of it.'

'I won't have any money to save if *she* takes it all.'

Doris shrugged. 'One day you'll get your wages. Parents usually take young maids' money, you know.'

'*She* isn't my mother, though.'

'She's the nearest you've got now, and she's doing you a favour with this. You'll understand that one day.'

She waited for her words to sink in, then continued, 'Just make sure you follow my advice. Once you're twenty-one, things will change completely. And by the time you're eighteen you can ask for a share of your wages, because by then you'll have enough experience to get another job if they don't agree. Though I think they will. The Daltons are very decent with those they employ.'

She grinned. 'Don't tell Winifred I told you how to get out of this later, but fair's fair. Just make sure you prove yourself a good worker, so they'll want to keep you on.'

'But I won't be twenty-one for another five years!'

'I thought Winifred said you were fifteen. It'll be longer than that.'

'I'll be sixteen soon.'

'Hmm. You look younger.' She studied the girl. Though she was quite tall, Harriet had a child's innocence on her face still, and an unhappy child at that. 'Five years isn't long. It'll soon pass. Now, let me show you your room.'

Doris heard the girl cry herself to sleep and felt an unexpected surge of sympathy. Not enough to get her out of bed to comfort her young visitor, though.

When Harriet woke, it was fully light and later than usual for her, after the weeks at the bakery. Afraid she'd be in trouble for sleeping in, she got up and washed quickly in the cold water from the ewer, then dressed and hurried downstairs, taking her slop bowl with her.

There was no one in the kitchen and the fire wasn't lit, so Mrs Miller wasn't up yet, thank goodness.

First things first. She needed to empty the slop bowl

and go to the lavatory, which was down at the back of the house, past the scullery and coal store. It was inside, not at the end of the yard, which seemed a great luxury on a rainy morning.

When she'd taken her slop bowl back to her bedroom, she decided to light the fire, hoping that would please the old lady. She found a hessian pinafore hanging on the wall next to the coal store, and put that on to clean out the grate. Soon, the fire was burning brightly.

Afterwards she washed her hands and made sure there was water in the kettle before pushing it over the hottest part of the stove top.

She turned as she heard footsteps on the stairs.

Mrs Miller came into the kitchen, moving slowly and stiffly. She was wearing a long woollen dressing gown, with her white hair hanging down her back in a thin plait. 'Good. You had the wit to get the fire going.' She went across to hold her hands out to its warmth.

They were gnarled hands, Harriet noticed, hands that had worked hard. Still worked hard, judging by how clean everything was here. She waited, clasping her own hands in front of her.

Mrs Miller sat down at the kitchen table. 'Cup of tea first. You can make it for us. Use my ordinary tea in the red tea caddy. I'll tell you how I like it.'

There followed what Harriet soon realised was a lesson in the correct way to do things. And she had to admit that the tea tasted better than any other she'd had. As she set her empty cup down, she realised Mrs Miller was studying her once again.

The old woman repeated what Winifred had said, 'You're definitely going to be pretty when you grow up. You're like a colt at the moment, all legs and arms, with just a few curves starting. Did you want to go to that fancy school?'

Harriet nodded. 'Oh, yes. I like learning things. I was going to be a teacher.'

'Well, that chance has gone now, but you can still educate yourself. Anyone can read books these days. They're all over the place, not like when I was a girl. I use the public library and I buy cheap books from the market sometimes.'

It wasn't the same to read books as it would have been to be taught by well-educated people, Harriet thought sadly. She always had questions to ask about what she'd read. But it was no use protesting.

'Here's what we're going to do, young lady. I'll give you a few lessons in how to look after a house *properly* – there's a big difference between that and what most folk call housework – and if you show promise during this first week with me, I'll write to someone I know, to see if she can help you find a place. Mrs Stuart is the housekeeper now at Dalton House, took over from me. I trained her and she'll trust you if I vouch for you.'

'How can you vouch for me if you've only just met me?'

Mrs Miller laughed, a rusty sound as if she didn't do it often. 'I've trained a lot of girls. I can tell within the hour whether they're worth the bother or not. If *you* will only set your mind to it, you'll be well worth training.'

That thought warmed Harriet. 'I will do my best, I promise you. Where's Dalton House?'

'Near Reading.'

'How far away is that?'

Mrs Miller gave her a knowing smile. 'Far enough for your purpose. Norris won't find it easy to get to you there.' She waited. 'Well, is that a bargain?'

Harriet hesitated. 'Do you and Winifred have to take *all* my wages? I'll need to buy more clothes and underwear. I'm still growing in . . . places.' She could feel herself blushing.

Mrs Miller pursed her lips. 'Yes. I suppose you will need something.'

'Winifred won't let me keep any money at all.'

'No. She's greedy, Winifred is. Always was. Doesn't know when to stop grabbing. That puts people's backs up. So we'll not tell her exactly how much you're getting and we'll leave you a shilling a week of your own.' Mrs Miller tapped her nose. 'What she doesn't know won't upset her.'

'It's still not much.'

'It'll be enough if you're careful. In a house like that you'll get tips now and then from guests. All the general tips go into a pot and even the youngest gets a

41

share of those every quarter, plus a few shillings extra at Christmas. Now, let's have our breakfast. I like two slices of toast with jam, but I daresay a growing girl like you will want more.'

'I do get a bit hungry. Sorry.'

'There's plenty of bread and some apples as well. I like a nice juicy apple.'

Once they'd eaten and cleared up the kitchen, Mrs Miller said, 'We'll go upstairs and I'll show you how to make the beds *properly*. You've just dragged the covers over yours. Slovenly, that is. Then you can show me your clothes.'

'They're not very nice and I haven't got a lot of stuff.'

'Doesn't matter because we'll make a list and I'll get the money from Winifred to buy what's needed. After that, you should learn to make your own clothes. It's much cheaper.'

'The teacher at school said I'm not very good at sewing.'

'How hard did you try?'

Harriet wriggled uncomfortably. 'Not very. It's not very interesting, sewing.'

'No, but it comes in useful. So that's another thing you'll need to learn *properly*. You should start making a list.'

'How can I learn to sew better if I'm working as a maid?'

'There'll be somebody to help you at Dalton House.

All the girls sew. Most of them make their own clothes. Some make stuff for their bottom drawer, others like to embroider. The family used to have a sewing and mending woman come to the house one day a week, probably still do. Make friends with her and ask her help. If she's willing to teach you, ask the housekeeper to make time for you to learn. She won't say no, because you'll be able to do simple mending for them then.' She waited. 'Well, is that agreed?'

'Yes. And thank you for helping me, Mrs Miller. I don't know what I'd have done without you.' She shivered.

The old woman snorted. 'I'm no saint. I'm earning good money from helping you. Mind you, that said, I'd definitely rather do good than evil in this world. Makes life pleasanter all round.'

By the time Harriet went to bed that night, her head was full of new ways of doing things, new ways of looking at the world, and if she'd heard the word 'properly' once, she'd heard it a hundred times. Still, the day had flown by, at least.

Mrs Miller said you should learn anything you could, whether you liked doing it or not, whether you thought you'd need it or not. That made sense.

And though he was in the same town, there had been no sign of Norris prowling round this house. Harriet had looked out of the window to check several times after he'd have stopped work for the day. You couldn't be too careful.

She thought Mrs Miller had noticed what she was doing, but the old lady hadn't commented. Mrs Miller seemed to notice everything. She was all right, though, under that sharp way of talking. Kind, even.

Strange to think she was a relative of Winifred. They were like chalk and cheese. Winifred was a horrible woman and Harriet hoped she'd never see her again as long as she lived.

Norris sat scowling into the fire, slippered feet resting on the fender.

'You're a fool,' his mother said suddenly.

'I'm a man, with a man's needs. You can't turn me back into a lad.'

'Well, men who have a bit of sense in their heads don't mess in their own backyard.'

'Harriet's been egging me on.'

Winifred slammed her hand down on the arm of her chair. 'Let that be the last time you lie to me about that.'

Their eyes met and he was the first to look away.

'Harriet has *not* been egging you on. She's young for her age, won't be ready for a man for a year or two yet, if I'm any judge. Comes of all that damned book learning.'

'I'm going to have her one day.'

'Then you're an even bigger fool than I thought. She'll never want you after what you did to her. Now, enough of your sulking. Help me make a list of what we can sell. I'm not keeping James's things, but I'm not giving them away, either. Those damned horse brasses will be the first to go.'

'Why don't we take a casual stall at the market? We'll get more money for them that way, even after paying for hiring a stall.'

'I thought about that, but if we do, these snooty neighbours will notice and gossip. We're keeping our noses clean from now on, you an' me, my lad. We're going up in the world and appearances matter. Not that it wasn't a good idea to take a stall, and I'm glad to see you have some brains in your head.'

'I *am* your son.'

'Yes. But you're your father's son, too, and that's the half that worries me.'

Norris let her organise the evening and mostly kept his mouth shut, but he'd meant what he said about Harriet. No lass was going to get the better of him, not now and not in the future. Besides, he wanted her. There was something about her that he had to have.

But for the time being, his mother held all the power, because she had the money. She also had the wit to keep the money safe and see the future more clearly than he'd done so far. It had made him think when he found her bank book and saw how much she had saved.

Norris was fed up of his stinking job, wished he'd worked harder at school and got a better one. His mother wasn't the only one with a desire to improve her life. He intended to look around for something else, but he was going to make sure this time he found a job that suited him.

His mother had done well for someone who'd grown up in the slums.

Norris intended to watch her more carefully and learn how she did it.

Doris was very scornful of Harriet's clothes. She picked through them, holding them as if they were full of fleas or lice.

'They're not dirty,' Harriet protested. 'I keep myself clean.'

'They might as well be dirty, such ugly, lumpy, *cheap* things. I bet the dye runs when you wash them. Yes, I thought so. You won't do me any credit wearing those.'

'Winifred won't spend much money on me, you know.'

'She'll spend what I tell her. There's some writing paper in the top drawer of the bureau. Fetch it here, and my pen too. I'll write her a note, then we'll make our list.'

She sat chewing the end of her pen, then dipped it into the ink and began to write.

'You have lovely handwriting,' Harriet said.

Doris smiled down at the page. 'Shows a lot about the writer, good handwriting does. What's yours like?'

'Not bad. I got top marks for penmanship at school.'

Doris shoved a piece of torn paper at her and

selected another pen from the box. 'Show me. Write a few sentences.'

There was silence for a few minutes, apart from the scratching of their pens on the paper, then Doris stopped writing, read through what she'd written and nodded. 'She'll come round when I send her this.' She held out her hand. 'Let me see yours.'

Harriet passed over the paper, waiting anxiously while the old lady studied the poem she'd written.

'That's good handwriting. One thing I won't have to teach you, at least.'

More praise, Harriet thought and tears came into her eyes.

'What's upsetting you now?'

'It was just – that's the second time you've praised me.'

Doris's voice softened a little. 'No one praised you at home, did they?'

'Not after Mum died.'

'Well, I only give praise when it's due. But if it *is* due, I always give it.'

Harriet nodded, swallowing hard and fumbling for her handkerchief to wipe away the tears.

'Right, then. I'll go next door. Might as well give young Jimmy a halfpenny to deliver this as spend a halfpenny on postage. When I come back, we'll make a proper list.'

While she was gone, Harriet washed up the dishes and let her thoughts wander.

Fate seemed to have offered her a second chance of making something of herself, though she'd far rather have become a teacher. She'd never met anyone like Mrs Miller. 'Shrewd', that was the best word to describe the old woman, though she wasn't unkind with it.

It wouldn't hurt to learn how to be shrewd.

Chapter Three

Two weeks after Harriet's arrival, Mrs Miller received a letter with a job offer for her guest. She read parts of it aloud. *Trust in your recommendation, as always . . . the mistress sends her regards . . . have enclosed a postal order for the train ticket.*

Harriet would have to travel to her new job by train because Dalton House was over in the next county. 'I have to go on my own?'

'I'm not coming with you to hold your hand. You have a tongue in your head. Just ask for help if you don't know what to do.'

When she was ready to leave, Mrs Miller studied her, head on one side. 'Turn round. Yes, you'll do. Now, I've done my best for you. It's up to you after this, my girl. Work hard, be honest and cheerful, and you won't go far wrong. And remember, always do your best, whatever it is you're doing.'

'I will. And thank you for all your help.' Mrs Miller had been kind to her, and had even bought her a new

49

hat as a present when Winifred insisted her old one would do. The new one was a neat felt with a small brim, navy blue to match her new coat. Yes, and the old lady had helped her trim it with some ribbon she said she'd had 'put by'. So it looked nice, which helped give Harriet confidence.

She had a sudden urge to hug Mrs Miller, but didn't quite dare.

The old lady gave her a quick pat on the cheek, then stepped back. 'You'll be all right, girl. They don't eat their servants for dinner.'

The boy next door was waiting outside with his father's wheelbarrow loaded with Harriet's tin trunk, bought second hand at the market, with the faded old suitcase balanced precariously on top. The trunk had her name painted on the side now. Mrs Miller had done that herself in white and it looked lovely.

There weren't enough clothes to fill both trunk and suitcase, but that had left enough space for all her parents' books in the trunk. She would have to change trains three times to get to Dalton House. Mrs Miller had told her how to manage this, so at each station she found a porter, watched anxiously as her trunk was unloaded from the luggage van onto his trolley, and tipped him the amount Mrs Miller had said would be right.

No one else got off the third train. It was a small country station and for a minute Harriet panicked when the train left and she couldn't see anyone except herself and the porter. Then, as the cloud of steam from the train cleared, she saw a grey-haired man appear at the station entrance.

When he saw her, he came forward, pulling his cap off politely. 'Harriet Benson?'

'Yes.'

'I'm Bert Billings. Groom and general dogsbody at Dalton House.'

He laughed at his description of himself as he put his cap back on again and that made her relax. He had lovely twinkling eyes, surrounded by wrinkles, so he must be quite old.

'I've been sent to fetch you. Let's get your luggage loaded on the brake.' He pointed to a vehicle with two horses, both busy eating from their nosebags.

The porter helped him with the trunk and when she pulled out her purse to tip the porter, Bert shook his head. 'Save your pennies. I'll see to that. You're on family business now.'

She put her purse away, grateful to save even threepence from the nine shillings and twopence halfpenny, which was all she had in the world. She carried the suitcase across to the brake and the men brought the trunk.

Bert spoke differently from the people she'd grown up with, his speech slower. She realised he was waiting for her and blushed for keeping him waiting.

But he didn't seem annoyed. He indicated the driver's bench seat. 'Up you hop, young Harriet. We won't put you in the back with the luggage. You'll see more if you sit next to me.'

Once they'd left the station yard, he let the horses find their own pace and smiled at her. 'Nervous, are ye?'

'Yes, I am a bit.'

'How old are you, lass?'

'Nearly sixteen, Mr Billings.'

'Just call me Bert. They all do. Is this your first place?'

'What? Oh, you mean my first job.'

He clicked his tongue in a disapproving way. 'Don't let Mrs Stuart hear you calling it a *job*. She thinks that word sounds common and she'll give you one of her dark looks.'

'Oh. Right. I'll remember that.' He was so kind, she dared ask, 'Um . . . what's it like working at Dalton House?'

He took a moment to think, head on one said, then said, 'It's a good place to work. The family live quietly mostly when they're down in the country, because their children are all grown up. The master and mistress stay up in the London house a lot of the time. When they're here, they entertain the local gentry now sometimes, so we get a bit of company in the servants' hall.'

He hesitated, before adding, 'It's partly because of Mr Joseph that they live so quietly here and don't hold house parties.'

'Who's Mr Joseph?'

'Youngest son. Been an invalid most of his life, poor

lad. Look! We're almost there.' He didn't say anything else about Mr Joseph and somehow she didn't like to press him for more information.

A short time later Bert laughed as the horses began to slow down. 'See that. These two know their own way home. I don't have to tell them where to turn, do I, my lovelies?'

Dalton House was far bigger than Harriet had expected. From the drive she saw a long, rambling building – with other buildings behind it. Goodness, how many were there?

It was a mixture of the styles of architecture she'd learnt about in one of the books she'd borrowed from the library. She'd taken the book out because she liked looking at the pictures of big gardens full of flowers. There weren't any flowers at all in her street.

Dalton House sat among lovely green lawns, like the ones in the park at home. Fancy having all that grass just for one house. She'd always wanted to walk barefoot on the grass in the park, but of course you couldn't go on it, even with shoes on, or the park keepers would throw you out.

The big house seemed to be smiling at the world, and it looked like a home, even if it was a posh one. It was a mild day and there was a white table at one side of the grass, under some big shady trees. A young man was there talking to a lady standing next to him. She was carrying a basket full of flowers.

The man was sitting in a chair with big wheels on

it, like bicycle wheels. Harriet squinted to get a better view of it and saw that it had rims sticking out from the wheels, which he used to move it slightly. There were smaller wheels at the front. She'd never seen a chair quite like it.

'That's the mistress with Mr Joseph,' Henry said. 'He sits out when she'll let him. And he moves that old chair all over the place when she's not down here. Eh, she fusses over him like a hen with one chick, because they nearly lost him a time or two when he was younger. She has four other children, three more boys and a girl, but they're grown up and married now, got their own homes. Mr Joseph is the youngest. I doubt he'll ever marry, poor lad.'

He hadn't looked all that bad to Harriet. He wasn't pale or listless like other invalids she'd seen. He'd been talking animatedly to his mother, waving his arms around and laughing at something.

They drove round to the back of the house and Bert drew up by some double doors.

'Us servants don't use the front door.'

She nodded. 'Mrs Miller told me about that.' She'd been warned to say *Mrs* Miller here.

'How is she? We were sad to see her go, though Mrs Stuart does pretty well. Best housekeeper we ever had, Mrs Miller was. She never missed a thing, but she was fair.'

'She's well. She has a lovely little house and she helps at the church, visits her friends.'

'Well, if you write to her, as I dare say you will, tell her Bert sends his regards. Now, hop down. I'll get the lad to help me carry your things in. What've you got in that suitcase, rocks?'

'Books.'

'Ah. A reader, are you?'

'Yes. I love reading.'

'Tell the housekeeper. The mistress lets servants borrow books from the old schoolroom, but most of them aren't interested in books. The maids would rather giggle and gossip. But if you like reading, you'll find plenty of it up there.'

When she went into the kitchen, everyone stared at her and she could feel herself blushing again. Then the young woman nearest said, 'You must be Harriet Benson. I'll take you to Mrs Stuart straight away. I'm Jenny.'

Harriet couldn't summon up a smile.

'We aren't going to torture you, you know,' Jenny whispered.

'It's just . . . I've never been in service before.'

'We all have to start somewhere.' She knocked on a half-open door. 'The new maid's arrived, Mrs Stuart.'

The housekeeper was plump, with a rosy, pink face. She was wearing a black dress with cream lace collar and cuffs, very grand. 'Come in here, child. How's Doris?'

'Mrs Miller's well. She sends her regards.'

'She taught me all I know. If she recommends

someone, we always hire them if we're needing more help. Now, tell me about yourself.'

By the time Jenny was sent for again to show the newcomer up to her bedroom, Mrs Stuart knew all about what had brought Harriet to Dalton House, even though she hadn't intended to tell anyone about Norris's attacks. But somehow, Mrs Stuart was so kind and motherly, it all tumbled out, and Harriet had a little weep.

Mrs Miller hadn't wanted to know the details. Mrs Stuart did.

'You'll be safe here, child,' Mrs Stuart said. 'We don't allow that sort of thing to go on at Dalton House. Ah, Jenny. Can you take the new girl under your wing?'

Jenny looked at Harriet's tear-stained face in surprise but didn't comment till they were up to the attics. 'Were you in trouble about something?'

Harriet blushed. 'No. The trouble was at home. I don't know why I told Mrs Stuart, but somehow it all came out. My stepbrother was . . . making a bit of a nuisance of himself. I don't even like to think about what he tried to do.'

'He sounds a rotter. And everyone tells her their troubles. Mrs Miller was a good housekeeper, but Mrs Stuart's a motherly person with the younger maids. Pity she never had children. If you ever need help, go to her.'

They stopped at a long narrow attic room with a

sloping ceiling, one dormer window and three single beds. The trunk and suitcase were already there, waiting to be unpacked.

'This bed will be yours,' Jenny said. 'And you get that chest of drawers. It's missing a leg, so you have to leave the brick under it, but it's all right apart from that. And these are your hooks. Let's get your things put away, then I'll take you down and start you off.'

When they'd done that, they left the empty trunk and suitcase near the bed. 'I'll send someone to take them up to the top attic.'

Jenny hesitated, then said in a softened voice, 'Um, I just wanted to say: not all men are like that stepbrother of yours. I'm walking out with a farmer's son and my John's a real gentleman. Wouldn't do a thing to upset me, if you know what I mean. It's because I'm leaving in the autumn to get married that they need a new junior, so you got the job. You'd miss out on a lot if you didn't find yourself a fellow one day.'

Harriet tried not to shudder at that thought. 'I'll do my best to please.'

'I'm sure you will. Come on. We've a lot to get through. They're having guests to dinner tomorrow, just a few neighbours, but everything has to be perfect for the mistress.'

And so it began . . .

* * *

57

From his seat under the tree, Joseph watched the new maid arrive. 'That girl's got a sweet face, Mama. Doesn't she look nervous, though?'

His mother peered short-sightedly across the lawn. 'She's from Mrs Miller. The girls she sends us are always good workers. She'll soon settle in.'

Joseph changed the subject. His mother left all the management of the servants to the housekeeper, but he liked to know everyone who worked in the house. Sooner or later he'd find time to chat to the new girl.

She had beautiful hair, russet not ginger. He'd seen and loved that hair colour in a book of paintings by Dante Gabriel Rossetti. Which one did she remind him of? He'd have to check.

'Are you sure you're not cold, dear?'

He stifled a sigh. 'It's a sunny day, Mama. I'm very comfortable out here.'

'Will you be all right if I leave you for a while, then? You have your bell? Good. You can always ring if you need help.'

'Yes, of course. But I'll be all right.' He let the sigh out as he watched her walk towards the house. He wished she didn't fuss so much. Then he smiled fondly. No one was as elegant as his mama. She always looked as if she was floating when she walked, while he had an ugly limp and had to move quite slowly. He could move, though, and wished they'd let him be more active.

As he grew older, he felt to be in better health,

hardly wheezed at all, wasn't in as much pain from his hip, didn't come down with heavy colds in winter. But he could never persuade his mother to give him even half the freedom his brothers had enjoyed.

She always quoted Dr Macleod, but *he* did just what Joseph's mother wanted, including telling her that her son must live a quiet life.

It suited Joseph in one way, because he had no desire whatsoever to go up to London and join the social round, but things could be too quiet! He sometimes felt he would go mad with boredom here. Which was ungrateful of him when he was surrounded with such loving care.

But there you were. He was twenty-one and considered himself a man grown, though his family didn't accept that and still treated him like a boy. Unfortunately, he had developed a man's physical longings and needs during the past year or two. That tormented his dreams sometimes and kept him awake, but there was no way he could see of satisfying such needs. What woman would want a man with a twisted body like his?

He couldn't afford to marry, anyway. He'd supposed his father would set up a trust fund for him once he turned twenty-one, as he had for Joseph's brothers, but he wasn't equipped to earn a living and provide for a family like his brother Richard, who was a lawyer, or Thomas, who was in banking. Unless they bought him a house he'd have to stay here. He couldn't laze away his life in a wheeled chair, reading or chatting to his family. He didn't want to. There must be something else he could do with his life, something more worthwhile. He'd find it one day.

Harriet had never worked as hard in her life, not because her employers were slave drivers, but because she had so much to learn and wanted to prove herself. She didn't tell anyone when it was her birthday soon after her arrival. Why bother? There was no one here who really cared.

In June, the master and mistress went up to London, taking some of the staff with them.

Before they left, Harriet heard Mr Joseph insisting that the main rooms should be shut down while they were away. She didn't mean to eavesdrop, but he had such a lovely voice that she liked to listen to him speaking.

'Mama, dearest, you know I never use those rooms when I'm on my own, and you usually have to hire extra staff in London. It's such a waste of time keeping so many servants here just for me. I infinitely prefer my small sitting room when I'm not in the library, you know I do.'

Infinitely prefer, Harriet mouthed to herself, liking the phrase.

'Are you sure, Joseph?'

'I'm absolutely certain, Mama.'

'Well, we'll try it just this once. After all, Jenny can

let us know if she needs more staff. She's not leaving to get married for a while yet.'

Harriet felt a sudden surge of guilt at standing around eavesdropping and went off to dust and clean the housekeeper's room. She spent most of her time cleaning up after the servants, and it'd been explained to her that new maids didn't serve the family until everyone was sure they wouldn't make mistakes.

She thought about what she'd overheard, though, when she went up to clean the servants' area in the attics. To her, it had sounded as if Mr Joseph was a bit impatient about the way everyone fussed over him. Not that he was ever impolite. He seemed to have a very sweet nature. He was roughly the same age as Norris, but so unlike her stepbrother.

He spent every fine day sitting on the lawn and a couple of times, when Harriet had been cleaning the attic windows, she'd stopped to watch him for a moment or two. For some reason he fascinated her.

When his mother came out and gestured to the sky, then towards the house, he'd closed his eyes as if summoning up all his patience. After that, he'd shaken his head and said 'No, mama!' quite emphatically.

Harriet couldn't hear the words, but could tell what he'd said from the way he shaped his mouth. She'd seen him disagree with his mother once or twice before.

'He's not going to do as he's told for ever,' a voice said behind her.

She turned to see Jenny standing behind her. 'I didn't hear you come in.'

'No. You were too busy staring out of the window.'

'I'm sorry. It won't happen again.'

Jenny smiled. 'You work hard and if you want a breather for a minute or two, I reckon you earn it. Anyway, it's what us servants do, isn't it? Watch the family, I mean. Because we're away from our own families.'

'I suppose it is.'

'I miss my family. I'll see a lot more of them after I'm married.'

'I haven't got any family left now, not close enough to count, anyway.'

'Well, the other servants are like a big family, aren't they?'

Harriet didn't contradict her, but it wasn't the same. She still missed her mother and father dreadfully. She realised Jenny was saying something and tried to concentrate on her companion.

'I've been here for eight years and I've seen Mr Joseph grow up. He used to be ill all the time, but in the past year or two he's seemed a lot better. And he's started making his own decisions. The mistress doesn't like that. She still wants to baby him.'

'He doesn't look ill.' She didn't like to say the word 'crippled'. It was such an ugly word and he seemed to be too nice to call a cripple. 'It's only when he walks that you can tell he has . . . um, problems.'

For a minute or two longer they both watched Mrs Dalton argue, then spread her arms wide and stare at the sky as if giving up the attempt. Shaking her head, she walked back to the house and entered through the big French windows.

Behind her, Mr Joseph rested his head against the back of his chair as if weary. When he straightened up, he looked round furtively then threw off the blanket they always insisted on covering his legs with, before standing up.

He took a few slow steps round the table then walked back to the chair again, holding onto its back. Then he let go and moved across to the nearest tree, turning to beam triumphantly at his wheelchair.

'He's like a child learning to walk,' Harriet breathed. A neighbour's little son had been just the same, venturing further each time and beaming at the world as if it was a great accomplishment to get somewhere new.

'I didn't know Mr Joseph could walk so far without support,' Jenny said. 'And what are we doing gaping out of the window when we should be working? We've a lot to do before the family go to London.'

Harriet was sorry to move away. She'd like to have seen where Mr Joseph went next and how he managed. But she did as she was told, because she wasn't paid to watch other people. 'Are you sorry not to be going with them this time, Jenny?'

'Not at all. London's dirty and busy, and I never

feel safe walking the streets. If it's not pickpockets, it's people bumping into you, they're in such a hurry. I'd much rather be in the country, near my John. There's still a lot to do before my wedding. I've all sorts of things to sew.'

'If you want any help . . . I can do plain sewing.'

Jenny smiled. 'Bless you, that's kind. We'll see how I go.'

But she didn't ask for help and Harriet knew why. Try as she might, she couldn't sew neatly. She got lost in her thoughts and put in crooked stitches. It was worrying her how she'd replace her clothes if she grew any more.

Not much else was worrying her, though. Dalton House was a happy place to work and she was so relieved to be here.

She hadn't heard from her stepmother, but when she'd written to Mrs Miller to thank her for her help, she'd received a reply, one asking questions that needed another letter to answer.

She was hoping Mrs Miller would write again, because it was lovely to receive a letter like the other servants sometimes did, made her feel less alone in the world.

At the end of September, Jenny left to get married. The mistress gave permission for a special afternoon tea in the servants' hall to bid her goodbye.

Everyone had bought her a present, but Harriet

didn't dare spend her remaining few shillings and she wasn't skilled enough to sew anything worthy to be called a present, either.

Mrs Stuart found her sniffling over the fire she was lighting one morning and persuaded her to reveal why she was upset.

'I don't want them to think I'm mean,' Harriet sobbed into her duster.

'I have a book someone gave me. I've never opened it, because I'm not fond of reading. Why don't you have that and give it to her? No one will be surprised at you giving her a book.'

'But it won't come from me. Not really. And she doesn't read much.'

'She'll be getting it because of you, though, and that's what's important. It's a pretty book and she'll put it on show in her parlour.' She patted Harriet's shoulder. 'You're right to save your money, child.'

'I still won't have enough to buy new clothes. I've grown already since I came here, the food's so good.'

'I can help you there. We have quite a few things other maids have left behind, those who married well. They're only lying around in a box upstairs. If you don't mind second-hand clothes, I'm sure I can find things for you when you grow out of those.'

'Really? You won't mind?'

'No, dear. You're a hard worker and already I can trust you to do a job properly without me breathing down your neck. That's worth a lot to me.'

Harriet blew her nose. 'Thank you.'

'It's my job to help the maids. Now, I came to find you because I have something to tell you – good news, I hope. We have a new maid starting on Monday, as you know, and I want you to hand over your present jobs to her. You can take over Mabel's duties and she'll do Jenny's.'

Harriet let out a huge sigh of both relief and pleasure, because she'd hoped for this, but hadn't dared ask. She didn't mind at all when Mrs Stuart laughed at her. It would be lovely to have a bit of a change.

The new duties weren't any more interesting than the old ones, but at least they took Harriet into the front part of the house more often and she had the pleasure of cleaning the beautiful rooms the family used, places she'd only popped in and out of before when helping Mabel or Jenny.

If it hadn't been for the books, Harriet would have been unhappy in spite of people's kindness. She couldn't help being frustrated with the monotony of her days. And when she had her monthly day off, she had nowhere to go if it rained, but if she stayed in the house someone was sure to ask her to 'just help for a minute' with a job.

In the end, she began to take refuge in the old summer house. No one used it any more and it was looking distinctly shabby, its white paint faded and blistered, and there was a leak in one corner of the roof. She was surprised that the Daltons didn't do something about it, but it wasn't the only part of the gardens that was being neglected.

The head gardener found her there and looked at her in surprise. 'What are you doing here, lass?'

'I've nowhere to go on my day off and if I stay in the house they find me something to do, Mr Gunson.'

'The other maids go into town and look round the shops.'

'That costs money, and I don't have much.'

'I see.' His expression softened. 'You look cold.'

'I am a bit.' She was beginning to worry about what she'd do when winter brought ice and snow.

'Well, the family don't use this place any more, that's for sure, an' they're not likely to, neither. They spend more time in London these days. Tell you what, lass. I've got some old horse blankets. You could wrap yourself up in those for an hour or two.'

'Thank you so much.'

He walked away, shaking his head and muttering to himself.

She went back to her book, finding it hard to turn the pages with her gloves on, but even harder if she left the gloves off and let the chill air stiffen her fingers.

She was grateful when Mr Gunson came back with the ragged old blankets.

Later that day, he walked past again, stopped to stare at her and once more came across to speak to her. 'You still here?'

'I'm all right now I have the blankets. I like to sit and read.'

'Did you have anything to eat at midday?'

'I . . . um, wasn't hungry.'

'Hmm.'

He came back a short time later with a wrinkled apple and a stale piece of bread. 'It's not much, but it'll fill your belly.'

'You're very kind.'

'You're the same age as my daughter. I'd not like her to spend all day on her own like this.'

'I'm not on my own. I've got a book.'

'Books! It's people you should be with at your age.'

She didn't say it, but she was happy to be away from people. It was lovely to sit quietly like this, even in the cold weather, so she just repeated, 'I'm fine, really I am.'

As Christmas approached, the other servants wrote to their families and spent their time making little presents. Harriet felt so left out, she asked Mrs Stuart for some leftover bits and pieces of material that the mistress's maid was throwing away. She found a nice square piece and hemmed a handkerchief out of it for Mrs Miller. The sewing wasn't very neat, however hard she tried, but it was the thought that counted.

To her surprise, she received a postal order for five shillings and a book from Mrs Miller in return.

She walked round in a glow all day. She'd saved up some money from the weekly shilling from her wages, and from the Christmas bonuses. It wasn't much, just under two pounds, but it was a start.

After Christmas, life settled down.

Well, it did until the 22nd January when the Queen died. Victoria had been on the throne for as long as most people remembered.

Dalton House went into instant mourning, of course, with the family wearing black and the servants black armbands.

Harriet stared at her armband. She hadn't had anything black to wear when her mother died, and even Winifred hadn't worn more than a black armband for her husband, and that only for a week.

The Queen had died at Osborne on the Isle of Wight, but Mrs Stuart read out to the servants a description of her coffin being brought back to London on the royal yacht *Alberta*. It came from the master's newspaper, which was passed to the housekeeper once he'd finished with it.

She also read out to them the details of the funeral on the 2nd February.

The mood lightened after the grand funeral and everyone expressed hopes for a happy reign for Victoria's son. Edward the Seventh had waited long enough to get to the throne. Let him enjoy it while he could, Mr Dalton said.

It seemed that the Daltons had met him in London,

which made Harriet look at them with awe for a day or two.

She had expected there to be a coronation for the new king almost immediately, but it wasn't to take place till the following year.

The household routine fell into its usual predictable patterns of behaviour.

Chapter Four

As spring approached, another problem rose for Harriet. She'd now read all the books in the schoolroom, a few of them more than once.

Thinking of how many books there were in the library, she plucked up her courage and went to consult Mrs Stuart, asking if there were any other books she could borrow. 'I've read all my own books several times. And I'd look after the books, you know I would.'

'I've never seen such a reader as you.'

'I enjoy finding things out.'

'I'm told you sit in the old summer house on your days off, reading away.'

She blushed. 'I didn't think anyone would mind. No one else uses it now.' She waited, holding her breath. What would she do if she was forbidden to go there?

Mrs Stuart looked at her thoughtfully. 'Leave it with me. I'll ask about the books. And make sure you don't catch your death of cold out there.'

'Mr Gunson's given me some old horse blankets and a piece of canvas. I'm really very snug.'

'It's a pity this isn't a big enough house for us to have other maids of your age. You need friends of your own age.'

'I'm fine as I am, Mrs Stuart, honestly I am.'

'Well, ask Cook to make you some sandwiches next time and . . . I'll ask about the books.'

'Thank you so much.' Harriet let out a sigh of relief. It'd make such a difference to get some new books.

When she had her morning consultation with the mistress the following day, Mrs Stuart raised the matter.

'Well, Harriet doesn't seem cheeky or forward, but it's a strange request from a servant. I hope she's not neglecting her duties.'

'She's a very hard worker. And Harriet isn't at all cheeky. If anything, she's too quiet for someone her age. She can't afford to buy books because her stepmother takes most of her wages.'

'Hmm. What do *you* want to do about her request?'

'I was thinking about asking Mr Joseph to help, ma'am. He's been rather restless lately, hasn't he? I hope I'm not speaking out of turn, but I can't help noticing.' She waited, head on one side. The mistress didn't like to be hurried.

'You're right, Mrs Stuart. Joseph is getting rather

restless. I know he's better than he used to be, but I still worry about him overdoing things.'

Mrs Stuart didn't mention how much walking Mr Joseph did, up and down the first-floor corridors and round the quieter parts of the garden, even in the cooler weather. He still had a crooked, awkward walk, but he seemed much quicker and stronger these days.

Not only wasn't it her business what he did, but she didn't blame the poor young man. No one had discussed this, but all the servants were keeping quiet about his activities, even his manservant Pollins. They were glad to see him improving because he was never anything but polite to them.

At last Mrs Dalton said slowly, 'What do you think Joseph can do?'

'I wondered if he'd be interested in helping Harriet find some more reading material from the library and even, if he has time, answering any questions she raises. She's asked me if I could explain several things she's found in books, and I must confess, not being much of a reader, I couldn't answer all her questions. I'm sure Mr Joseph would know the answers, though. He reads even more than Harriet does.'

'I don't know what the world is coming to when servants read the same books as their employers and ask questions.'

'We're in a new century now, ma'am, with a new king. Ways are bound to change.'

Mrs Dalton sighed. 'I suppose so. Still . . . since you say she's such a good worker, I'll ask Joseph what he thinks. I'm not promising anything, mind, and if it tires him, of course it must stop at once.'

'Of course. Thank you so much, ma'am. It's always good to keep the staff happy. That way, they work harder and we don't lose the ones we've trained. Mrs Miller always made a point of that, if you remember.'

Mrs Dalton shrugged and went off to consult her maid about an alteration to one of her gowns. She clearly felt enough had been said on the subject.

Mrs Stuart could only hope her mistress would remember to ask about the books.

That evening dinner was just a family gathering. Joseph wasn't hungry but tried to eat enough to stop his mother nagging him. It had been a long rainy day and he hadn't been able to get outside or walk about much.

'Are you not feeling well?' his mother asked once his father had dismissed the servants.

'I'm fine, Mama, just a little bored today. My new box of books should have arrived.'

'Stop fussing over the boy, Sophie!' his father barked.

'I'm not fussing, William. But a mother notices these things. Oh, I forgot to mention earlier, Joseph dear, that Mrs Stuart asked a favour today – or rather, she asked me if *you* might consider doing her a favour by helping out with something. But of course you must say no if it's too much for you.'

He waited, sure it would be something and nothing.

'That young maid, Harriet, is apparently a great reader and has finished all the books in the schoolroom, though I find that hard to believe. Mrs Stuart wondered if we had anything in the library we might allow her to read.'

'She'll probably just want some rubbishy novels,' her husband said at once. 'She won't find anything like that in our library.'

'If the girl really has read every book in the schoolroom, then she's read a couple of shelves of textbooks as well,' Joseph said, his interest piqued.

'Well, I doubt whether a girl like that could have read so many books in just a few months. She probably skimmed through the difficult ones. But still, it's a harmless occupation and a quiet one, so I'm inclined to humour her. Happy maids stay with you, and that makes life so much easier. Servants are getting very uppity these days.'

Joseph really liked the idea of helping Harriet, but shrugged, knowing better than to show great interest in this, or his mother would start to worry that it was too much for him. 'I could quite easily select a few books for her. It'd only take me a few minutes. Though I'd rather do that during the daytime than wait until she's finished her duties in the evenings. Perhaps she could be spared for a few minutes to tell me about her interests.'

His mother let out a little puff of irritation. 'Of course she can be spared. She must come at a time that's convenient to you. That isn't the point. I don't want you wearing yourself out.'

'I'm in the library most of the time anyway during the colder weather, and as I said, it'll only take a few minutes. I'll speak to Mrs Stuart tomorrow.'

'Then that's settled.' His father changed the subject to their next visit to London and his mother joined eagerly in the discussion about when they would move to town.

Joseph leant back and let them talk. It didn't bother him to be the only family member in residence here. In fact, he preferred it. When his parents were away, he found life at Dalton House far more congenial.

He smiled at the thought of helping Harriet. He'd enjoy that and feel he was doing something worthwhile for a change. She seemed a very nice young woman.

He'd worked out which painting she reminded him of: *Sancta Lilias* by Dante Gabriel Rossetti. He had a print of it in a book about Pre-Raphaelite artists. He didn't always like Rossetti's faces, but this one was lovely, and very like Harriet now she didn't look so gaunt.

That same year Norris Harding found himself a more interesting job, working in a rather special sort of club, in charge of keeping order.

'You've got a job in a house of ill repute!' his mother exclaimed, scandalised. 'But we agreed to stay respectable.'

'It's a very exclusive place, and I'll be making five times the money I do now.'

There was dead silence for a moment or two and he waited, not allowing himself to smile at her astonishment, but relishing it nonetheless.

'Five times as much!'

'Yes. Such places bring in a lot of money, if they're discreetly run. The women there are a better class of whore, clean and pretty. And the customers may not be gentry, but they're self-made men who have plenty of money.'

Her voice turned suddenly harsh. 'I forbid it. I'm trying to *rise* in the world, not let you drag us down to the gutters and associate with . . . with such females.'

'Think I don't know your own mother was a whore?' He used the word deliberately.

She turned pale. 'How did you find that out?'

'From my new friends. One of the older fellows knew her.'

'Well, I haven't followed her example. She saw to that, did everything she could to keep me respectable.'

'Let's face it, Ma, I'll never make my fortune by working for someone else, and we don't have the connections for me to do much else. I'm going to take this job.'

'I could give you the money to start a shop – one in

a decent area, not one with poor clientele. You could build it up and—'

'I do not want to run a shop. I'd go mad fiddling about with bits and pieces of paper all day and kowtowing to idiots. I'm not fond of getting up early, either, so even the hours will suit me better in this new job. Anyway, I've already given notice, so it's done now.'

'Oh, Norris! What will people think?'

'I don't care what people will think. I care that I'll have a chance to make real money. For you, bettering yourself means being respectable and making money; for me, it's making a lot of money, the more the better. Money's what gives you power to do as you please.'

She scowled at him. 'I'll never be considered respectable if my son works in a place like that.'

He sat down beside her and took her hand. 'You've tried, Ma. You married two respectable men, and weren't they bores? Little dictators, telling you what to do and not to do.'

He got a smile out of her with that. 'And you've lived in a respectable street for three years now. That hasn't made you happy, either, has it?'

'I like this house.'

'I'll buy you a better one in a few years.'

She reached out to pat his cheek. 'You're as wilful as your father was. I won't have much choice about your new life, will I? You've seen to that.'

'I want this money, Ma. And I'm going to have it.'

'I don't know what my friends will say. They're bound to find out.'

'Your friends won't mind what I do. And maybe we'll find you another house once I'm settled into my new job, one where the neighbours aren't such damned snobs.' He laughed suddenly. 'I'll tell you a secret: the man who owns the house of ill repute is well known in the town and he's anxious to continue keeping his involvement quiet.'

'Who is he?'

'Swear never to tell anyone.'

'Of course I won't. Do you think I go round looking for trouble?'

'It's Councillor Clifford Grayson.'

She gaped at him. 'I don't believe you!'

Norris leant back in his chair and smiled, enjoying shocking her. 'It's the truth. But if you say one word about this, we'll both have to leave town within the hour. Yes, really. Grayson's managed to keep his other little businesses quiet for years. An upstanding gentleman, our Mr G., pillar of the church, talked about as a future mayor.'

'Why did he tell you about it?'

'He didn't. I found out from a fool who was upset about something and was going to blab about it. So I shut him up and earned Mr Grayson's gratitude.'

'How did you do that?'

'I knocked a bit of sense into the idiot and made

sure he left town that same day. You'll keep your mouth shut, won't you, Ma?'

'You'd not have told me if you didn't know I can keep my mouth shut better than most.'

'Yes. You're not stupid, like most women. That's why I came to you. I'll need some money to buy better clothes. Got to make a good impression.'

'Let me think about it.'

'You've got plenty of money. You don't need to think.'

'I do. I always need to think.'

But she'd lend him what he needed, he knew that. And he'd look after her, because she'd been a good mother to him . . . except in the matter of Harriet. Well, he'd learnt to keep his temper under control now, most of the time. But he'd find Harriet again one day. He'd promised himself that.

He was going up in the world, but he knew he had a lot to learn first. Harriet would keep. She was safe, still working in that big house. He'd got his mother to ask Auntie Doris about her. He'd take Harriet away from it when he was ready.

He might even marry her.

Ma would throw a fit, didn't have a good word to say about Harriet, except that her wages made a nice little present every quarter.

Joseph rang the bell and waited until his manservant arrived with his morning cup of tea. Pollins had been with him since he grew too old to be cared for by Nurse. He'd still needed help getting around in those days, so he'd been given his own servant. Pollins was still a big, strong fellow, but Joseph refused physical help, just let Pollins do the jobs any manservant would, keeping his clothes in order, tidying up the bedroom, bringing up his hot water.

'Good morning, Pollins. It looks fine enough for a walk or a drive, so I think I'll wear my country clothes today.'

'Mrs Dalton is expecting guests for luncheon, Mr Joseph.'

'She doesn't usually expect me to attend her luncheon parties.'

'She's invited Mrs Jeffcott and her daughter. And . . . um . . . your mother asked me to make sure you wear your new navy-blue suit.'

'She's not—' He broke off, staring in dismay at Pollins.

'I think she's found a young woman who might suit you.'

Joseph groaned, remembering other luncheon parties where his brothers had been matched with young ladies. It had started as soon as each brother had finished studying or training, and found what his father called 'a decent job'. Each brother had complained and resisted, but in the end they'd been pushed inexorably towards suitable matches.

Only Selwyn, the eldest, had chosen his own

bride, but of course, she'd come complete with money and connections in the county, so she'd been very acceptable. He was living in the next county now, in the house she'd inherited. He hadn't needed to find a profession, with the prospect of inheriting Dalton House.

Most of the matchmaking had taken place in London, though Joseph had heard all about it from his brothers' complaints. It had continued unremittingly until his parents found young ladies for each of their sons.

'Has she found me a matching cripple, perhaps?' Joseph couldn't help the edge to his voice.

Pollins didn't even try to answer that.

'Sorry. I shouldn't be sharp with you, Pollins. It's not your fault. But I have no intention of marrying unless I feel some affection for the lady in question. And even then, what lady would want a man like me?'

'One with a true heart, Mr Joseph. One who can look beyond the obvious. As I've told you before.'

'I think I'm coming down with the influenza.'

'You're not usually a coward. What would it hurt to meet this one, lad? And any others she brings here? You might find one to your taste.'

When Pollins called him lad, it reminded Joseph that his manservant had been with him since he was a small child, and knew him better than anyone. It also meant Pollins was offering him advice, something he didn't often presume to do.

'I don't want to be paraded for inspection.' He heard how sulky his voice sounded, but couldn't help it.

'Neither do the young ladies, sir. Just meet them. You never know, you may even like one of them.'

'Damn you, stop being so reasonable. Oh, very well. Get out the blue suit.'

Pollins smiled, the special smile he only allowed himself when he'd won a point about something.

Miss Christina Jeffcott and her mother were visiting some neighbours, who also attended the luncheon party.

Joseph drew in a sharp breath when he entered the room and saw the dismay on Miss Jeffcott's long, thin face at the sight of him. He'd have sold his soul not to wheel his chair across the room in front of strangers but there was no getting out of it.

By the time he reached the guests, Miss Jeffcott's dismay had turned to badly masked revulsion.

He felt equally repelled by her. Sometimes ugliness came from the soul, rather than from the arrangement of a face. Miss Jeffcott had little good to say about anything. She prodded her food as if suspecting poison. She avoided looking directly at Joseph and answered his polite remarks in monosyllables.

The guests weren't encouraged to linger.

'I don't like that young woman,' his mother said when they were alone.

'Thank goodness. Nor do I. Look, Mama . . . I don't want to be paraded for inspection like this.'

'No young man does, but it's how our society works, matching young people into pairs, so that they can create new homes and families.' She laid one hand over his. 'There's no reason you can't marry too, Joseph, now that you're so much better.'

'Isn't there? Did you see the revulsion on her face?'

The silence told him his mother couldn't find the words to deny that. In the end, she just repeated, 'Well, I don't like her, so she won't do. But keep an open mind about others, hmm?'

He had a sick certainty that she wasn't going to stop till she found him a wife, and he was equally certain that only the most unappealing young women would even consider him.

He did what he always did when upset, sought refuge in the library, which no one but him used.

But he couldn't settle to reading, or sketching, or doing anything, so he decided to have a chat with the young maid about her reading. Helping someone was a more positive way to spend time than moping about.

He got up and pulled the bell, waiting by the fireplace for someone to answer. It was Mabel, who never allowed herself to get into conversation with him or any member of the family, so he merely said, 'Would Mrs Stuart be free to speak to me for a few moments, do you think?'

'I'll go and see, sir.'

The housekeeper was there within two minutes.

'I hope I haven't taken you away from something important, Mrs Stuart.'

'Not at all.'

'It's about the maid who needs something to read. Would it be convenient to see her this afternoon?'

'If you're sure you have time, Mr Joseph.'

'I can always make time to help a fellow reader.' He moved too quickly and had to grab the bookshelf to steady himself.

'Should you be standing up for so long, sir?'

'Yes, I should. I need to move about in order to strengthen my muscles.' He smiled at her and said coaxingly, 'But we don't need to tell my mother about me nearly falling just now, do we? She does worry so.'

Mrs Stuart smiled back at him. 'As you wish, sir. I'll send Harriet down in a few minutes. How long do you need her for?'

'An hour, maybe? I want to do this properly.'

'Very well.'

While he waited, he limped across to the shelves which contained his own additions to the family library and ran his fingers along them, pulling out books he thought might suit and clearing a shelf for them.

Books. Was that all he would have to fill his life? His parents were very generous about buying him any book he fancied and two booksellers in London sent him lists every month. But collections of paper couldn't replace real life and he was itching to do something more than sit and read.

He'd tried writing a novel, but it was far harder than he'd expected and the result was dull and flat. He simply didn't have a gift for storytelling. He'd tried doing research about the family history, thinking to compile a book about the Daltons, to be published privately, but that soon palled. They weren't a very interesting family on either side. Minor gentry, some connections to commerce and the professions, no scandals that he could unearth. No achievements, either.

He realised someone was tapping on the door, so called, 'Come in.'

Harriet stepped into the room, but stayed near the door, looking extremely nervous.

'Please close the door and come over here.' He wouldn't put it past his mother to eavesdrop, just to make sure he wasn't being treated disrespectfully. Harriet came closer and stood waiting.

'Do sit down.' When she hesitated, he said, 'If you don't sit, I have to look up at you and that makes my neck ache.'

'Oh. Sorry, Mr Joseph.' She pulled up a chair and sat down on the edge of it, looking ready to flee if he so much as twitched.

'Tell me about the books you've read. Which ones have you enjoyed most?'

She looked reluctant, so he coaxed her. 'I can't find you more books to read if I don't know what pleases you.' He gestured around them. 'As you can see, we have thousands to choose from.'

'I read anything I can get hold of, sir.'

'But what do you *like* most?'

After a short silence, she said, 'The ones that teach me something about the world. There was a book about the history of Britain in the schoolroom and one about the Empire. I'd heard some of the stories at school, but when I read the books, I could understand the . . .' she waved her right hand in the air, as if seeking words, then came out with, 'the patterns of history.'

He was surprised at this perceptive remark. 'I know exactly what you mean. I felt like that when I read the same books as a child. What else have you enjoyed?'

Suddenly her reserve seemed to fade and they started chatting like old friends, comparing their favourite books. But the minute he asked her about herself, her answers became monosyllabic and she started to look uncomfortable, so he went back to books.

He kept an eye on the wall clock, because if she stayed too long it'd upset the housekeeper and possibly his mother. He decided to share that with her. 'I'd better not keep you too long or Mrs Stuart will be upset.'

Harriet at once jumped to her feet. 'I'm sorry, sir. I shouldn't have talked so much.'

'Please sit down again for a minute or two. You

haven't talked too much. It was me. I've enjoyed chatting to you because no one else here is interested in history. Or in finding out what the rest of the world is like. I get lonely sometimes, even in a house full of people.' He surprised himself with this confidence, but she was so easy to talk to, it had just slipped out.

'So do I.' She clapped one hand to her mouth, as if afraid of having spoken out.

'Then we have that in common. The second thing I want to say is, I'll put some books for you on the end shelf.' He got up and limped across to it, sneaking a glance at her face and seeing no signs of revulsion. But, of course, servants wouldn't dare let themselves betray such feelings about their employer's family. 'You may choose from them and change your books as often as you like. Any that you've read, lay on their side at the end, like this, and I'll put them away again.'

He turned to a nearby shelf and selected a few more books to add to the row. 'Come and choose your first one.'

She came as timidly as a wild animal, her eyes on the books. The minute she got to the shelf, he might as well not have existed. After studying every single title, and making little crooning noises of pleasure, she chose a book about Scotland, then stood there with it clasped to her chest. 'This one, please, Mr Joseph.'

'Better take two. In case you run out and can't get back in here to change them.'

'Really?'

This time she chose a novel, then caught sight of the clock and gasped. 'I'd better get back now, sir. I've been here nearly *an hour*.'

'Yes, of course. Perhaps you'll come again when you've read the book and tell me what you think of it, or you could ask me questions if anything isn't clear?'

'Really?'

'Really and truly.'

She beamed at him. 'I do wonder about things sometimes, so if I'm not troubling you, sir, I'll do that. If Mrs Stuart allows it, of course.'

'I'll tell her it cheers me up to talk to you about books.'

She looked at him very solemnly, then said quietly, 'I didn't think people with families could get lonely.'

'We can all get lonely. That's why we need to make friends.'

It was almost a whisper. 'I don't have any friends now.' She didn't wait for an answer, but moved towards the door, the books clutched tightly to her chest.

Half an hour later, the housekeeper came to see him. 'Am I interrupting, Mr Joseph?'

'No, of course not.'

'I just wanted to check that everything went all right with Harriet.'

'Oh, yes. She's a very polite young woman and I enjoyed chatting to her. You know, I think I'd have enjoyed being a teacher. I'm going to plan a course of reading for her. Would you mind if she came to spend an hour with me two mornings a week? I'd enjoy it so much.'

She looked surprised, then uncomfortable. 'You'd have to ask your mother about her coming to talk to you regularly. Borrowing books is one thing, but that's . . . well, different.'

'Oh. Yes, of course. I wasn't thinking. I'll speak to Mama. But it wouldn't upset your routine too much?'

'We're here to serve the family, Mr Joseph, whatever they need.'

'Well, thank you for letting Harriet come to me. It cheered me up no end to be able to talk to someone about books.'

There! Mrs Stuart went back to the housekeeper's room and closed the door to signify that she wasn't available. She wanted to think about this, but it was easy to understand, because she'd already guessed: Mr Joseph was growing restless because he was so much better nowadays. She'd heard of that before, lads growing out of their weakness if they survived childhood, though of course he'd never be able to walk steadily, poor young man. But why they thought he should choose a wife only from ugly or ill-mannered young women, she didn't know. He had a very sweet nature, Mr Joseph did.

Opening the door slightly, in case anyone wanted to speak to her, she got on with her work. But she kept thinking about Mr Joseph, remembering the times they thought they'd lost him as a child, and realising how well he was looking these days.

Later, she snorted loudly right in the middle of sorting out the linen, making Mabel jump in shock. As the maid stared at her, she said hastily, 'Sorry, dear. I was just remembering something that had annoyed me. Nothing to do with you. It happened years ago. Let's get on with checking the linen.'

But later she saw Mr Joseph make his way back to the library after a solitary evening meal in the breakfast parlour. The master and mistress should make more effort to introduce him to neighbours and people his own age, not just occasional suitable young women. He should make friends and go out on his own. Why did they discourage this so persistently?

She sighed. It was the way he walked. It did look rather ugly. They were ashamed of it and that made him ashamed, which had turned him into a recluse.

It wasn't right. There was nothing wrong with his brain and he was as kind as you please. And he wasn't bad-looking, either, with that soft brown hair and those dark brown eyes.

Well, if permission was given, she'd make sure Harriet was allowed to spend time with him. She could trust that girl not to be cheeky. And if teaching the maid could put that bright, interested look on Mr Joseph's face again, it'd please her greatly.

As she was getting into bed, Mrs Stuart decided that if Mr Joseph continued to get better, and if they continued to keep him too closely confined, there would be trouble ahead. He was a young man, after all, and young men did rebel at times.

But pleasant though she might be, Mrs Dalton wasn't the sort of mistress you could talk to frankly, or offer advice to, especially about the family.

Only, servants couldn't help noticing things. Sometimes they noticed far more than their employers did.

Chapter Five

When Joseph's parents returned briefly from London, he joined them for luncheon, feeling a lift of his spirits when he saw his new box of books being carried towards the library from the rear of the house.

His father was in a good mood, smiling at him across the table. 'I forgot to ask you. How did it go with the young maid last week? Did you find her some easy books to read?'

'She's an intelligent young woman, Father. She doesn't need easy books, only something to feed her brain.'

His father snorted. 'Servants don't need brains; they need brawn and stamina, even the women.'

His mother chimed in unexpectedly. 'They do need brains if they're to rise to the higher positions in a house like this, William. Take Mrs Stuart. She's a clever woman, who manages the household accounts and all the details of running a big house extremely efficiently. I'm sure I could never do such a job half as well. Mrs Miller was intelligent too. In fact, I've been very lucky with my housekeepers here.'

'That's because you treat your staff well, Mama, so they work better for you. And you're right about brains, too. Did you know that just before she came to work here, Harriet won a scholarship to grammar school which would have enabled her to train as a teacher?'

She looked at him in surprise. 'Then why on earth did her family not let her take up the scholarship?'

'Her father died suddenly, and her stepmother wanted her out working and bringing in money.'

'How did you find all that out from the girl so quickly?'

'Oh, I didn't talk about personal things to *her*. We only discuss books. Mrs Stuart and I had a little chat afterwards. She has her eye on young Harriet for advancement, thinks we've got a treasure there. She keeps in touch with Mrs Miller, as you know, and *she* is a relative of the stepmother.'

'Well, we must be sure we keep the girl happy, then. I know it'll be a bore, but if you can spare time to continue helping her select books, do it for me, there's a dear. Good servants are getting harder and harder to find these days. When I hear the tales some of my friends in London tell about impertinent maids, it makes me shudder.'

As the meal ended and the servants cleared away the final dishes, Joseph began to ease his wheelchair away from the table. His parents exchanged quick glances and his mother said, 'Don't go yet, Joseph. Your father and I would like to have a little chat with you.'

He stopped moving, guessing what this was about.

'We've been thinking that we ought to take you out and about more, now that you're so much better. And . . . we need to think seriously about your future.'

'I'm not exactly an asset to a social gathering. I can't even stroll round someone's gardens, let alone dance or play tennis.'

'Nonetheless, you need to meet people your own age and make friends. It may even be useful for you to go up to London to broaden your circle of acquaintances.'

'You know I never feel well there.' It had been true in the past, but Joseph doubted it'd be true now. However, if a lie got him out of going up to London, he'd tell it willingly. He didn't enjoy crowds and the thought of the social round his parents described made him shudder.

'We can think about London later. For the moment, your father and I will spend more time here and entertain more frequently.'

'Mama, if this is about finding me a wife, I don't even want to think about that.'

His father said loudly and firmly, 'Joseph, you *need* to find a wife, so do as your mother tells you.

She knows how to set about it, after helping marry off your brothers and sister.'

'What if I don't meet anyone I can grow fond of?'

His mother's voice was sharper than usual. 'You won't if you decide against it in advance.'

There was silence and he wondered if he dared leave now, but she moved her chair closer to his and took his hand. 'We all have to be practical in this life, Joseph. Marriage for people of our class is as much about the *business* of living as about affection. It's time you began to look for a wife because you're going to *need* one. We won't always be here to care for you.'

He could hire someone to care for him. You didn't have to marry for that. But he didn't say it. Sometimes it was better to listen, nod and go your own way.

His father took over, clearing his throat noisily. 'There's something you don't know, Joseph. I'm afraid the family finances never recovered from the reverses of the eighties and nineties. In fact, they've been stretched pretty thinly over the past few years – establishing three sons in good occupations, giving your sister a dowry and providing a decent income for my heir, especially now that Selwyn has a wife to support.'

Joseph had heard his father complain about money before, but had paid little attention because he'd seen no sign of his parents making any economies in their lifestyle. How short of money could they be?

It suddenly struck him that they'd probably not expected to need to support him as an adult and had made no provision for it. He'd nearly died a few times as a child, when he couldn't breathe properly, but that had gradually stopped happening as he grew older.

'I'm sorry to disappoint you, Father, but I could never live with a woman I didn't like, let alone touch her in bed.'

'Watch how you talk in front of your mother!' his father snapped.

'Sometimes it's better to be frank and we *are* talking about marriage, after all.'

'*Sometimes*, my boy, you should heed the advice of those older and wiser than yourself without arguing. Frankly, if you wish to continue living in comfort for the rest of your life, you need to find a wife with money. Now, don't say anything you may regret. We'll talk about this again in a couple of days' time, once you've had the chance to consider your lack of other financial alternatives.'

His mother let go of his hand, which Joseph took as a sign that he could leave. 'I'll get back to my books, then.' He rolled his wheelchair towards the door without a word, but he knew that nothing they said or did would make him agree to marry a disagreeable young woman like Christina Jeffcott.

And he was quite sure that no charming, pretty young woman would look twice at a penniless cripple like him. He didn't mind considering a wife who wasn't pretty, but he wouldn't tie himself to a person he disliked.

He sighed. The conversation had shown only too clearly what a low value his parents placed on him. Well, he'd known that, really, but he didn't normally allow himself to dwell on it.

He looked down at his twisted body and grimaced. He might be walking more strongly these days, but it was an ugly way of moving and people still averted their eyes from him. He didn't even know whether he could father children, because he'd never had the opportunity to get close to a woman in that way.

But once in a while he grew restless and found himself staring at images of women's bodies in books, finding some of them attractive, responding to them. So perhaps he wasn't totally useless in that respect. He'd probably never find out, though, because he didn't think he could face the humiliation of trying and failing.

Moving his chair across to the window, he sat for a while, staring out at the rain-soaked landscape. Spring had been very wet and even the summer had seemed grey and overcast. The colours outside were as dull as his mood.

What would he do if his parents insisted he marry some girl he detested? Would they threaten to disown him? Carry out the threat? He was totally dependent on them financially.

No, they wouldn't do that because it'd be embarrassing for the family. But they could make his life very difficult. He was only too aware of that.

The following day his mother came into the library during the afternoon. 'Not reading, my dear boy?'

Joseph jumped in shock. He hadn't heard her come in. 'Sorry, Mama. I was miles away.'

'You spend far too much time inside that head of yours.'

'It's quite a pleasant place, with a well-furnished brain to play around in,' he mocked, 'however poor my body is physically.'

She sat down beside him. 'We upset you yesterday, didn't we?'

He chose to misunderstand her. 'About what?'

'I can still tell when you're prevaricating, Joseph. You have a very open face.'

'If you've come to persuade me to marry a woman I dislike for the sake of her money, you're wasting your breath. I couldn't do it, Mama. I just . . . could not.'

'But what alternative is there, darling? This house has to go to the oldest son, and you've never got on with Selwyn, or he with you, so you'll have to move out when your father and I die. We're in our sixties now, so we have to plan for the worst. And you'll only have a couple of thousand pounds plus anything Selwyn can add to it. *If* he'll make you an allowance.'

'I'd not take anything from him.' Selwyn had tormented him as a child, not casually like his other brothers, but unremittingly. Now Selwyn tried to ignore him as much as possible, which suited Joseph just fine. He frowned at her. 'I didn't even know I'd have that much money.'

'My mother left it to you. It's increased a little, I gather. Compound interest, whatever that is. Your father's man of business looks after that sort of thing. It won't be nearly enough to maintain you in any sort of style, though. You won't even be able to buy a house, because you'll need the capital in order to live off the interest, so you'll have to take rooms.'

'Then I'll take rooms and live cheaply, Mama. There are public-lending libraries, so I could still read.'

'And Pollins? What about his wages? How would you manage without his help? Not to mention a maid or two to do your housework?'

He didn't answer, knew she'd hit a sore spot there. Pollins had been with him for years and was far closer to him than most servants were to their masters. And Joseph would definitely need help with the daily chores needed to run a home. Shopping, he supposed, preparing food, washing clothes. How ignorant he was of how most of these things were actually done!

'I'd find a way,' he muttered. 'Others live in lodgings, after all.'

'You'd hate it. No privacy.'

'I'd still have a room of my own.'

She studied his face. 'You're as obstinate as your father, do you know that?'

'Am I? Poor you, then.'

'Your father gets exactly that look on his face when he turns mulish about something. At least promise me you'll give our candidates a chance.'

He hesitated, then said, 'I'll meet them, yes, and be polite to them, but unless I *like* someone, I won't marry her.' Love he didn't expect, but surely liking wasn't too much to expect.

'Thank you, dear.' She stood up and bent to drop one of her light kisses on the top of his head. 'I'll have to think about it very carefully. We must be able to find a young woman you can get on with, if we try hard. Or at least one who won't give you any trouble. As long as you don't expect her to be beautiful.'

She moved towards the door, leaving a sigh drifting behind her. The faint smell of the perfume she always wore lingered in the air after she'd gone.

As did her final words.

The thought of being put on display to miscellaneous spinsters horrified him. How could he bear it?

How could he stop it happening, though? He couldn't be rude to his mother, because, apart from the fact that he loved her, she was only trying to help him in her own way.

And he did have to think about his future. He could at least consider it, as he'd agreed.

But if he had some money of his own, maybe he could build a life somewhere else. A terrifying thought, but . . . also an exciting one.

He'd insist on managing the money himself from now on. Why on earth had they kept the information about it from him?

Because they didn't consider him an equal.

Over the next few months, Joseph was dragged to every house in the neighbourhood. He met the few young ladies who lived nearby, and other young or not-so-young ladies who were connections of the neighbours and who were sent for to visit.

Somehow word had got out that the Daltons were looking for a wife for their youngest. Failures from the mating season in London were being lined up for a last desperate attempt to win a husband, any husband.

As the summer and autumn passed, he grew used to being watched as he limped around parlours.

He grew used to seeing the visiting ladies avert their eyes.

He found it hard to chat to them, not only because he'd led such a sequestered life, but also because he had so little in common with them. None of them seemed very intelligent, or even well read. If they'd read anything, it was poetry or novels. And few expressed opinions of their own, agreeing with whatever he said, or parroting clichés.

And always, always, he was conscious of the way they avoided looking at him when he moved. That was the main factor that decided him against them, all of them.

It was a relief to take refuge in the library when he came home and immerse himself in books. Or just sit and stare into space, worrying, trying to think of a way of persuading his mother not to do this to him, trying to work out a way of *earning* money.

The visit to the library twice a week by Harriet never failed to cheer him up and stimulate him. She was always full of questions about what she'd been reading, or what she'd seen in his father's discarded newspapers. He'd now won permission for her to read these once the housekeeper and cook had finished with them.

Her opinions were her own, some of them giving him a very different view of life.

'Do none of the other servants want to read the newspapers?' he asked idly.

She flushed. 'Mrs Stuart and Cook glance through them. The others don't. They think I'm only pretending to understand them.' She sighed. 'And it's true. I don't understand a lot of what's reported in the news because I've never been anywhere. Could you explain about . . . ?'

And they'd be off. She challenged him mentally. She made him laugh.

She had become . . . a friend in all but name.

His mother came in one day when they were laughing and raised her eyebrows.

Harriet was up from her chair instantly, bobbing a curtsey and edging towards the door.

'Don't go,' his mother said to the maid.

He wished she hadn't, waited in dread for what she'd say.

'Tell me what you're reading, Harriet.'

'The newspaper, ma'am. Mr Joseph is explaining things to me.'

'And do you understand them?'

'Not always, ma'am. But I try.'

'Well, I'd like to chat to my son now . . .'

Harriet picked up her new books and the newspaper, thanked Joseph for his time and trouble, and was out of the door very quickly.

'Do you think she should sit down as if she's your equal, Joseph?'

'She said that, too, when she first came. But it hurts my neck to look up at her, so I told her always to sit down when we're talking.'

'This is the second or is it the third time this week she's been here? Is it really necessary for you to spend so much time with her?'

He spoke slowly, searching for the sort of argument which would convince her. 'I can't do much charity work, Mama, not like you do, but I consider this one way of helping those worse off than myself. It makes me feel a little better about my useless life.'

She looked at him sadly. 'Is that how you feel? Useless?'

He nodded.

'Well, then, keep helping the girl. She always seems very quiet and polite, I must admit. I wonder how old she is now?'

'She was seventeen in June, though she seems older, perhaps because she's been through some hard times in the past year or two. The other servants made a special tea for her. They always do that on someone's birthday, apparently. They clubbed together to give her a present. She hasn't had many presents in her life and the thought of her new box of handkerchiefs made her cry when she told me about it.' He smiled reminiscently.

'Seventeen. Yes, and she's growing fast, isn't she? She was very childlike when she came here, now she's a young woman. Just . . . don't get too personal with her, Joseph.'

He let out a sniff of bitter laughter. 'I couldn't even if I wanted to. *She* is far more aware of the differences in our stations than I am. She'll talk about books till the cows come home, and ask dozens of questions about the world, but she'll hardly say a word about herself. She says it's not proper.'

His mother looked a little happier. 'Oh, well, if *you* regard it as a charity, and *she* knows her place, that's all right. I was worried you might start to develop an affection for the girl. You're a young man at a vulnerable age, after all.'

He flushed and prayed for forgiveness for what he was about to say. 'Develop an affection for a *servant*, Mama? I think not.'

Her whole body relaxed. 'Good. See you don't change your mind about how you should deal with her. I'd not like to lose such a hard-working maid. And you are, after all, a gentleman born and bred.'

'Gentlemen raised by you would never tamper with the servants, I promise you. None of my brothers ever did, either.'

She smiled. 'No. You're right. Your father and I care very greatly about setting and maintaining standards. Now, what I came to tell you was that we're going up to London at the weekend. Do you mind?'

'Not at all. You and Mrs Stuart have the house running so smoothly, I shall be perfectly comfortable.'

'Not . . . lonely?'

He shrugged and avoided a direct answer. 'I'm used to being on my own.'

But he was lonely. The better he felt, the more he wanted to do something with his life.

He had the money he'd inherited tucked away in his own bank account and was adding to it bit by bit, because his father gave him an allowance still. Not nearly as much as they'd given his brothers, but every little helped. Since his father still paid for his boxes of books and he'd stopped spending his allowance on anything but necessities, he was adding to his capital.

He didn't tell them that, of course. He didn't tell anyone else, either, not even Pollins. Well, he didn't have any friends with whom he could exchange confidences. Only Harriet, and he had to tread a very careful line with her.

Chapter Six

1903

In the spring of 1903, Joseph's parents came back from London looking grim. But they refused to discuss what was upsetting them.

His mother stayed at Dalton House for longer than usual, claiming she was worn out by town life. But his father kept going up to London every few days on business.

What business? Joseph wondered. His father usually left that to his man of business or his lawyers.

His mother took him out to meet a couple of young ladies, one of whom turned out to be not so young.

He'd hoped that had fizzled out, but apparently it had been revitalised by whatever was causing his father's bad temper.

He didn't like these ladies any better than the previous ones he'd met. Each had some unpleasant traits, or at least it seemed so to him – even if it was only a way of tittering that would drive him insane if he had to live with it.

* * *

Of course, the servants were well aware of what was going on.

'I'd marry money in a jiffy,' Mabel said. 'Even if it was an old man. Or a cripple.'

'What if you didn't like him?' Harriet asked.

'I'd console myself with his money. Being rich would make me happy enough.'

The kitchen maid laughed. 'You've got a man. Leave the rest of them for us.'

'And be careful with that Jack Porter. Got a bit of a reputation, he has.'

As Mabel blushed bright red, everyone smiled – not nastily, though.

Harriet carried on with her work thinking about the rumours. Mr Joseph might be a cripple, but he was so kind and pleasant, what did that matter? Surely there would be some young lady who could see his virtues and be happy to marry him?

In May Harriet would turn nineteen. It was hard to believe she'd been at Dalton House for three years now but she felt quietly happy there. Her sessions with Mr Joseph made such a difference to her life.

Only one thing about her life upset her, but it upset her a lot: her stepmother was still receiving nearly all her wages and she had nothing to buy new clothes with, so Mrs Stuart had had to find clothes for her, and shabby, old-fashioned clothes they were too.

Her shoes, also second hand, pinched because they

were too small, and there was a hole in one of the soles. And there were so many darns in her stockings, it was a good job they were black and the darns didn't show too badly. She might not be good at sewing but she had had to become a skilful darner.

It wasn't fair. She didn't feel she owed the wages to her stepmother, who had taken all her dad's money and possessions. That should have been enough.

Mrs Miller had advised her to wait until she was eighteen to try to change things. But when Harriet had tried last year, Mrs Stuart had refused to consider it, because her stepmother was her legal guardian till she was twenty-one.

Harriet couldn't face another two years of scrimping like this.

On her nineteenth birthday, she got up as usual, but Mabel stayed in bed. She'd had an upset stomach for the past week and had been sick several times. She'd begged Harriet not to tell anyone.

That had worried her. Being sick in the mornings could be a sign of other problems, and Mabel hadn't had her monthly courses for several weeks. You couldn't help knowing something like that when you lived so closely together.

Just as she was finishing pinning up her hair into the bun she now wore, Mrs Stuart came to the bedroom. At that moment Mabel vomited into the slop bowl.

The housekeeper stood by the door, watching, then turned to Harriet. 'Has she been sick before?'

She hesitated, then nodded.

Mrs Stuart folded her arms. 'Well, there's only one thing it can be and she can't hide it any longer.'

Mabel turned white as a sheet, her eyes rolled up and she crumpled on the floor in a faint.

'Let's get her on the bed.' Mrs Stuart took Mabel's feet and they lifted the unconscious young woman up.

As she began to recover, Mabel saw the housekeeper's grim expression and burst into tears.

'I'd have thought you'd have more sense, Mabel Ashton!'

The sobs grew louder.

Harriet backed towards the door. 'I should leave you and—'

'No, stay. I shall need your help.' Mrs Stuart turned back to Mabel. 'Whose is it? Will he marry you?'

'It's Jack Porter's and we're engaged. I'd not have done it otherwise. I was going to give notice at the end of the month on quarter day, to leave at the end of September, so that I could earn some more money.'

'Well, you'll have to leave earlier now, won't you? You couldn't have hidden it until then, anyway. You'd have been too big. The mistress won't want a pregnant maid staying on, let alone opening the door to people. You'd better write a note to your Jack and I'll send Billings over to the Porters' farm with it. Ask your young man to come and fetch you straight away.'

Mabel mopped her tears and nodded, seeming suddenly resigned.

111

'In the meantime, Harriet will help you pack and, since the mistress is away, we'll skimp on the housework for once. Your wages will be paid up to yesterday.'

They waited till her footsteps had faded on the stairs, then Mabel sat up, spots of red in her cheeks. 'Miserable old devil. She might have let me work a month longer, at least.' Her stomach rumbled loudly and she looked at Harriet pleadingly. 'Could you get me something to eat, do you think? Now I've been sick, I'm ravenous.'

'But you're all right? About marrying Jack and everything, I mean. He *will* marry you?'

Mabel shrugged. 'We're engaged, aren't we? His parents won't be best pleased at us having to get married in a hurry, but they'll cheer up when I present them with their first grandchild.'

In the kitchen Cook swung round. 'Is it true?'

Harriet stopped in surprise. 'Is what true?'

'That Mabel's in the family way and has been dismissed.'

How had they found out so quickly? 'She's leaving to get married, yes.'

'Well, it's one way of catching a husband who's younger than yourself. He'll inherit the farm one day, that Jack will, so she's done well for herself in one way, at least.'

'You sound as if you don't like him.'

'A leopard doesn't change its spots. He likes the women too much, that one does. He'll give her grief.'

'Can I take Mabel something to eat, please? Then Mrs Stuart says I have to help her pack and stay with her till she leaves.'

Jack arrived within the hour, plonked a cheerful kiss on his betrothed's cheek and got Billings to help him get her trunk down the back stairs.

Mabel turned at the bedroom door, grinned and pulled off her maid's cap, screwing it up into a ball and throwing it at Harriet. 'Here. You take it. I'm never wearing such a horrid, old-fashioned thing again. Slaves, that's what servants are. Nothing but slaves!'

Some would say Mabel had disgraced herself, but Harriet envied her. Mabel would have a husband and family. *She* wouldn't be on her own in the world.

Then Harriet squared her shoulders. She was doing all right, wasn't she? Earning her living, had the respect of the rest of the household.

But now it was time to take a stand about her wages. Only then would she feel right about her life here.

Harriet raced through her tasks, doing as much of Mabel's work as she could, wondering if her sessions with Mr Joseph would be cancelled till they found a replacement maid.

When it came time to go to the library, she went to

see Mrs Stuart first. 'Do we have time for me to talk to Mr Joseph today? There's still a lot to do.'

'Since Mr and Mrs Dalton are in London, and it's Mr Joseph's needs we're serving, I think it's more important that you see him.' Her eyes were twinkling as she gestured towards the fancy, lace-trimmed aprons hanging ready for those serving the family. 'Wash your hands and change. Don't keep him waiting.'

Mr Joseph was standing by the window staring out at the gardens. He turned as Harriet knocked and went in. 'Happy birthday.'

'Thank you. How did you know?'

'Mrs Stuart told me.' He looked at her hair and nodded. 'I see you've decided you're grown up now.'

'I think I've been grown up for a while, but I couldn't be bothered to change. My hair will only slip out of the pins.'

'You're always very correct, aren't you?'

'I try to be.' But she thought of what she intended to do tomorrow and her heart lurched in her chest.

'What's wrong?'

'Nothing.' She tried to smile.

'There is something. Tell me. You know what they say – a trouble shared . . .'

She hesitated, then couldn't help it. She desperately needed to talk to someone. 'It's about my wages.'

'What about them? Don't we pay you enough?'

'Oh, no, no. It's not that. It's my stepmother. She takes all my wages except for a shilling a week, and she'd take that too if she knew about it. Mrs Miller suggested to Mrs Stuart that I keep just a little back.'

'That explains it!'

She looked at him in puzzlement. 'Explains what?'

'Why you never wear any other clothes than your uniform, even when you've got your day off, and why your stocking are more darns than original stockings.'

'Oh.' Shame sent heat into her cheeks.

His voice was gentle. 'I can't help noticing things. I spend a lot of my time watching people. Don't you have any money apart from that shilling a week?'

She shook her head. 'Just the tips, only there haven't been as many of those lately, because it's been very quiet here.'

'That's not fair, them leaving you so little money when you work so hard.'

'I was thinking . . .' Once again she hesitated, then the rest of it tumbled out. 'I thought I'd ask Mrs Stuart if she could pay all my wages to me from now on, then I could buy new clothes and save something for a rainy day.'

'It seems very reasonable to me.'

'Really, truly?'

'Yes. Really, truly.' He limped across to the desk and picked up a parcel wrapped in brown paper. 'Anyway, I bought you a present.'

'Oh! You shouldn't have.'

'It's only something small. Go on. Open it.'

She'd guessed what was in the square package

already. A book. But she found it was two, a novel by Marie Corelli, *A Romance of Two Worlds*, and one by Rudyard Kipling, *Kim*. She looked at Mr Joseph uncertainly. 'I thought . . . I'm sure I heard the mistress say that Marie Corelli was a shocking person.'

'Mama has never read any of her books – well, she isn't much of a reader. If anyone complains about what you're reading, tell them Miss Corelli is the Queen's favourite author and Her Majesty owns all her books.'

'Goodness. Does she really? I'm in excellent company, then.'

'And no one can complain about you reading Mr Kipling. He's very popular. This is a fairly recent book.'

'You still shouldn't have done this.' People would talk if they knew.

'I wanted to. And I thought you should enjoy some light reading. You read some fearsomely difficult books.'

'I like to learn things.' She stroked the covers of the books, then looked at him. 'Thank you. It was very thoughtful of you. I shall always treasure them.'

'Good.' He moved back to the desk.

She dared say something personal. 'You're using the wheeled chair far less during the day. I do hope you're feeling better.'

'I'll never walk straight, but I can move about now. Mama – well, she'd wrap me in cotton wool, if she could.'

He scowled suddenly, adding as if speaking to himself, 'Or marry me off to a rich fool, and I won't agree to that.'

'You should only marry someone who's intelligent,' Harriet said. 'That'd be a proper match for you. You have a fine mind.'

'Thank you for the compliment. I really value it, coming from you.'

This conversation was getting dangerously personal, she thought, and tried to think of something else to talk about.

Mr Joseph must have agreed because he changed the subject. 'Well, tell me about your reading. Have you finished that book?'

The personal confidences were at an end. She was relieved. Though it had been nice to chat.

Almost as if they were friends.

When their hour finished and she left the library, Harriet went to change out of the fancy apron, but before she could do it, one of the other maids came to find her, 'Mrs Stuart wants to see you. At once.'

'I'll go right up to her room.'

The housekeeper's door was open, so Harriet knocked and peered in.

'Ah, there you are. How was Mr Joseph?'

'He seemed well.'

'What's in your parcel?'

'Mr Joseph gave me a birthday present. Is it all

right to keep them?' She held out her two treasures for inspection.

'Books? Oh yes, that's all right. He's such a kind young man. All the servants like helping him. Now, come and sit down. I want to talk to you.'

When Harriet was seated at the other side of the desk, Mrs Stuart studied her. 'You look older with your hair up, and that's a good thing, given what I'm going to say.'

She waited, hands clasped loosely in her lap.

'I'm going to offer you a try as head housemaid.'

'Me?'

'Yes. You know the work and I know I can rely on you.'

'Have you found someone else already for my job?'

'Yes. I started looking round when I guessed about Mabel. A girl from one of the nearby farms is starting tomorrow. Lyddie's only fourteen, but she's strong and willing. We need someone else as well, really, but I shall look around. You can't be too careful these days.' She cocked her head on one side. 'It'll mean a rise in wages, of course.'

Harriet took a deep breath. 'I was going to speak to you about my wages and ask you not to pay them to my stepmother from now on.'

'I'm sorry, but as I told you last year, I can't do that until you're twenty-one.'

'How can I be head housemaid, when I don't even have proper clothes to wear? My stepmother wasn't married to Dad for long and never did anything for me. I shouldn't have had to give her anything.'

'Hmm. I tell you what I'll do. We'll go on paying her the same amount, and you can have the difference between that and your new wages.'

Harriet shook her head. 'I'm sorry to disappoint you, but I feel very strongly about this, and if necessary I'll leave and find a job elsewhere. Mrs Miller agrees I should get my wages now.' And had offered to give her a reference because she said Winifred had disappointed her. She wouldn't say why, but after that one comment she'd stopped mentioning her niece at all.

'She agrees? Well . . . I'll consult the mistress when she comes back.'

'Thank you. That's very kind of you. I do appreciate it. I don't want to leave.'

'I don't want to lose you, but that doesn't mean you've won. Get back to work now.'

When Harriet had gone, Mrs Stuart sighed. She didn't blame the girl, but she could see trouble ahead if the stepmother made a fuss.

She'd do it if it were left up to her, but she could change nothing without Mrs Dalton's approval. She was not the employer here.

Joseph's mother came into the library and sat down beside him, saying brightly, 'You and I are going to have tea with General Mortimer, his sister and her husband tomorrow. And his niece.'

Joseph didn't groan aloud, but he wanted to. He didn't like the general at all, who always spoke to him slowly and clearly, as if he were an idiot, and barked orders at those he considered his inferiors.

'You'll behave yourself, won't you, dear?'

'Don't I always?'

'You become very quiet in company. I do wish you'd chat more.'

'They stare at me when I move. I feel like an animal in the zoo. Animals aren't famous for chatting.'

'Nonsense. You're too sensitive. And even if they're a little . . . surprised at first, they'd soon get used to you if you gave them the chance.'

But would he get used to them averting their eyes when he walked across a room, he wondered? 'What's this one like?'

'Pleasant but a little stupid, I gather. Do be kind to her.'

What did she mean by 'a little stupid' he wondered? None of the young women had seemed very intelligent to him. Oh well, he'd soon find out.

The following afternoon Joseph followed his mother and their host into the house. His stomach began churning with the usual nervousness as all eyes turned to watch him walk across the room. For once, the young woman stared solemnly, didn't shudder, didn't look hastily away.

Was that a good thing or bad?

The general introduced them to Mr and Mrs Baudrey, then to their daughter Geraldine, who was fair-haired and pretty enough to make him wonder why she hadn't found a husband already.

They seated him next to her on the sofa. Could anything have been more obvious?

She continued to smile and he quickly realised it was a rather vacant expression.

When he addressed a remark to her, she replied to his platitudes with her own, speaking as if she'd learnt the phrases by heart.

'Fine summer we're having, Miss Baudrey.'

'Oh, yes. Summer is a very nice time of year.'

'Do you live nearby?'

'We live near Bournemouth. We're visiting my uncle. Bournemouth is a very popular seaside town.' A pause, then, as her mother flapped a hand at her from across the room, she added, 'Do you live nearby, Mr Dalton?'

Surely they'd told her where he lived?

She listened to his reply with that same fixed smile, didn't continue the conversation, sat smiling vacuously. It was beginning to worry him how like an automaton she was.

Her mother interrupted, starting them off on a discussion about Miss Baudrey's pet dog. Again, it was as if the daughter had learnt the responses by heart.

As the conversation limped along, he realised that Miss Baudrey was more than a stupid young woman.

They might dress her womanly body in fine clothes, but her mind was still that of a child. And not a very clever child at that.

Her eyes gave away her anxiety. She turned again and again to her mother to check that everything was all right.

He was relieved when tea was brought in and the conversation became broader. Afterwards the general suggested sitting in the garden, and to Joseph's relief, Geraldine ignored her mother's frowns and plumped down on the grass to make daisy chains.

He let the other adults do the talking and watched the poor girl fiddling with the flowers, then hanging one chain of daisies round her wrist.

Her mother was looking daggers at her, so he bent down and asked her to make him a chain, putting it on his own wrist. That at least seemed to please the mother.

When it came time to leave, she put her arm round her daughter's shoulders and expressed a hope that they'd see him again soon.

He didn't share her hope, so merely inclined his head.

There was no point in trying to talk frankly to his mother in the carriage, since it wasn't a long drive and they had the top down, so could be overheard. It was an effort to hold his anger in until they got back.

'I see your father's returned. Come and join us in the sitting room, Joseph dear,' his mother said when he'd dragged himself up the steps and through the front door to where she was waiting for him. 'Ah, here's Pollins with your wheelchair. You must be tired now.'

He was tired, and his back and hip were aching. He wanted nothing more than to lie down with a hot-water bottle and rest. But he couldn't refuse to join his parents, so followed his mother into the sitting room, guessing what was coming.

His father gave one of his harrumphs and took up his favourite position in front of the fire.

'Did your business in London go well, William?'

'No. Things were worse than I'd expected.'

'Oh dear.' His mother sat down in her favourite armchair.

'How did your tea party go?'

'Geraldine's a charming girl, isn't she, Joseph? Pretty, too.'

He shrugged, unwilling to agree to make any complimentary remark about the general's niece in case it gave them ammunition for their arguments.

'We're hoping you'll see your way to getting better acquainted with Geraldine, Joseph dear. She'll come into a substantial amount of money when she marries, a very nice sum indeed. And though she can't afford to be picky about a husband, because she *is* rather stupid, her parents are concerned to find her a *kind* husband, one who'll look after her.'

'I'm not interested in the job, thank you very much. And I'm picky about a wife.'

His mother made a gentle shushing noise. 'Don't speak hastily, my dear. Remember, it'd set you up for life in great comfort if you married Geraldine.'

Joseph looked from one to the other. 'Even if I intended to marry – which I don't – I could never marry someone like her. She's a child still, and always will be. Stop pretending she's merely stupid. It's far worse than that and living with her would bore me to tears . . . if it didn't drive me insane first. And what if the taint passed to her children?'

'You needn't have children by her.'

'That is surely one of the main purposes of marriage?' And watching one of the gardeners with his son over the past year or so had made Joseph realise that he'd like to have children. That had surprised him.

'I'm not going to get angry at you,' his father declared, 'because I can see this has come as a shock. We'll give you time to get used to the idea.'

'I shall never get used to the idea of marrying that poor helpless creature for her money – nor could I sentence myself to a life with her.'

His father looked across at his mother. '*You* talk to him! He's obviously in one of his moods. I've been patient long enough. This must be sorted out. Especially after what I found out in London.'

When his father had gone, the silence was deafening.

Then his mother said quietly, 'Your father is quite determined about this.'

'So am I.'

'Think about it, my dear boy. You'd have your own home.'

'With Geraldine.'

'You needn't see her except at mealtimes. She has a devoted maid who looks after her and a dog to play with.'

'Dolls as well, I suppose? What sort of marriage would that be? A travesty. People would laugh at us and we'd be social outcasts.'

He rolled his chair back. 'No, Mama. There is no argument you can bring to bear on me that will make me agree to marry her.'

Chapter Seven

The other servants were full of it. Mr Joseph had quarrelled with his parents and the master was furious, snapping at everyone, family and servants alike, not caring who heard what he said to his son.

Harriet listened to the gossip, wondering how much of it was true. Mr Joseph was so quiet and polite, she couldn't imagine him quarrelling with anyone.

'Has Mr Joseph said anything to you?' Cook asked.

'No, of course not. We only ever talk about books. I'd not presume to discuss his personal life, let alone ask him embarrassing questions, any more than he would ask me such things.'

Mrs Stuart came into the room. 'Quite right, Harriet. And the rest of you shouldn't be discussing the family's business, either.'

But that didn't stop the gossip when the housekeeper wasn't nearby, and though she didn't join in, Harriet couldn't help overhearing the titbits of information they'd overheard and then passed round in whispers.

The quarrel was because the master had found a young lady for Mr Joseph and they were determined that he'd marry her.

The young lady had a lot of money, no one had any idea how much.

No one knew what she was like, but they guessed ugly, or why else would she marry a cripple?

Joseph watched his parents get out of the carriage which had brought them from the railway station and enter the house. They'd gone rushing up to London two days previously after receiving a telegram.

They both looked tight-lipped as he ran his wheelchair into the drawing room to greet them. His mother was standing holding one hand to her forehead, an ominous sign. When he went across, she reached out to grasp his hand briefly, then flung herself down in her favourite armchair.

'Didn't you enjoy your visit this time, Mama?'

'Not all of it.' She looked at her husband as if asking him to take over the conversation.

'We've run into a bit of trouble, I'm afraid. Well, more than a bit. It's Selwyn – to cut a long story short, he's been spending too much and needs his debts paying. We're going to find it hard to do that.'

Joseph could feel himself stiffening. He hoped this wasn't leading round to him. And trust Selwyn to overspend. He already had a huge allowance but used the excuse of being the heir to a country mansion to indulge himself in whatever took his fancy, without counting the cost, not to mention gambling on anything that moved.

'We shall have to rent out the town house to some rich Americans or some rich industrialist.'

'That's . . . terrible.'

'As a result, we really need to sort out your future once and for all, to make sure you're secure. Just in case Selwyn does it again.'

Joseph felt angry at that. Why should his life be dictated by what Selwyn did? 'Oh? Who are you going to introduce me to next?'

'We saw the Baudreys in town. They're still interested.'

'Well, I haven't changed my mind.'

'They'll agree to you having your own quarters if you marry Geraldine. You'll only need to see her at breakfast and dinner.'

'And even that would be too much. I feel sorry for the poor girl, I really do, but I'm not tying myself to her for the rest of my life.'

'You're not likely to find anyone else to marry who can offer you as much.'

Joseph stared at him in amazement. '*Offer me as much?* She can't offer me anything I'd want from a wife.'

'Then you're a fool. You need money and she can offer you plenty of that.'

'I don't want to get married at all. I know what

I am.' He looked down at his twisted body with a grimace.

'I'm sorry, but I must insist.'

Joseph looked at his father. 'You can't insist. I'm over twenty-one.' He wondered suddenly if he could get a job as a tutor. He was enjoying teaching Harriet, seeing her mind develop. It might be worth looking in the newspapers, seeing what sort of tutoring jobs were advertised. If he could earn his keep, he could let the interest on his small inheritance build up over the years.

How much did it cost to live simply, in a small house, anyway? He didn't even know that.

A hand on his shoulder made him glance sideways. Only his mother touched him like that. He'd not noticed her coming to stand beside him. 'Joseph dear, I'm afraid I agree with your father. We need to get you settled.'

'But not imprisoned in an unbearable situation, surely?'

She looked across at her husband. 'Perhaps we can look round for other possible matches, William.'

'People prepared to put up with a cripple don't grow on every tree, dammit. You've been looking for two years now. And you know we agreed to stand firm about this, Sophie.'

Joseph dug his fingers into the palms of his hands. *Cripple*. How he hated that word. And though he already knew and was hurt by the way his father was ashamed of him, it wasn't usually brought out into the open so brutally.

'But we can surely give Joseph time to consider his future more carefully? Get used to the idea?' his mother pleaded, squeezing his shoulder gently.

'We've given him time, dammit all.'

His father did that, too, Joseph thought, talked as if he was too stupid to understand. He shouted, 'I'm here with you and there's nothing wrong with my hearing. If you have something to say, say it to me, not to my mother.'

He was pleased to see his father look shocked at this, opening and shutting his mouth as if he didn't know what to say.

Joseph was so furious he turned his chair round and wheeled it out of the room. They didn't try to stop him so he paused outside the door to eavesdrop, not ashamed of doing it, either. Sometimes it was the only way to find things out.

He saw his mother's reflection in the hall mirror. She'd gone across to her husband and was standing close to him. Her voice sounded clearly.

'Well, let's give him a little more time, William. It's a big step to take. I'll talk to him again when we're all calmer, reason with him gently.'

'He's beyond reason. What we need to do is threaten him with what will happen if he doesn't do as we ask.'

Joseph could just imagine his father glaring at her, jutting out his chin in that stubborn way he had.

'He'll come round. He's a reasonable boy and—'

'*Boy?* He's a young man now, turned twenty-three as he just pointed out! You baby him too much. I'm going to threaten him with a dose of reality. I've had enough of soft words and coaxing. He needs stronger medicine.'

Joseph decided he'd better make his way to the library. He didn't want one of the servants to catch him eavesdropping, or worse still, his father.

Harriet too had heard much of what her employers had been saying, because sounds carried in the spacious hall and stairwell. Why they so rarely bothered to close the doors, she didn't understand. Did they think the servants were deaf?

She shouldn't have been listening, but with them going on at Mr Joseph, she couldn't help stopping on the landing above just for a moment.

When he came out of the drawing room, he stopped to listen too, and she didn't blame him for eavesdropping. Her heart went out to him, he looked so unhappy.

She didn't move until he'd continued on his way and closed the library door behind him.

Then she went quietly about her work. At one point, she stopped to shake her head at the Daltons thinking they were short of money. She'd consider herself rich beyond her wildest dreams if she had even a hundredth of what they possessed.

It wasn't likely she'd ever be rich, but if she was, she wouldn't waste it on living so extravagantly and selfishly. She'd live in modest comfort and take great satisfaction in helping others.

But she wasn't rich, so she'd better get on with her work.

Mrs Stuart was called to her mistress's small sitting room. 'Welcome back, ma'am.'

Mrs Dalton gestured to a chair. 'It's good to be here. I don't know why, but London seemed so grey and dirty, far worse than usual. Is everything all right?'

'Well . . . there's something else I need to tell you, ma'am. It's Harriet.'

'Never tell me she's in trouble too?'

'Oh, no, ma'am, certainly not. She's not at all interested in men and she's still one of the best workers we've ever had. I know she's young, but I've taken it upon myself to promote her to head housemaid, as we discussed. I wouldn't have done it in London, but in a country house her age is not as important. It is about getting the work done, after all.'

'I don't mind at all.'

'There's a small problem, though, and I've not been able to persuade Harriet to let this matter drop. We've been sending most of her wages to her stepmother and Harriet wants that to stop. We turned the same request down last year, but perhaps we should reconsider now. Apparently the woman was only married to her father for a short time and there doesn't seem to be any love lost between the two of them.'

'Then let the girl keep her wages.'

'She's under twenty-one. The stepmother could make a fuss, claim she's the legal guardian – though I don't know whether she is. But she could make a nasty fuss and cause gossip, and I know how you'd hate that. I suggested not telling the woman about the promotion and continuing to send her the same amount of money, but giving Harriet the rest.'

'That's a good idea. Do it.'

'Harriet won't hear of it. She says if she's not to get her wages, what's the point of working so hard and she'll go and find a job elsewhere.'

Mrs Dalton let out a sigh that was more like a groan. 'The servant question raising its ugly head! I thought I was safe from that sort of thing here in the country. What is the world coming to when a young woman of nineteen tries to tell her employer what to do?'

'I can see her point.'

'Yes. But as you said, we can't go against the law and we definitely don't want gossip just when we're trying to arrange Joseph's future. Tell Harriet she must do as you suggested.'

'And if she still won't . . . if she leaves?'

'Then she'll have to leave. We've been more than

kind to her, letting her study with my son, promoting her at a very young age. No. She must do as I say. I'll not be dictated to by a servant. As if it isn't enough for my son to defy his father.'

She hesitated, then leant forward to confide her troubles.

Mrs Stuart sometimes thought that if they had been of the same station in life, they'd have been good friends. But she never let herself forget that she was only the housekeeper. There was always something to sort out in a large household, but Mrs Stuart was a bit worried about the stubborn look that had accompanied the girl's refusal to compromise.

She wished Mrs Dalton had given in on this.

When Harriet went to see Mr Joseph later, he noticed that her eyes were puffy and red-rimmed, and her usual eager smile was missing.

'What's the matter?'

'Nothing.'

'I think there is. Tell me, Harriet.'

'They won't pay me my wages, Mr Joseph. And I've been doing my sums. I don't have enough money to live on if I try to find other work.'

His heart went out to her. The world was full of injustices. 'How much would you need to live on temporarily if you left?'

'I don't know. About five pounds, I suppose, just in case I have trouble finding another place. There is a shortage of servants . . . but I wouldn't have a reference from my employer, only from Mrs Miller.'

'If necessary, I'll forge one for you, pretend I'm my mother.'

She gaped at him. 'Really?'

'Yes, really. But I hope this can be settled without you leaving. I should miss you greatly.'

'I'd miss . . . our lessons together.'

He smiled at her. 'It's a bit more than that, isn't it? I feel that you've become a friend now.'

He saw from her face that she felt the same. Their times together were the high points of his week. 'Don't you agree?' he prompted softly, wanting her to say the words.

'Yes. We are friends. You're the only real friend I have.'

'Then you must allow me as your *friend* to give you money in case of emergencies.' He limped across to his desk, opened the top drawer and pulled out a coin purse. 'There you are. Five sovereigns. Just in case.'

When she didn't move, he walked across to her and tipped them into her hand, closing her fingers round the coins. 'Put them somewhere safe.' He didn't want to let go of her hand, but he forced himself to do so.

'I shouldn't accept.'

'Five pounds is very little to me.' Though that might change.

'I'll pay you back once things settle.'

'You don't have to.'

'I do. I'd not respect myself if I didn't.'

She put them in her apron pocket. 'I'm afraid I don't feel like talking about books today, Mr Joseph, if you don't mind. I can't seem to settle to anything until I know what's going to happen to me.'

'Then let me ask for your help instead. I'm trying to gather some information because I've got problems too.'

'About marrying Miss Baudrey?'

He looked at her in surprise.

'We servants can't help overhearing things the family say, because they leave the doors open and speak so freely.'

He explained in more detail about Geraldine, feeling angry all over again at what his parents wanted him to do.

'You'd be unhappy with her,' Harriet agreed.

'I do have some money, because I inherited two thousand pounds. It's not a fortune and I don't know whether the interest on that will be enough for me to live on. Do *you* know how much a small house costs to rent, how much food costs every week, how much it'd cost to hire a general maid?'

Harriet felt happy to be able to help him in return and began to give him facts and figures. She was good at arithmetic, her teachers had always said.

As he listened, Mr Joseph rested his elbows on the

desk and clasped his hands under his chin. The gold cufflink nearest to her gleamed in the sunlight as if trying to send her a message.

She stopped talking and pointed to it. 'I've seen you wearing other gold cufflinks. Do they belong to you or to the family?'

'They're mine, of course. They were presents. I have quite a few sets.'

'And you have a pocket watch with a gold chain. That's worth a lot of money, too.'

He stared down at his cufflinks, clearly not having considered the value of his other possessions, so she waited to get his attention again.

When he looked up, he was beaming at her. 'You've given me the answer. I inherited my godmother's jewellery as well as having valuables of my own. There's quite a lot of it. She said in her will that she hoped I'd give it to a wife one day. She died when I was quite small, so she didn't see how twisted I grew. My father says a normal woman wouldn't even consider marrying a cripple like me.'

There was pain in his eyes as he looked down at himself. Harriet wished she could hug him and tell him he was as lovable as anyone else. 'That's not true! A lot of women would be happy to marry you.'

'You don't have to lie to me.'

'I'm not lying. Your father's wrong. You're a kind man and that's worth a lot. And your face is . . . nice to look at, gentle and . . .' She could feel herself blushing as she added, 'Your face is actually quite good-looking, Mr Joseph. It's far nicer than Mr Selwyn's. I think people's nature shows on their faces.'

His mother should have told him this sort of thing, to help build his confidence, Harriet thought. Or his nurse, only she'd died when he was thirteen, Mrs Stuart said. Since then, he'd had Pollins, who'd been promoted from gardener to manservant because he was strong and could carry Mr Joseph if necessary.

Mr Joseph didn't look as if he believed her, so she said firmly, 'I'm telling you the truth. Your face *is* good-looking.'

For a few moments their eyes met and he blushed slightly.

'You're giving me hope, Harriet, on all sorts of fronts.'

'If you don't need to marry a fine lady, I'm sure you'll find someone who'll care about you and not care about the problems you have, someone who'd enjoy being your companion and wife.' He reached out to pat her hand. She turned her hand in his and gave it a quick squeeze. Warmth seemed to flow between them, from the friendship they dared not acknowledge in more than whispered words.

Then the moment was over, and she was sorry.

'I did wonder if I could earn some money tutoring.'

'I don't think teachers earn much, not enough to live as the gentry do, anyway.'

'But anything I could earn would help, and it'd give me something to do. I get so bored.'

She gave him a wry smile. 'We servants have too much to do and you have too little, Mr Joseph. It's a strange world, isn't it?'

His mother walked into the library. 'Oh. Are you here *again*, Harriet?'

She stood up and began lying without even thinking about it, anxious only to protect him. 'Mr Joseph was just finishing. Would you like a tea tray, ma'am?'

'Yes. Good idea. And bring some cake.'

She turned her back as if the maid had already vanished.

Harriet walked out feeling the extra weight in her apron pocket as it bumped against her leg. That money might make the difference between freedom and working for almost nothing.

If she'd given him hope, well, he'd given it to her as well.

His friendship meant the world to her. She hoped nothing would happen to separate them.

When the maid had gone, Joseph's mother said shrewishly, 'You spend far too much time with that girl.'

'She *is* one of our maids. Am I not allowed to send for a tea tray?'

'You know what I mean. She was sitting down in your presence.'

'We already agreed that she should do that, because it makes my neck ache to look up for long.'

She let out a little sniff of irritation. 'I think we'll restrict Harriet's visits to a few minutes from now on, just to borrow books and she must remain standing. It'd be unfair to stop her reading in order to punish you.'

He was surprised at how upset he felt at the thought of missing his little chats. Then he realised what his mother had said. *Punish*. As if he were a child.

'Did you hear me? She can come for five minutes to change her books, and that's it.'

'Because you feel the need to punish me, she must suffer. And are you going to continue paying her wages to her stepmother, Mama?'

'Of course.'

'Why?'

'Partly because I'm not having a servant threaten me, but mainly because she's under twenty-one, however capable she is. We certainly don't want the stepmother coming here and making a fuss. What would people think?'

'Who cares what people think? I happen to agree with her. I don't think it's fair that Harriet should work so hard for nothing.'

'Are you getting fond of that girl, Joseph?'

'Not in the way you mean, Mama. She *is* after all a servant.' He hated speaking like that about her, but it was necessary to protect her.

'Yes, and *she* should remember that, too. Giving me ultimatums, indeed. I never heard the like.'

She waved one hand dismissively. 'But I didn't come here to talk about a maid. It's you I'm concerned about. You simply must face facts, Joseph. We all have to do that. Your father and I will have to make some serious economies in our way of life from now on. We're even thinking of selling the London house, though I should hate to do that, so we'll try renting it to someone first. We can't sell Dalton House, because it always goes to the eldest son, but I'd rather live here anyway, in the circumstances.'

'Are things really that bad financially?'

'Yes. We keep telling you.' She dabbed at her eyes. 'If Selwyn doesn't keep his promise about not getting into any more debt, your father will have to put a notice in the papers that he will not be held responsible for his heir's debts. Imagine the shame of that! If it happens, I could no longer show my face in London.'

He had never seen her so upset. 'Is there anything I can do? I can stop ordering new books, for a start.'

'It'd be much more helpful if you married Geraldine. Your father didn't tell you, but they're prepared to make a payment to the family, as well as setting you up in your own home with her.'

It annoyed him all over again that *he* should be asked to make up for the money Selwyn was wasting. 'I couldn't marry her, and nothing you say or do will change my mind about that.'

'Joseph, please reconsider. For the family's sake.'

'I'm not marrying that poor child, Mama. She isn't fit to be married. And even I, cripple though I am, deserve better than a half-wit wife.' He stared at her without flinching, hoping she would believe him once and for all.

She obviously did.

'Your father will be furious.' With a sob, she ran out of the room.

Sophie ran back to her husband, weeping, not caring that Harriet was just bringing the tea tray to the library.

'I've changed my mind, William. I don't think Joseph will be won over by reason. You'll have to . . . deal with him. I've already forbidden him to hold those sessions with the maid, but it made no difference.'

'I shall do a lot more than that.' But his wife wasn't listening.

'As if a female like that needs educating anyway. She was probably only pretending to read those boring books of his. I'm sure I wouldn't understand half of what's in them – or want to. I only allowed it because it made him happy. Now, I'm wondering if he's grown fond of her. He denies it, of course, but I'm going to keep a closer eye on things from now on.'

'The maid's certainly pretty, though she doesn't flaunt it at you like some. You sound as if you're angry with her as well.'

'Because she's defying me and I *won't* have a servant do that.'

He blinked in shock. 'I beg your pardon?'

She explained, ending, 'And apparently, she's threatened to leave if we don't pay the money to her.'

'Sack her immediately.'

'I would, but it's getting really hard to find properly trained maids. I wondered . . . William, I know the servants are my business, but if *you* had a word with Harriet, a very stern word, then surely she'd stop making a fuss?'

'I'll be happy to do that. No time like the present, eh?' He went across to the bell pull and when Harriet answered it, he said curtly, 'Fetch Mrs Stuart and come back with her.'

After a quick look of shock, her face became expressionless. 'Yes, sir.'

When she went out, she met Joseph in the hall and stepped aside for him to pass.

'What's the matter now, Harriet?'

'I have to fetch the housekeeper and go back with her. It'll be about my wages.' She didn't wait for an answer, but hurried to the rear of the house.

He hesitated, then wheeled himself into the small room next to the front door. When the two servants had gone into the drawing room, he'd come out and eavesdrop again, much as he disliked doing that.

He waited, wondering why so many bad things were happening at once. He had a sense of foreboding, as if something terrible was going to happen. He'd had feelings like this before, and they'd always presaged unpleasantness.

But he wasn't going to change his mind and he suspected that Harriet wouldn't change hers, either.

Her friendship was the only good thing in his life and he wasn't going to abandon her. Somehow he'd find a way to help her.

He didn't intend to lose touch with her, either.

Harriet followed Mrs Stuart into the drawing room and remained standing next to the half-open door while the housekeeper moved forward a couple of steps. Harriet waited for someone to tell her to close the door, but they didn't, so she didn't offer. She was beyond caring who overheard.

'I gather there is a problem with Harriet and her wages, Mrs Stuart,' Mr Dalton said. 'Has she agreed to be sensible or is she still refusing to do as she's told?'

'I . . .' The housekeeper hesitated, looking at Harriet, then risked a small lie. 'She's decided to be sensible.'

The master moved to stand in front of Harriet, looming over her.

'Is that so, young woman? Have you decided to be sensible and do as you're told?'

'I'm afraid Mrs Stuart must have mistaken something I said. I can't work for no wages. Look at my stockings!' She stuck out one slender ankle.

'They're nothing but darns. I have no decent clothes. And I work as hard as anyone could. I pride myself on that.'

'She's telling the truth about that, sir,' Mrs Stuart put in quickly, seeing the master turn a dark-red colour. 'I've had to give her old clothes from the attic.'

His voice was harsh. 'That's not the point. I won't tolerate disobedience from my servants. Either you agree to accept the increase in the wages, as Mrs Dalton has ordered, or you leave my employment.'

'I'll have to leave, then, sir, though I'll be sorry to do so.'

'Then I shall take you back to your stepmother myself. Be ready to set out with me tomorrow morning.'

Mrs Stuart gasped. What had got into the master? He had been very short-tempered and autocratic lately. 'Sir, please could you—'

'Quiet!'

'I don't need taking anywhere. I can find my own way,' Harriet said quietly.

'You're under age. Did you think we'd let you wander the country on your own?'

'I came here on my own in the first place and I was much younger then.'

'Don't be so impudent. I'll say it one final time: you're a minor. If you leave our supervision, you're under your stepmother's control still. Which is why your wages must be paid to her till you're twenty-one.'

That was when Harriet let her anger boil out. 'If you force me to go back to that house, my stepbrother will finish what he tried before and rape me.'

Mrs Dalton let out a little scream and covered her eyes with one hand as if to hide from the word.

'Don't be ridiculous.'

'He tried before. That was why I left.'

'He was probably fooling around, teasing you. You're making a mountain out of a molehill.'

She raised her voice. 'He ripped off my knickers, held me down and put his hand where he shouldn't.'

The silence seemed to throb with the shock of this statement. Mrs Stuart moved to stand beside Harriet. 'She's telling the truth about that, sir. Mrs Miller told me about it when she first wrote to ask if we could find Harriet a job.'

And suddenly, it was too much. The memory of that last day had given Harriet nightmares ever since. She burst into tears and ran out of the room, clattering blindly up the front stairs, seeking refuge in her bedroom.

What was she to do? How could she stop them? The master might be pleasant when he was getting his own way, but he was a very stubborn man once he got an idea into his head and he wouldn't brook opposition, especially from servants, but even from his own son.

Sobs shook her again, but she'd long ago learnt

that weeping didn't help, so she forced herself to stop, blowing her nose several times and scrubbing her face dry with the corner of her apron.

There was only one solution that she could see. She had to find a way to leave before Mr Dalton could carry out his threat. Thank goodness for the money Mr Joseph had given her. She was sure they wouldn't expect her to run away yet, so she'd go while they were still thinking what to do.

Her suitcase was on top of the wardrobe. She couldn't carry a trunk, but she could fill the case and slip out through the back of the house. It was the work of a moment to pull the case down and start shoving her clothes into it.

But though she worked rapidly, just as she closed the suitcase and turned towards the door, brisk footsteps came along the corridor towards her room.

Before she could hide what she was doing, Mrs Stuart appeared in the doorway.

Joseph waited until the housekeeper left his parents, then went into the sitting room to join them. 'Are you really going to carry out your threat, Father?'

His father scowled at him. 'What do you mean?'

'I overheard you threatening that poor maid.'

'I'll have to think about what to do. If I hadn't had confirmation that she was telling the truth about the stepbrother from Mrs Stuart, I would definitely have taken her there by force.'

'We can't expose her to danger like that, William.' Joseph's mother blushed.

'I don't know what the modern world's coming to,' he grumbled. 'All I know is she can't stay here unless she agrees to do as your mother wishes. I won't keep a disobedient servant, no matter what.'

Joseph realised it was more a matter of saving face for his father than of looking after Harriet or seeing she was treated fairly, which didn't surprise him. His parents were perfectly happy to let the stepmother continue taking most of their maid's wages.

What could he do to help her, though? He was as helpless as she was in many ways.

Or he had been. What Harriet had said today had given him hope. He did have things he could sell, some of them quite valuable. Maybe they would bring him enough to buy a small house somewhere. Pollins wouldn't mind that, he was sure. The older he got, the more Pollins had relaxed with him. In fact, his manservant and Harriet were the only people who treated him like a normal human being instead of a freak.

Perhaps Harriet could come with them as the maid? Would she do that?

All he could decide at the moment was that if his father was going to start laying down the law and enforcing it with threats, he'd have to have a plan in mind for leaving home at a moment's notice.

His feelings for his father, never warm, had grown

much cooler lately and had worsened again after the recent bullying of Harriet.

He wondered what she was doing at the moment? Had Mrs Stuart persuaded her to accept a compromise and stay?

Mrs Stuart came into Harriet's bedroom, not commenting on the suitcase. She sat on the bed and patted the space beside her.

Harriet sat down, sighing.

'Do you really want to leave Dalton House?'

'No, of course not.'

'Then you're going to have to accept a compromise.'

'But it's not right.'

'No, it's not. But life isn't always fair, as you've already found out. I've been thinking, though. What if I write to your stepmother and say that you don't have enough wages left to buy decent clothes and she'll have to let you keep more of the money each quarter?'

'She won't care about my clothes.'

'She might care if I said we couldn't continue employing you unless you were dressed decently.'

'She'd still get some of my money.'

'I know. But it's the best I can do. And she won't know about the rise in wages, will she?'

Harriet let the silence continue. She'd have to agree to this, but she wasn't jumping at it, wasn't going to pretend she liked it.

'Is it agreed, then?'

She let her voice go sulky. 'What choice do I have?'

'None. Good girl. Now, unpack that suitcase and come back to work.'

When Mrs Stuart had left the room, Harriet unpacked quickly. She hesitated over the five pounds Mr Joseph had given her, then hid it in a rolled up old stocking in her drawer. She'd keep it for a while. Just in case.

Chapter Eight

1904

As the weeks passed, the atmosphere at Dalton House continued strained, because Joseph remained at odds with his family. There had been several loud arguments with his father, who was still trying to compel him to marry Geraldine.

For a person like him to leave home took some thinking about, because he had never lived anywhere else but Dalton House, but he was thinking about it now, very seriously indeed. Planning for it.

Then they heard that Selwyn had incurred some more debts. Mr Dalton was forced to place an advertisement in *The Times* stating that the family would no longer be responsible for the debts of Mr Selwyn Dalton.

He turned on Joseph in an absolute fury after that. '*You* could have made this unnecessary if you'd only be sensible and marry Geraldine.'

'Marry to pay my brother's debts? Never.'

* * *

In the middle of January, the mail was brought to the breakfast table, as usual, for the master to distribute.

'There's a letter for Harriet.' He picked it up, staring at it as if it was poisonous. 'And it's from some lawyers, Harrington and Lloyd of Swindon. See!' He showed his wife the envelope, which had the name of the sender neatly embossed on the back flap of the envelope.

He turned it over in his hands several times. 'Do you think I should open it?'

Joseph stared at him in amazement. 'It's not addressed to you, Father.'

'It's come to my house.'

'I don't think you should open it, dear,' Mrs Dalton said.

Joseph added what he considered a clinching argument. 'In any case, it's unlawful to open somebody else's letters without their permission.'

'Then we'll get her permission.' Mr Dalton picked up the handbell from beside his plate and rang it loudly, scowling at his son.

It was Harriet who came in and stood waiting for instructions.

'Ah. Just the person I wanted to see. I have a letter here for you.' Mr Dalton held it out but didn't let her take it from his hand. 'I'm going to open it for you, because it's from some lawyers and you won't understand the language. Though why lawyers would be writing to *you*, I cannot understand. I hope you're not in trouble.'

While his father was speaking, Joseph got up from his chair and moved to the head of the table, snatching the envelope. 'I think Harriet can open her own letters, Father.' He passed it to her.

She immediately put it into her apron pocket, wondering what to say to the master, who was looking angry.

'Your father was only trying to help, Joseph,' Mrs Dalton said quickly. 'Harriet, once you've read the letter, if you have any difficulty understanding it, my husband will be happy to help you. Now, could you please bring us a fresh pot of tea, please?'

When the maid had left the room, Mr Dalton turned to his son, his face red with anger, his eyes bulging. 'If you *ever* do anything like that again, I'll throw you out of the house.'

'You won't need to. That was the final straw and I'm leaving.'

They both gaped at him and the silence continued for a few moments.

Then Mr Dalton gave a scornful laugh. 'Leaving! How can you possibly do that? You haven't got enough money to live on. And how would you manage on your own? I've made sure Pollins won't go with you. He knows which side his bread is buttered on.'

Which explained a lot about why his manservant had been looking unhappy lately and trying to persuade him to do as his father wished. Joseph felt his own anger rise to meet his father's. 'That's a dirty trick. But it won't stop me going. I can leave on my own.'

'Try it. You'll soon come running back. You have little experience of the world outside this house. Though maybe it'll do you good to suffer a bit. Maybe then you'll let those wiser than you guide your actions.'

'I'm not as stupid as you seem to think, Father. I'm sure I shall manage reasonably well, particularly since I'm not a spendthrift like my brother Selwyn.'

'You don't know anything about managing in the world out there. Haven't you been listening to me? Your money will run out within a couple of years at best. And in cheap lodgings you won't have the comforts you have here, or a library full of books. You'll be bored and friendless.'

Joseph didn't mention the jewellery. 'I'll manage the money very frugally, believe me.' A sense of relief flowed through him as the decision was taken. 'Nothing you say will change my mind. I'm not a child and I refuse to be treated as one.'

'Go, then. You'll regret it and beg to return – and it'll be under the same conditions.'

Mrs Dalton burst into tears and turned on her husband. 'Don't do this, William.'

He drew himself up even more stiffly. 'I can see that I need to remind both of you that *I* am master here and I intend to remain so until the day I die.'

Joseph rolled his chair towards the door without another word.

'Don't forget to leave that chair behind when you go,' his father yelled after him. 'It belongs to me.'

'William, this is beyond reason!' his wife pleaded.

Joseph stopped to look back at her. 'It's all right, Mama. I may look ungainly when I walk, but I can move around tolerably well. I won't take anything of yours, Father, I promise. I hope you enjoy using the chair.'

'I also own the books in the library.'

'Except for the ones that have been given to me as presents, of course. They aren't yours, and I know exactly which ones I own.' Joseph continued on his way, glad that the need to roll the chair along hid the way his hands were shaking.

He could hear his mother sobbing as he moved towards the stairs and got out of his wheelchair.

He couldn't hear his father comforting her, as usually happened.

He didn't deserve the scorn and bullying, wouldn't put up with them. His father had even taken from him the manservant who had looked after him since childhood, who had carried him up and down the stairs, sat up with him night after night. And refusing to let him take the wheelchair was petty in the extreme.

What threat had made Pollins refuse to come with him?

*   *   *

When she left the drawing room Harriet stopped to listen to the quarrel, praying they wouldn't drive Mr Joseph away. She couldn't bear the thought of not seeing him again.

And sadly, Mr Dalton was right. His son had no experience of the world, would be an easy target for villains and cheats.

It suddenly came to her that if Mr Joseph left, there was nothing to keep her here, so she'd run away too. This was the only home she'd known. Only . . . the main reason she loved being here was because of Mr Joseph.

Yes, she'd go too. But if she went, she wouldn't dare leave openly in case the master carried out his threat to take her back to her stepmother.

When Mr Joseph came out of the drawing room, she didn't attempt to hide the fact that she'd been eavesdropping.

'Come into the library,' he mouthed.

She nodded and followed him, closing the door quietly behind them. 'Are you really going to leave, Mr Joseph?'

'Yes. My father has left me no alternative.'

'I'm coming with you, then. You'll need someone to help you and he said Pollins wouldn't come.'

'I can't ask you to do that. You'd lose your job.'

'I'm not staying anyway if your father even expects to open my letters.' That reminded her and she pulled the letter out of her pocket, staring at it.

'Open it. I'll move over to the window and leave you in peace, then you can tell me what it's about or not, as you choose.'

She picked up the silver letter opener from the desk and slit the envelope neatly along the top. Inside it was one sheet of paper. She read it, frowned, then read it again, shaking her head in bafflement.

When she looked up, Mr Joseph was watching her, waiting.

She walked across the room and held the letter out to him. 'Your father was right. I don't understand what this means. Why would anyone leave me a legacy?'

He took the letter and read it quickly, then like her, he read it again more slowly.

Dear Miss Benson

We have pleasure in informing you that we are holding a legacy for you from one of our clients, who died recently.

We would ask you to visit our rooms at your earliest convenience so that we may deal with this matter.

Yours faithfully

Reginald Lloyd

'Can you guess who it might be?'

She shook her head. 'There's no one with anything to leave me, now that my father's property has gone to my stepmother.'

'Then you must go and see these lawyers and find out what this is about. It may be good news.'

She put the paper into her apron pocket. 'I doubt it. Anyway, it can wait a day or two. More important at the moment is what you're going to do, Mr Joseph. How will you manage without Pollins? Or your wheelchair?'

'I can manage in the short term, but I'll have to buy another wheelchair and hire another manservant if my father won't relent—'

He broke off as something else occurred to him. 'I don't even know whether they'll let me have the carriage. If not I'll have to hire transport from the village. Only, how can I do that? And afterwards, where shall I go? A hotel, I suppose.'

'There's one near the railway station in Reading, just across the road from it. I saw it when I came here.' She had a quick think. 'You can hire the trap from the village inn. I can bribe the gardener's lad to nip into the village and tell them.'

Joseph looked at her, his eyes sad. 'It's a poor lookout when a grown man doesn't even know how to leave home, isn't it?'

'That's why you'll need me. You will let me be your maid, won't you?'

'It wouldn't be fair to you, much as I'd welcome your help. People would get the wrong impression.'

'I don't mind that. I shall know we're doing nothing wrong.'

'You're absolutely certain you're going to leave here?'

'Oh, yes. I only stayed because you were still here.' He'd been as lonely as she had, but they'd had each other.

'You've been the best part of my life for a while now, Harriet. You mean a lot to me.'

They had never spoken so frankly. She smiled, treasuring his words, then glanced at the clock. 'I daren't talk to you for much longer or they'll get angry with me. I'll come to join you at the hotel tomorrow morning. I'll have to leave here during the night and catch the milk train to Reading.'

'Why during the night?'

'Your father threatened to take me back to my stepmother himself.'

'That was a while ago.'

'He meant it and he's very angry about all sorts of things, so I'm sure he'd still do it.'

'How will you get to the station?'

'I'll walk.'

She heard his mother's voice in the hall and looked at him in dismay.

'Hide behind the curtains in the bay window,' he said quickly.

She barely had time to conceal herself before the door opened.

Mrs Dalton came in and held out one hand, saying in a throbbing voice, 'Joseph, you can't do this to me.'

'I can't stay here now, Mama. Father has made that impossible.'

She pressed her handkerchief to her eyes for a moment, then said in a muffled voice, 'Your father's right about one thing: you don't have enough money to live on.'

'I've been planning it for a while and I've worked out what to do, how to manage.'

'Tell me or I'll worry.'

'If I do that, you'll end up telling Father, because he'll nag you till you do. You know you can never stand up to him.' He looked beyond her. 'And if you want to hold a private conversation, it's always better to close the door. Now, I have to go up to my room and start packing. I wonder if Pollins will be allowed to pack for me, and if I'll be allowed to use the carriage to take me to the railway station?'

She mopped her eyes. 'You're leaving because of a disobedient chit of a maid and that stupid letter of hers?'

He forced a light laugh, not wanting Harriet to suffer. 'This isn't because of Harriet, Mama.'

'Then why are you leaving? Your father's more upset about this than you realise. If you'd only apologise, he'd be quite happy to let you stay.'

'I've been considering how to leave for a while. And I think once the dust settles, we shall all be happier if I'm off your hands. I'm well aware that my father considers me a freak.'

He could see the sadness in her eyes at that and she didn't try to deny it. 'I'll be all right, Mama. And I promise to get in touch with you once I'm settled.'

She sat down on a chair and began sobbing bitterly. He had to comfort her before he could leave, but eventually managed to coax her upstairs to have a lie down.

All the time, he was conscious of Harriet listening behind the curtains. Would she really follow him to the hotel? Could she manage to escape? He didn't dare offer to take any of her luggage with his because the other servants might notice and report that to his father.

Harriet was right: he did need help. But it wasn't just that. She'd had become a necessary part of his life. Only now was he becoming aware that his feelings for her were more than those of a friend.

Could she think of him in that way?

This wasn't the time to consider that. He must be practical and get ready to leave.

He'd insist she go to the lawyer's in Swindon before they settled anywhere. Yes, they should definitely do that first. The legacy might give her a little more money to live on, make her life easier.

But how to keep her safe afterwards? Legally, she was still a minor, as his parents had pointed out. Would this stepmother come after her? No. Why should she?

But just in case, they must keep their final destination secret.

*　*　*

Once Mr Joseph and his mother had left the library, Harriet left her hiding place and hurried to the kitchen.

'Where on earth have you been?' Cook demanded. 'Mrs Stuart's looking for you and she's not in a good mood.'

'I was upstairs mending my hem. I caught it on my heel and it looked awful.'

She repeated the excuse to Mrs Stuart, surprised at how easily the lie slipped out.

'I see. Well, never mind that now. What were you thinking about, refusing to let the master help you with that lawyer's letter? I've never seen him so angry.' She leant forward, speaking earnestly. 'I thought you'd learnt your lesson last time, you foolish girl. If there's one thing the master won't tolerate, it's disobedience. Tell me at once what was in the letter and we'll take it to the master for his advice.'

'I'm sorry but it's private.'

The housekeeper gasped. 'Are you mad? You'll lose your place over this and then he'll remember his old threat of taking you to your stepmother.'

Harriet said nothing.

'You've got that stubborn look on your face again, and it won't do.' She sighed and her voice became almost pleading. 'We servants can't afford to be proud or stubborn, Harriet. You know that.'

'I'm sorry if what I've done upsets you, or the master, but sometimes things are . . . private. Even for servants.'

'Well, don't say I haven't warned you.'

'No, I won't. Thank you for trying.'

'Well, you'd better get back to work now. There are bound to be orders flying. The master will be making sure we all know he's in charge.'

Before she did, Harriet nipped up to her bedroom to hide the letter, then went about her work.

She couldn't help worrying about Mr Joseph and wondering how he was getting on, but the housekeeper kept her too busy to go near him, let alone help him.

After he left Harriet in the library, Joseph watched his mother climb the stairs, then went into the breakfast parlour and rang for a pot of tea and a scone. He'd not eaten much at breakfast, because of his quarrel with his father.

After he'd finished, he made his way slowly and painfully up the stairs. When he got to the top, he looked down regretfully at his wheeled chair standing to one side in the hall. Pollins usually took it up and down the stairs for him several times a day.

He'd miss the chair greatly because he got tired when he walked around. However, he was stronger than he used to be. He had to remember that. He'd cope. Other people did. He wasn't a fool.

His manservant was waiting for him in the bedroom. 'You should have rung for me, Mr Joseph. I'll go and fetch your chair up.'

'Thank you.'

When Pollins came back, Joseph sat down in the wheeled chair with a sigh of relief. 'You'd better sit down for a moment. I have something to tell you: I'm leaving and I have to go today.'

His long-time companion turned pale, looking anguished.

'Father's already told me you won't be able to come with me. I know that's not your choice. What did he threaten to make you agree to that?'

'He said he'd turn my brother and his family out of their cottage, and dismiss Vic from his job on the estate. My mother's old and infirm. She lives with them now my father's dead, as you know. If it was just me, I'd not mind what the master did, but it'll hurt them.' He shook his head sadly. 'He's changed a lot lately, the master has. I think it's Mr Selwyn's troubles have caused it.'

'Yes. And your brother has five children depending on him, too. I do understand why you daren't disobey Father. I shall miss you greatly, though.'

'Is there no way you can stay, Mr Joseph? No compromise possible?'

'None. I won't marry that poor Baudrey girl. Now, I'd better get started. Will you help me pack a couple of suitcases? And then pack everything else in a trunk or two until I can let you know where I am? I'll go down to the library once we've finished here and pick out my own books. I'll take a few with me but the rest will have to be stored in the attic till I have somewhere to house them. Can you see to that for me?'

'Yes. I can at least do that for you. You'll write to let me know where you are, Mr Joseph? In case I can ever join you? I wouldn't need wages.'

'You'll always be welcome to work for me.'

'You'd better write to me care of my brother Vic, then. We all heard about the master wanting to open Harriet's letter.'

'Disgusting, isn't it? Father's still living in the dark ages, I think.'

'Money's a very powerful thing. I wish you had more of it.'

The two men began sorting through the clothes and underwear. Soon two suitcases were full and Pollins went to get help in bringing down some trunks.

While his manservant was away, Joseph took his godmother's jewellery from its hiding place and put it in one of his suitcases.

When Pollins came back, he sent him to the stables to ask if the brake was available. This was where things would become extremely difficult if his father refused to let him use the family vehicles.

But Pollins came back to say Bert Billings would be waiting for him at the back of the house.

'Does my father know I'm using the brake?'

'No, sir. And the vicar has come to call, so the master will be occupied for a while. We could take your trunks down as well if you go straight away. Then you'd be sure of keeping all your things.'

'I don't want to get anyone in trouble.'

'Me and Bert have decided to plead ignorance if the master questions us about helping you. After all, he hasn't given us any orders about *not* helping you, has he? Now, I'll go and see if the coast is clear. And . . . I think you should take the wheelchair with you as well. We'll hide it under a blanket. I can say I've taken it up to the attics if the master asks.'

'Thank you. I shall miss you greatly, Pollins.'

The older man nodded, his eyes suspiciously bright. 'Where are you going?'

'To Reading.'

'And after that?'

'Who knows?'

It was amazing how the servants banded together to help him leave. The groom helped with the suitcases and trunks, the gardener stood at the corner of the house, keeping an eye out to make sure the coast was clear as they left. But the vicar's gig was still at the back of the house, so they felt fairly confident they could get Joseph away while his parents were still entertaining their visitor.

Most of the servants came out to offer their best wishes for Joseph's future happiness, all except Mrs Stuart. But she didn't try to stop the others from saying goodbye, or tell the master what was happening.

Harriet came out with the cook, her eyes saying

what she couldn't put into words, that she'd see him tomorrow.

In spite of how well this was going, Joseph felt nearly sick with nerves as he hauled himself up beside Bert on the seat of the brake.

His father was right. He'd lived a very cocooned life and knew little about how to manage in the world, apart from what generalities he'd read in books, newspapers and magazines.

He prayed Harriet would get away safely. Surely she would? No one would expect her to creep out during the night. He needed her in so many ways.

Bert coughed to get his attention. 'I hope you don't mind, but seeing as you're without help now, I sent a message to my nephew Frank, Mr Joseph. The poor lad's restless and was going to leave the village and look for work in a town. If you'll just pay his fare into Reading, he'll help you on your journey, deal with your luggage and other things. That way you'll both benefit.'

'What a good idea! I can't tell you how grateful I am. Do you think your nephew would stay with me temporarily and take Pollins's place until I'm . . . more settled? I'll pay him decent wages, of course.'

'We can only ask him. But I 'spect Frank will agree. As long as he's out of the village, he'll be happy. The girl he loved upped and married someone else and he's very cut up about it. He never did like his job, though.'

At the station a young man came forward to greet

Bert, who took him aside and started whispering.

Frank beamed at him, then came across to Joseph, smiling. 'I'll be happy to work for you for a few weeks, Mr Dalton. Very happy.'

'Thank you. I'm grateful.' He looked at Bert. 'How do we find out when the next train leaves?'

'There's one in fifteen minutes,' Frank said. 'I asked. In case.'

'Good. I'll buy us both tickets. Frank, you'd better travel with me first class in case I need help.'

All too soon the train arrived and his new servant helped Joseph on board, while Bert followed them with the two suitcases and the trunks were loaded into the luggage van.

The guard stood there impatiently as Frank lifted the wheelchair into the luggage van as well, lodging it carefully in among packages and boxes and two mail sacks so that it couldn't move about. As soon as the compartment door was closed, the guard blew his whistle and the train chuffed slowly out of the little station, gathering speed.

Joseph leant back and closed his eyes for a moment, then looked at Frank. 'So. That's done. I've left home.'

'Good for you, Mr Joseph. So have I.'

'I'm sorry about your girl marrying someone else.'

Frank chuckled. 'I don't mind at all. I didn't want to get married yet, you see. It made a good excuse for leaving, that's all. Even my Mam said she understood.' He shrugged and pulled a wry face. 'I didn't like deceiving Mam, but she wanted to keep me tied to her apron strings till she passed me on to a wife. It's the twentieth century now, and I intend to see more than one small village before I settle down.'

'We have a lot in common, then. My mother and father wanted to wrap me in cotton wool and keep me shut away.'

'You didn't get into the village much, did you?'

'No. Or anywhere else, come to that. Until recently.'

The train rattled along, the rhythm of its wheels very soothing.

'Where are we going, sir?'

Joseph wondered what to tell him, then decided on the truth. 'Apart from a few nights at a hotel, I haven't a clue.' But he was in charge of his life now, wasn't relying on his parents, didn't have to answer to anyone but himself, so he could decide later.

And that felt good.

Chapter Nine

During the evening, Harriet managed to sneak up to her bedroom on her own for half an hour while the other servants were sitting chatting over a cup of cocoa. At the moment she shared a bedroom with Amy, a new girl who slept like a log every night and had to be shaken awake in the mornings. Harriet doubted she'd have any trouble leaving the bedroom unnoticed during the night.

She packed her things quickly and systematically, cramming her suitcase with as much as she could fit in. After that she filled an old sacking bag she'd made herself and used for storing oddments and books.

If you owned as few possessions as she did, you didn't want to lose a single one. Sadly, she'd have to leave her books behind. She hesitated . . . Well, all but the family Bible that had been her mother's. She valued this more than any of the others and somehow felt it to be important to her, she couldn't imagine why.

She hid the case and bag in the mop cupboard on the landing. Not much risk of them being discovered at this time of day. She hung up her best clothes there, too, ready to change into for her escape.

When everyone came to bed, she got undressed, keeping her underclothes on beneath her nightdress without sleepy Amy noticing.

Harriet had no trouble staying awake after the lamps were turned off, all except one burning dimly on the landing, in case of an emergency. She felt extremely alert, and was sure her eyes were wider open than usual. Excitement seemed to be sending her blood racing through her veins, and she had great difficulty lying still.

As the house grew quiet, she could hear, very faintly, the big clock in the hall two floors below, striking the hours and quarter hours. When she'd first come to Dalton House, that clock had disturbed her sleep, but now, like everyone else, she was used to it and hardly noticed its melodious chimes.

Tonight she counted every one.

At half-past one she got up and went out onto the landing, where she pulled the nightdress off and stuffed it into the sacking bag. Then she slipped into the skirt, blouse and threadbare jacket she wore to church on Sundays. Her hat was already in the bag because she didn't want it blowing off as she walked, and anyway, it was only an old navy felt.

Through all this, the other servants slept peacefully,

the clock chimed again and the old house creaked around her. Once something rustled in the distance and Harriet froze, alert for other movements. But there were no other sounds, no footsteps, no doors opening.

She crept down the back stairs, carrying her suitcase, then came back for her bag. They were heavy and awkward, but she would just have to manage to carry them both once she got outside the house. She needed absolutely everything in them.

On her second journey down the stairs, she stopped on the first floor to leave a note for Mrs Stuart on her desk, then she carried on down to the kitchen.

The outer door was locked, of course, and the big key made a lot of noise, so she didn't go that way, but the scullery door was fastened only by two bolts. She slid them back slowly, inch by inch, relieved when they made the faintest of snicking noises.

As she opened the door, something touched her ankle and she let out a squeak of shock before she realised it was only the kitchen cat. After lifting her bags outside, she shooed the animal inside again, and closed the door.

She took a deep breath to steady her nerves. This was it. She really was leaving. Picking up the bags, she set off across the stable yard. Not far to go now, she told herself, and she'd be off the estate.

When a figure loomed out of the darkness in front of her, she stopped dead with a gasp, her heart thudding in her chest. Disappointment speared through her. How had she been discovered so quickly? How had she given herself away?

'What are you doing out at this hour, lass?'

'Oh, Bert! You gave me such a shock.' Now that her eyes were used to the darkness, there was enough moonlight to see him staring at the suitcase. She prayed he wouldn't feel it his duty to give her away.

'Come round here where we won't be overheard.' He took her into the tack room, where his deep voice was a comforting rumble in the darkness. 'Running away, aren't you?'

She reached out to clasp his arm. 'Yes. I have to, or the master will take me back to my stepmother and my stepbrother . . . touches me. *Please* don't give me away, Bert. I'm afraid of him.'

'He must be a brute. Don't worry. I won't give you away. Those bags of yours look heavy. Is someone coming to help you?'

'No. I have to go into the village, because I want to catch the milk train into Reading. I can manage.'

'Have you got somewhere safe to stay, friends to help you? I don't like to think of a pretty lass like you wandering around on her own.'

She hesitated but she trusted Bert, who never said a hurtful word and did many kindnesses for his fellow servants. 'I'm going to work for Mr Joseph.'

He chuckled softly. 'Ah. That's all right, then. Though I don't know whether you'll be looking after him or he'll be looking after you. I think he'd make a better master here than anyone else in the family, even if the poor lad can't walk straight.'

'He's a very kind person – doesn't deserve to be so badly treated by his parents. They wouldn't even let him take his wheelchair. That's cruel.'

Bert chuckled. 'They didn't tell us who work in the stables about that, did they? So it got put into the back of the trap, that old wheelchair did.'

'I'm glad. He does need it.'

Bert picked up the suitcase. 'Come on, then. Let's be getting you to the station. I'll carry the case, you take the bag. Heavy, isn't it?'

'I'm taking everything I can, though I had to leave most of my books behind.'

'You're like Mr Joseph, love your books. Me, I never bother with anything but the Sunday newspaper. Now, walk on the grass as we go down the drive. The gravel's noisy.'

'I don't like you to lose your sleep.'

'A man my age don't need as much sleep as a young 'un, and since I haven't got a wife to nag me, I reckon I can do as I please, night or day. I often go for a walk early in the morning, so the others are used to me coming and going. I'll probably get back without them waking, anyway. In any case, I won't need to mention seeing you.'

Tears came into her eyes. 'Oh, Bert, I was dreading lugging my bags to the station. I'm so grateful for your help.'

As they turned out of the gates and onto the lane that led into the village, he leant closer to murmur, 'We should keep our voices down, even now. Someone may be up with a sick child, for all we know. Now, best foot forward. We need to get you to that station.'

When she saw the light of the single lantern that was always left burning overnight outside the small branch station, Harriet's spirits lifted.

Bert set down the case next to the wooden bench on the platform and looked round in disapproval. 'You're going to be cold, waiting out here.'

'It'll be worth it.'

'Did you leave a note?'

'Yes. On Mrs Stuart's desk. I'm leaving her in the lurch and I'm really sorry about that.'

'She'll understand. Want me to ask her to hide your books in the attic? Maybe you can get them back one day.'

'Do you think she would?'

'I've always found her very fair.' He started to leave, then turned back again. 'See you get as far away as you can from here, lass. You don't want the master catching up with you. He's turned nasty lately, especially if he's defied. Thinks he's above the law.'

'I'll try. It depends on Mr Joseph.'

'Tell him I said to get you away. Remind him that his father's good friends with the local magistrate and has used his friendship before to get someone charged and locked up unfairly.'

'Mr Dalton wouldn't do that to his own son.'

'No, not to his son, but he wouldn't hesitate to do it to you.'

'Oh. I'll remember your warning.' She took two quick steps towards him, stood on tiptoe and kissed his bristly cheek. 'Thank you, Bert. I hope we meet again.'

'So do I.' He patted her shoulder then walked quickly away.

She stood watching him go, staying there even after he'd disappeared from sight. Eventually, she looked round and shivered, feeling very alone in the darkness.

No use feeling sorry for yourself, my girl, she thought, looking up at the station clock. It said twelve minutes past two in the morning. Three hours to wait and the night was chilly.

She sat on the rough wooden bench, watching the moon come and go behind the clouds, but after a while she felt so cold, she began to walk up and down. But there was nowhere to shelter from the wind. It wasn't a strong wind, but it was damp and chilly, sucking the warmth from her body.

Every now and then she went to the front of the small building to check the station clock, but its hands seemed to be moving painfully slowly.

Her main worry now was whether the stationmaster would make a fuss about her leaving. He'd think it a bit strange because he knew she worked at Dalton House, and they'd normally have sent her here in the brake. Well, if he tried to stop her, she'd tell him she'd been sacked and pretend to cry, if necessary.

Other worries filled her mind until she realised she was letting this get her down. She'd got away from the house, hadn't she? And she'd soon be away from the village, too.

After that, who knew where she'd end up?

Had Mr Joseph meant what he'd said, about . . . valuing her? She hoped so, couldn't bear the thought of not staying with him.

Was she being a fool, expecting too much of him? She didn't know.

Where was he now? Sleeping comfortably in the hotel, she hoped. Waiting for her to join him.

She forced herself to walk briskly to and fro to warm herself up, though she felt so tired that what she really wanted to do was to lie down and sleep.

Four o'clock. Only another hour to wait.

No one at the hotel stared when a lame man turned up in a wheelchair, with a servant to help him with his luggage. They even found him a room on the ground floor, a comfortable one used for older and infirm clients.

Frank was very happy about escaping from the village and his high spirits cheered his master up. Joseph's bad hip was aching and he was exhausted by the time they were installed in the bedroom, but he was used to that.

He had to tell Frank to unpack a clean shirt and hang it up, and to get out his nightclothes. Then he explained that Frank would be able to get meals in the hotel's servants' quarters and should stay away from the guests' area except for coming to this room.

'Do you mind sleeping in here with me on the truckle bed? I think it'll be easier if we stick together. You aren't used to servants' ways and they might get suspicious.'

Frank went across to try the narrow bed. 'This'll do me fine. Nice to have a bed to myself.' He looked across apologetically. 'I ent used to servants' ways, I know, so I hope I don't give offence if I do something wrong, Mr Joseph.'

'I'm not my father. I don't stand on my dignity and I don't get upset when someone's honestly doing their best.' He frowned. 'Oh, and I forgot to say, I'll pay you the same wages as Pollins for helping me.'

'Fine by me. I won't lie to you, though. I don't want to be a servant for ever. I got other ideas. Bicycles. I'm good with them, want to set up to sell and repair them. But I don't mind staying with you for a few weeks. It'll let me get my bearings and I'll be able to save a bit more money. I've not spent much time out of the village because my pa's an old stick-in-the-mud.'

'I've as much to learn as you have, probably more. I've spent most of my life shut up in Dalton House, except for an occasional visit to London, when I was whisked to and from the station then hidden from view.'

Frank looked at him, opened his mouth then shut it again.

'If you want to say something, say it. I'd prefer us to be honest with one another.'

Frank was inexperienced enough in the ways of servants to take him at his word, and Joseph found he liked that frankness.

'We all think it's a shame how they've locked you away, Mr Joseph. You're not the only lame man in the world, after all. Nothing wrong with your brain or face, is there? Besides, if you don't practise walking, how will your legs get stronger? You was all white and wambly when you was a little boy, but your face is fair rosy now.'

Joseph stared at himself in the mirror. When he could see only his head and shoulders, he looked perfectly normal, in good health even. He wished the rest of him matched. Frank was still speaking.

'Why didn't Mr Pollins come with you today? Everyone knows he's devoted to you.'

'My father threatened to throw his brother and family out of work and their cottage if Pollins came with me.'

'Well! I never heard the like. That's downright mean, that is. An' I don't care if he is your father – Mr Dalton shouldn't have done it.'

'It is unfair. Very. And I'm not upset by what you've said. My father isn't . . . I'm not close to him. Or he to me. The only one he really cares about is my mother.' His brothers had always been ashamed to be seen with him.

'That's sad for you, sir. I may want to leave home, but I'm fond of my ma and pa, an' I know they care about me.' Frank frowned, as if getting his thoughts in order. 'I'm talking too much, speaking out of turn.'

'No, you're not.' Joseph laughed suddenly. 'I enjoy chatting to you.'

'Well, I'll tell you this, then, as well: if you were like your father I'd not have worked for you, whatever Bert said. But he told me you talk to servants as nice as you please and I can see he was right.' He gave Joseph a shrewd look. 'Odd sort of servant I am, eh?'

'Just right for an odd master.'

Frank went to pull out his own nightshirt and put it under his pillow. 'Nice feather pillow, this.' He turned to survey the room with some satisfaction, ambled over to the window, examined the ornaments on the mantelpiece and smiled at Joseph again. 'Proper luxury, this is, for me. Shall I fetch you some food now?'

'I'm not hungry.'

'You should eat something and I'm famished, even if you aren't. I could wheel you out for a walk afterwards, if you like. Get a bit of fresh air.'

Joseph shook his head. 'I'm tired. And I don't want

to be seen. I didn't tell my parents where I was going and I'd prefer to slip out of the district as quietly as I can.'

'Makes sense, in case your pa goes on the warpath. Just have a bite to eat, then, sir. You need to eat if you're to build up your strength.'

'You're as bad as Pollins. All right. Fetch me some food and order something for yourself – anything you like.'

Joseph sat back when he was on his own, feeling a sense of wonder and pride. He'd done it, left home. And the way the servants had helped made him feel humbled and warm. How kind they'd been!

But then, servants had always been kind to him, doing extra without complaining. Why his father grumbled so much about them, he'd never understood.

As he got ready for bed, he wondered what Harriet was doing now and prayed she'd escape without any trouble.

He felt happy at the thought of spending more time with her.

At long last, Harriet saw the hands of the station clock start to approach five. Twenty minutes to go, fifteen. It was still dark, apart from the one lantern that hung over the station entrance. She made another tour of the platform and station. Soon, very soon, she'd be away.

When footsteps sounded outside, she went to face the stationmaster. But it was his wife.

'Hello, dear! I didn't expect to see any passengers here at this hour. My husband's not well, so I've come to do the job. Don't tell anyone. I'm not supposed to sell tickets, only clean the station.' She turned round as a wagon drew up outside.

'Morning, John.'

'Morning, Ginny. Your old man still sick?'

'He is. Getting better each day, though.'

The man who collected the milk from the farms nearby got down and began to roll the churns on their round bases from his wagon onto the platform. He nodded to Harriet but all his attention was on the big metal cans of milk.

The stationmaster's wife opened up the ticket office. She didn't show the slightest interest in why Harriet was catching the train, only yawned widely and excused herself. She took the money, handed over a ticket, then dealt with the milk delivery.

Harriet couldn't help glancing towards the entrance, still worried that someone from Dalton House would come after her, though they'd only just be waking up there.

It wasn't till the train pulled out of the station that she could release the last of her anxiety in a long sigh and let her head fall back against the seat. She was alone in the compartment, alone in the world if Mr Joseph wasn't there at the hotel.

But she'd manage. She had no choice now but to manage. She'd burnt her bridges, and whatever happened, she couldn't go back.

But it wouldn't be the same if she wasn't with him.

In the early morning, when only the servants were up and about, Mrs Stuart waited for Harriet to come down, surprised the head housemaid hadn't started work yet. When there was no sign of her, she asked Amy where her room-mate was.

The girl looked at her in surprise. 'Isn't she down already? She got up before me, an' she didn't wake me, neither. If Susan hadn't of shook me awake, I'd still be asleep.'

Mrs Stuart exchanged startled glances with the cook, a woman her own age.

'She wouldn't—' Cook began, then looked at the young maids and didn't finish the rest of the sentence.

When the two older women were alone, she asked bluntly, 'Do you think she's run away?'

Mrs Stuart nodded slowly, regretfully. 'She might well have done. She was very upset yesterday. I think I'll just check her room.'

She found Harriet's half of the wardrobe empty, as were the drawers, except for the books in the bottom one.

Mrs Stuart plumped down on the bed. 'She's done it. Oh, dear, the master will be furious.'

She walked slowly down to her own room,

wondering why Harriet hadn't left her a note. It wasn't like that girl just to leave without a word.

There was nothing on the desk, but when she went round to the other side of it, she saw the corner of an envelope on the floor, sticking out from underneath the drawers at one side. It must have fallen off.

She picked it up and saw it was addressed to her in Harriet's elegant handwriting. 'Oh, dear!' She opened it and read the three brief lines of apology for leaving so abruptly. 'I wish you well, my dear,' she murmured, tears coming into her eyes.

Then something else occurred to her. 'I wonder . . .' Had Harriet's sudden departure got anything to do with Mr Joseph leaving? No, surely not? She could have sworn there was no budding romance between the two of them, because she'd kept her eye on them. There had been no touching and most of their conversations had been about books. 'No, surely not.'

Only . . . they were good friends now, completely at ease with one another. You couldn't help noticing that. She hadn't thought too much of it because she and the mistress were the same – good friends as far as their different stations in life allowed.

Feeling rebellious, she decided not to wake the mistress yet to tell her that Harriet had run away. Let Mrs Dalton find out later and let her tell the master after he got back. She would have the best chance of calming her husband's rage before he turned it on the rest of them.

When Mrs Stuart went down to the kitchen, she found Cook alone. 'Her things are gone.'

'I don't blame her.'

'No. Nor do I.'

'He'll be furious.'

'Yes.'

Cook chewed her thumb, then said, 'He was planning to go out shooting this morning. I've orders to pack him a snack and have a late breakfast waiting for him when he gets back.'

'He'll be in a hurry to set off. We won't slow him down with servant problems.'

With a nod, they separated and got on with their work. They were doing all they could to give Harriet time to get away, but both women were worried. They knew what their master was like if he felt himself slighted.

Later that morning, Mrs Dalton looked at her housekeeper in dismay. 'Harriet's run away? No, she can't have!'

'See for yourself, ma'am. She left me this letter, apologising for the inconvenience.'

Mrs Dalton read it in silence, then handed it back. 'I told my husband he was going too far.' She groaned. 'Oh, dear! I'm *not* looking forward to telling him.'

Since her mistress didn't seem to think of it, Mrs Stuart didn't suggest that Harriet might have gone to join Mr Joseph. She felt that was probably what had happened, but she'd let her employers work it out for themselves. Or not.

When the master came back from shooting, yelling for his breakfast, Cook had everything ready and the morning room table was set for him.

Doors opened and shut upstairs, then he came running down again. Cook and Mrs Stuart waited in the kitchen, nerves on edge.

A few minutes later the bell started pealing, on and on, as if the person ringing for service was angry.

Amy stared at it in near terror. 'It's the master. What's wrong now? I ent done nothin' wrong. I ent, Mrs Stuart.'

'I know.' She couldn't send the poor girl off alone to face the master in a rage. 'I'll go.'

When she went into the morning room, the master was pacing up and down, face nearly purple with rage. The mistress was sitting at the table looking upset, dabbing at her eyes.

'Why didn't you tell me earlier about Harriet leaving, Mrs Stuart?'

'You went out so early, I didn't find out till after you'd left, sir.'

'It's a disgrace. I don't know what the world's coming to when a servant just ups and leaves. Well, all I can say is, that damned girl will regret doing this. She had no *right* to leave without my permission.'

Mrs Stuart had to try. 'She was upset at the thought of being taken back to her stepmother's and I don't blame her. If that stepbrother was trying to have his way with her, Harriet was only doing what any decent girl would do and staying away from him.'

Mrs Dalton emerged from her handkerchief. 'I agree. I *told* you that was the cause, William. Pretty young women can be at risk from a certain sort of man, however virtuous they are, and our duty is to protect our maids, not throw them into the fiery furnace.'

He glared at her. 'If you can't say anything helpful, keep quiet.'

'Don't you dare speak to me like that!' His wife stood up and walked out, her shoes clicking more loudly than usual on the tiled floor of the hall.

Mrs Stuart followed her. The bell rang again before she'd gone into the servants' quarters and she hesitated. Reluctantly, she turned back.

Mr Dalton glared at her. 'I haven't finished talking to you. Where do *you* think Harriet's gone?'

'I haven't the faintest idea, sir. She said nothing to anyone and must have left during the night. I don't think she has any other family apart from the stepmother.'

'But you must be able to guess where she'd go.'

'I have no idea whatsoever, sir.'

He glared at her so fiercely, she wondered if he was going to dismiss her next. But she looked him straight in the eye, hoping her scorn would show. She didn't think the mistress would allow him to dismiss her, anyway. Mrs Dalton could occasionally stand up for herself if driven into a corner.

'Bring me some fresh tea,' he said. 'And some hot food. I think better on a full stomach.' He picked up a bread roll and tore a piece off it, slathering on butter thickly and cramming it into his mouth.

He eats like a pig when he's on his own, she thought. And for him, being with a servant was being on his own.

She walked out, not hurrying, hoping she looked calmer than she felt.

Chapter Ten

Harriet got off the train in Reading, letting the few other passengers overtake her. She felt her stomach churn with anxiety as she walked along the platform.

Would she find Joseph at the hotel? Had she remembered where it was correctly?

It was still quite early, but she hoped to get out of public view as soon as she could. She didn't think there would be anyone in Reading who would recognise her, but you couldn't be too careful. Anyway, Mr Joseph always woke early, all the servants knew that, so she doubted he'd mind her arriving before breakfast.

A porter in railway uniform came up to her. 'Need help with your luggage, miss?'

'No, thank you.' She didn't dare spend even sixpence on such a service until she knew whether she had a new job.

She started to move slowly towards the exit, weighed down by her suitcase and the shabby sacking bag. She put them down for a moment to study the street, relieved when she saw that the hotel she'd remembered from her one and only visit was indeed just across the road.

When she tried to go inside, the commissionaire at the door barred the way and asked her business.

'I've come to join my employer, Mr Dalton.'

'Your name, miss?'

'Miss Benson.'

'Ah, yes. Mr Dalton left word that he was expecting you.' He smiled at her in a fatherly way. 'You should really have used the servants' entrance at the back, but there's no one around to see, so I'll let you in this time. You'll need to speak to the clerk at reception.' With a click of the fingers, he beckoned to a pageboy, who put her luggage on a trolley.

She went across to the counter and repeated her request to see Joseph.

'I'll send someone to see if Mr Dalton is up yet.' The man looked down his nose at her, then beckoned the same pageboy.

Harriet nearly said Joseph was always up by this time, but stopped herself, because that would sound bad.

The lad returned a couple of minutes later. 'Mr Dalton says he'll meet Miss Benson in the dining room in five minutes. He says she can have breakfast with him.'

The man behind the desk pulled an even sourer face at this breach of normal behaviour.

Harriet turned round. 'What about my luggage?'

'It'll be kept for you in the luggage room, miss. You have only to ask for it when you return from breakfast.'

She looked at him doubtfully.

He rolled his eyes briefly towards the ceiling, as if she'd said something utterly stupid. 'Your luggage will be perfectly safe there, I assure you.' He gestured to a seat behind a big potted plant. 'You may sit over here to wait for your employer.'

Exactly five minutes later, the pageboy came across. 'Mr Dalton is waiting. It's this way, miss.'

When Joseph got the message that Harriet had arrived, he beamed at the pageboy and tipped him a whole shilling.

'I was worried they'd stop her getting away,' he said to Frank when they were on their own again.

'Well, she's here now. My uncle thinks a lot of Harriet. I knew she'd not let you down. Shall I wheel you into the dining room, sir?'

'Yes, please. Then go and get yourself a good, hearty breakfast in the servants' area.'

The guests' dining room was nearly empty at this hour of the morning, except for an elderly man reading a newspaper in one corner. He looked up briefly as they entered, then looked away quickly at the sight of the wheelchair.

Joseph chose a table by the window and watched the doorway eagerly. He saw Harriet stop to look round. Her face lit up when she saw him and he could feel himself beaming too. He beckoned her over.

The pageboy followed her, as if unsure whether to leave her there. 'Do sit down, Harriet. We'll have breakfast together and plan what to do next.' Joseph indicated the chair opposite him and the lad pulled it out.

She hesitated. 'Are you sure it's all right for me to join you in here?'

'It is if I say so. Anyway I'm hungry and I want to know how you got on, so we can eat as we talk.'

The pageboy walked away, turning in the doorway to stare at them.

'Aren't you hungry, Harriet?'

'I am now I've got this far, yes. But I still don't think I should be in here. It's for the gentry, not for servants.'

'And for the gentry's guests.' If she were dressed in fine clothes, she'd look every inch the lady, Joseph thought. She had a quiet, self-contained way of holding herself that was very attractive. At the moment, however, she looked shabby and nervous. He must buy her some decent clothes . . . if she'd let him.

Oh, she was here, she was really here!

'Let's order breakfast first, then you can tell me every single detail of how you got away.' He raised one finger and a waiter hovering to one side came across.

By the time she'd finished her tale, they'd both cleared a plate of ham and eggs, and were spreading butter and jam on pieces of toast.

'I don't think I've ever enjoyed a meal as much,' he said.

'You don't usually eat that much, sir.'

'I'm not usually free. It adds savour to the food, being free, don't you think? And it's partly due to you.' He took another big bite of toast, making a little murmuring noise of enjoyment.

'Due to me?'

'For reminding me that I have valuable things to sell, for telling me how much money I'd need to live simply. I'm so ignorant of normal people's lives that I hadn't understood that.'

'Oh, well, I'm glad I could help.'

When he'd crunched the last corner of toast, Joseph said thoughtfully, 'Bert was right. We should get further away from my father than this, or he'll be trying to interfere. I suggest we start by going to Swindon and finding out about your inheritance, then I'll try to find a little house to rent in a quiet village somewhere.'

After another moment's thought, he added, 'And if I like the looks of your lawyer, I'll ask him to act on my behalf as well, if you don't mind. I need to sell some of my grandmother's jewellery and I don't intend to use the Dalton family lawyer. Aside from the fact that I can't stand the fellow, he wouldn't dare do anything to upset my father.'

'Oughtn't we to find you a new home first? I'm sure my legacy won't be anything much.'

'Then best get it dealt with, so we're free to go where we choose.' He grinned. 'I'm the master now, so you must do as I say, young Harriet.'

She said, 'Yes, sir,' mockingly. Joseph had never been the sort to order people around, master or not. That was when she realised she was thinking of him as Joseph now, not Mr Joseph.

Things had changed between them.

He wiped his fingers on his napkin and laid it on the table, and she followed suit. When he pushed his wheelchair back from the table, he clicked his tongue in annoyance as it bumped into a chair from the next table.

'Could you push me out of here, please, Harriet? It's a bit difficult to move the chair myself among so many pieces of furniture.'

Once in the lobby, he took over again, wheeling himself towards the desk. 'We'll ask about trains to Swindon.'

Harriet stood behind him in a dutiful servant's pose, hands clasped in front of her, listening to him organise their departure. He seemed different here, more sure of what he was doing, a man rather than a boy, if that wasn't too fanciful a thought.

Could a person change so quickly? Joseph had done now he'd left his parents' roof.

She felt guilty for delaying him and hoped it wouldn't take long to sort out her legacy, which would be something and nothing, perhaps a memento from one of her father's cousins – though she wouldn't have thought any of them rich enough to need a lawyer to deal with their legacies. It was puzzling.

They caught a train on the Great Western Line at ten o'clock, getting the large pile of luggage on board with the help of two porters and Frank.

Joseph insisted his servants join him in a first-class compartment, because he didn't want to sit alone, so they did that.

Frank whispered gleefully to Harriet that they were seeing a bit of life, weren't they? She nodded, but sat stiffly in her seat, knowing she was out of place here with her shabby clothes.

No one else joined them in the compartment, though one lady glanced in and gave them a disgusted look, as if she could tell at a glance that two of the group were only servants.

Then the train set off and Joseph smiled at her. 'Don't look so scared.'

Harriet couldn't summon up a smile in return. The more she thought about what they were doing and how much there was to sort out, the more she worried.

'Tell me what's upsetting you.'

'Whether your father will come after us.' She hesitated. 'After me, especially, since you're over twenty-one.'

'That's why we need to see a lawyer, and if we don't like this one, we'll engage another to help you, if needed.'

'I think you'd be better off without me. I should just . . . disappear.'

'Promise me you won't do that.'

He looked at her so fiercely, she murmured a promise. Heaven help her, she hated the thought of leaving him.

'Good. I would definitely *not* be better off without you. I can't run a house without help, and there are so many everyday things of which I'm ignorant. I don't think Frank could run a house, either.'

Joseph seemed so positive about their future that Harriet pushed her worries aside and turned her attention to the countryside they were passing through. She'd never been so far west before, wondered where they'd all end up. She couldn't help yawning after a night without sleep, but excitement helped her stay awake.

Swindon station was busy and the narrow street outside it was equally crowded, with carts, carriages, bicycles and people on foot coming and going as if they were all in a tearing hurry. 'We'll leave our things in the left-luggage office,' Joseph decided. 'Then we can take a cab to your lawyer's.'

Once again, his money and gentle air of confidence seemed to sweep away all obstacles from their path. Or was it his personal charm and friendly manner, she wondered?

He joked with the cab driver about fitting in

three people and a wheelchair, and the man smiled at them benevolently as Frank managed to attach the wheelchair to the luggage rack.

When they arrived at the lawyer's rooms, there were steps, so Joseph sent Frank inside to find out if Mr Lloyd could see Miss Harriet Benson. He tipped the cab driver handsomely to wait for them.

Frank came back with the lawyer's clerk, who looked only at Harriet, begging her to come inside. He waited for the wheelchair to be carried up the three steps and Joseph installed in it again, then ushered her inside, letting the others follow.

She was surprised by this.

In the reception area, he turned to Joseph. 'May I ask who you are, sir?'

'I'm Harriet's employer, Joseph Dalton.'

She nodded. 'I asked him to come with me to see Mr Lloyd.'

Joseph smiled at the clerk, but this time won no smile in return. 'My manservant will wait out here for us, if that's all right?'

'Of course, sir.'

But it was Harriet the clerk was studying, as if he knew something about her. Only . . . what could it possibly be?

At Dalton House, Joseph's mother was worried about her son. But she was even more worried about her husband, who seemed prepared to carry out a witch-hunt for their missing maid. The situation was annoying, but honesty compelled her to admit to herself that it hadn't been her maid's fault.

'What good will it do to pursue poor Harriet?' she asked her husband for the umpteenth time, exasperation sharpening her voice, something she didn't normally allow because with a husband prone to get into rages if thwarted, it was helpful for one person to stay calm.

'It'll teach her not to disobey an employer and a gentleman,' he snapped.

'But you don't want her back. Why not just let her go?'

'I want her put in her rightful place. Someone needs to do that or she'll never make a good servant.'

'You know what will happen to her if you take her back to her stepmother.'

'I know what *she* says will happen. My dear Sophie, young men don't attack virtuous young women, they only deal that way with females of a certain type. She's making up this tale.'

'Mrs Miller believed her.'

'Mrs Miller was an admirable housekeeper but she's getting old now and old people can become credulous and forgetful.'

She couldn't imagine Doris Miller getting like that. 'What can you do to Harriet, even if you do bring her back? She's not a slave, after all.'

'I'm about to find out about that from my old

friend Gypson. As a magistrate, he'll no doubt be able to advise me.'

She gave up, but when her husband had left the house, she summoned Mrs Stuart and shared her worries.

'Can't you stop him, ma'am? That poor girl doesn't deserve this.'

'Unfortunately, I can't get William to listen to me, whatever I say. Don't you think I've tried to make him see reason? He's always been stubborn, but I've never seen him so bullheaded about anything. The only good thing is that it's taking his mind off Selwyn's mess . . . and off Joseph. Do you think my son will be all right? He hasn't even got Pollins.'

'I'm sure he'll be fine, ma'am. He's nobody's fool, Mr Joseph isn't. The master has decided to let him find out for himself what the world's like and I think he'll do well. We all like serving him, you know.'

'I never realised how much.'

'He'll find help wherever he goes, I'm sure.'

With that Sophie Dalton had to be content, but she continued to worry about what her husband was doing, because a visit to his friend Gypson had left him looking smug, and he wouldn't tell her why.

An elegantly dressed man of about forty, with smooth iron-grey hair, came into the entrance area of the lawyer's rooms and smiled at Harriet. 'Miss Benson?'

'Yes.'

He came across, holding out his hand. 'I'm Reginald Lloyd. I'm delighted to meet you at last. Will you come into my private office?'

She stood up. 'Yes, of course. This is Mr Dalton, my employer. I'd like him to come too, if you don't mind.'

He looked at Joseph and inclined his head. 'Do you need any help, sir?'

'Only if there are awkward corners or stairs. Otherwise, Harriet can push me.'

'Very well. Come this way.'

When they were all three settled in the big, comfortable office at the end of the corridor, the lawyer got out some papers and tapped them with his forefinger. 'This is the last will and testament of Miss Agnes Latimer, who was a relative of yours on your mother's side, Miss Benson.'

Harriet frowned slightly. 'My mother's maiden name was Latimer, but she always said her relatives had disowned her when she married my father.'

'Miss Latimer continued to think very highly of her, I promise you. Now, let's get the details out of the way. First we have to establish your bona fides. Do you have anything to prove who you are? It's not that I'm doubting your word, because actually, you look like a Latimer. That hair runs in the family. But, in law, it's always better to have incontrovertible proof.'

'I have my birth certificate and my parents' wedding lines.'

'Do you have them with you?'

'No. They're in my suitcase. We left it at the station's left-luggage office. Oh, and I have my mother's family Bible too. It's very old.'

'Perfect. Would you let my junior clerk bring the suitcase here now?'

She turned sideways to look questioningly at Joseph.

'My manservant could go with your clerk. He knows which suitcase belongs to Harriet.' Joseph took out the ticket which identified him as the person who'd lodged eight pieces of luggage at the station. 'He'll need this.'

'Thank you. I'll send Perkins with your man, then.'

When the clerk had been despatched, Mr Lloyd sat down again. 'Let me sum up Miss Latimer's will for you, Miss Benson. It's not complicated. She's left you everything she owned, except for a small bequest to her nephew. Your inheritance consists of a house and some land, and there are also various investments, which will bring in enough money to live on and maintain the house.

'The capital can't be touched, nor can the house be sold. They must be passed on to your chosen heir who must be a female, and a Latimer or a descendant of one.'

Harriet gasped, so shocked by this information she felt as if the room was spinning round her. She couldn't form a single word and put up one hand to cover her mouth, feeling as if she had to literally hold her shock in.

Only when Joseph took her other hand and patted it gently did things seem to steady again.

Mr Lloyd was leaning forward, looking anxious. 'Are you all right, Miss Benson?'

'I'm . . . amazed . . . and confused. Are you *sure* it's me she's left all this to?'

'Oh, yes. She had us looking for you during the year or two before her death, and when we found you, she was very happy indeed, sure you were the one.'

'But why did she choose me?'

'Because she considers you the female relative most suited to look after the Latimer inheritance. It's a great responsibility and passes only to the females of the family.'

'But I'm not a Latimer.'

'Your mother was, so you have Latimer blood in you, and when she made enquiries about you, she decided it had bred true. She does ask that you change your surname to Latimer, which can be easily done. Would you mind?'

'Of course not.' She shook her head, still feeling numb with shock.

'Could you tell us more about the house?' Joseph asked.

'It's quite large and is in a village called Challerton to the south-west of Swindon. That's all I'm authorised to tell you till we get there. It's a tradition to pass on the house in a certain manner.'

Harriet kept hold of Joseph's hand because everything else felt so unreal. 'I still can't believe it.'

The lawyer gave her an avuncular smile. 'It's a pleasant surprise, though, I hope. Could I ask where you're staying?'

'We were going to see if you could recommend a hotel in Swindon. And we need your help with something else.'

Joseph turned to Harriet. 'I think we should tell Mr Lloyd how we both came to be here today.'

At her nod of agreement, he turned back, his expression solemn. 'I think Harriet is going to need your help on two other matters. And I would appreciate the services of a lawyer, as well.'

'Then let me ask my office boy to fetch us some tea and biscuits so that we can talk in comfort.'

When Mr Lloyd had left the room, Joseph smiled ruefully at Harriet. 'It sounds as if I'll have to find myself another maid.'

'No! I don't want to leave you. I'd be completely on my own if I did.' Then she had an idea. 'Why don't you come with me to the house I've inherited? If it's large enough, you and Frank can stay there, at least for the time being.' She looked at him anxiously. 'Unless you'd rather not?'

'I'm honoured that you'd ask me. You're still nervous about my father, aren't you?'

She nodded. 'Yes, I am. And now, there's not only your father to worry about, but my stepmother. If she finds I've inherited something, she'll come after me and try to get hold of it.'

Behind them Mr Lloyd cleared his throat. 'I think you need to put me in possession of all the facts. I know you're a minor in law, but I'd expected there to be a family member responsible for you until you reach your majority.'

It took them a full half hour to tell him their stories and his expression grew steadily grimmer as the confidences continued.

'With your permission, Miss Benson – no, let's call you Latimer from now on or we'll get confused when we change over. With your permission and as your lawyer, I'll act *in loco parentis* for the moment. That means—'

She didn't want him to think her stupid, even though she was only a servant. 'I know what it means, Mr Lloyd. And yes, that sounds a sensible thing to do. I meant it when I said I would run away again if anyone tried to make me return to my stepmother's.'

'I hope it won't come to that.' He cocked his head as there were sounds outside. 'Ah, that sounds like my clerk returning with your suitcase.'

Perkins brought it in and Harriet searched inside, taking a big envelope from the bottom, holding it out to the lawyer. 'These are my mother's family papers. My father gave them to me to look after when he remarried.' She began to unwrap a parcel, to reveal a very old Bible, its gold lettering rubbed and its leather binding dull with age.

Mr Lloyd picked up the Bible and opened it, nodding, then turned to the envelope. 'Ah, good. Here are more than enough things which prove who you are. I wonder . . . would you consider leaving these papers and the Bible with me? I think they'll be safer here until we've got everything sorted out and you've legally come of age.'

'I think that'd be a good idea.' She didn't even ask Joseph's opinion. She trusted Mr Lloyd instinctively and obviously Agnes Latimer had also trusted him.

The lawyer leant back in his chair, looking thoughtful again. 'It's a bit more of a legal tangle than I'd expected, but we'll work our way through it. Now, I have other appointments this afternoon, so as you're not in urgent need of money from selling the jewellery, Mr Dalton, I suggest we find you a hotel.'

'Might I leave my godmother's jewellery with you in the meantime?'

'Certainly. It'll be quite safe here. I can, if you like, ask a jeweller I know to value it.'

'Please do.' Joseph took out the package and the clerk was brought in to list the items it contained before they were locked away.

When that was done, Mr Lloyd looked at his watch again and stood up. 'I'll make arrangements to take you both over to Greyladies tomorrow.'

'Greyladies?'

'The name of your house, Miss Latimer. Didn't I tell you? How remiss of me.'

'It's a lovely name. I'm looking forward to seeing it. Is it pretty? Does it have a garden? Even a little one would be nice.'

'Miss Agnes asked me not to tell you anything about the house till you got there and could see it for yourself. It does have a garden, but the only other thing I'll say is that it's a remarkable old place. I know it quite well because my father used to take me along with him whenever he went to visit Miss Latimer, whose lawyer he was till his death a few years ago. My family has a tradition of serving the Latimers and I hope you'll continue to use our services.'

'I'm happy to continue with you,' Harriet said.

'Good. Now, for the moment, I'll get my clerk to find you and your man rooms at a hotel, Mr Dalton. There's one near here which is small but comfortable. And I'd like to invite you, Miss Latimer, to spend the night at my house. You'll find my wife very motherly and welcoming.'

She was about to refuse this, not wanting to be separated from Joseph, when Mr Lloyd added quietly, 'Apart from the proprieties, you needn't be seen again by anyone in the town if we do that. What do you think, Mr Dalton?'

'I think that's an excellent idea.'

Not until he and his wife were getting ready for bed that night did Reginald Lloyd voice his concerns. 'I don't know how long we can keep Harriet's existence secret once she goes to live at Greyladies.'

'Then you must work out a plan for getting her away if those relatives come after her,' his wife said at once.

'I'm a lawyer. I've sworn to uphold the law. If it's on their side . . .'

She smiled as she stood up from her dressing table and reached out to turn down the gaslight. 'As if you've never bent the law before in the cause of real justice.'

'That was when I was much younger and a bit rash at times. But still . . . I couldn't allow a Latimer to be bullied – or worse. No, I couldn't allow that.'

'Of course you couldn't.'

'I shall have to think about it, work out some contingency plans. Like Joseph Dalton, I don't feel Miss Latimer will remain safe from pursuit for long. I'll speak to him again about his father and ask his opinion about how far he thinks Mr Dalton senior will go. But I won't do anything else until after she's seen Greyladies.'

Chapter Eleven

It rained during the night, but when Harriet woke and went to look out of the window of the large town villa where the Lloyds lived, she was greeted by sunshine and birdsong. A narrow flowerbed, bare at this season, marked the boundary between the vegetable garden and the paved area at the back where someone had placed a small wrought iron table with matching chairs.

She'd have thought herself in paradise to own a garden like that, to simply sit there and look at the flowers.

There was a knock on the door and a maid poked her head in. 'Oh, you're awake, miss. The master asked me to wake you, so that you can get an early start. Would you like me to bring you a tea tray? I've just made a pot, so it won't take a minute.'

'Yes, please.' Harriet went back to sit in the bed, piling the pillows behind her and feeling very grand to be waited on like this. The maid returned almost immediately with the tea and a plate with two biscuits on it.

When she was on her own again, Harriet allowed herself time to appreciate the crockery sitting on a pretty tray cloth and the fine china with lovely red roses on it. How many times had she performed the very same task, taking in the early morning tea? And now someone had done it for her.

Mr Lloyd had said she'd have enough money to live on for the rest of her life. Imagine never having to worry about money or even having to work for a living again!

Only . . . what would she do with herself all day? Housework, she supposed. Even if you had plenty of money, there were still chores to be done. If she was a married woman, she'd have children to look after, only she wasn't married and she wasn't sure she ever wanted to be. A woman was so much at the mercy of her husband, as she'd seen with her own father and mother. He'd been very much in charge, the one to make all the major decisions. You'd have to trust a man absolutely to give yourself into his keeping.

She hoped the house would be big enough for Joseph and his manservant to live there as well, because she didn't want to be separated from her only friend in the world. After all, he did need somewhere to live. And he did seem to want them to stay together. She knew she wasn't mistaken about that.

If only . . . she cut her thoughts short, wouldn't

allow herself even to dream of something so impossible. She prided herself on being sensible, had needed to be ever since her mother died.

Joseph was as far above her as the sun in the sky.

When they picked up Joseph and Frank from the hotel, they continued in Mr Lloyd's carriage and he explained to her, 'We could have gone most of the way to Greyladies by train, but then we'd need a carriage for the rest of our journey, so I thought, if you didn't mind, we'd take longer and then Mr Dalton needn't be inconvenienced.'

'That's very kind of you.'

She stayed out of sight in the comfortable carriage while the coachman cheerfully tied the wheelchair on the back of it. Frank opted to ride outside with him, which left Harriet to chat comfortably with Joseph and Mr Lloyd as they travelled. She almost didn't want the journey to end, the time passed so pleasantly.

After they left Swindon, they travelled south-west into a more rural part of Wiltshire. The scenery was beautiful and so were the villages they passed through, with grey stone houses and often grey gabled roofs as well.

About two hours later Mr Lloyd said quietly, 'We'll be arriving soon, so I'd better tell you more about your inheritance, Harriet.'

She leant forward eagerly.

'Greyladies is built on the remains of a former

abbey. Even in its prime, it wasn't a big abbey, just a small foundation. You see, in 1536 the king decided that hundreds of other religious foundations all across England should be closed.' He looked at Harriet as if wondering whether to explain this further.

'Henry the Eighth and the dissolution of the monasteries,' she said. 'Yes, I know about it. I've read quite a lot of books about English history.'

His surprise at her knowing this was obvious, but he didn't comment. 'Good. At the time, about a dozen nuns lived at the abbey, spending their lives in prayer, offering help and kindness to those in need.'

'Is any part of the abbey still standing?' she asked, thinking it might be interesting to have ruins nearby.

'There are a few pieces of wall left and some lines of stones where the foundations were. The people in the village keep the grass around them mown because hikers come to see them and view the ruins, and then they usually spend money at the village shop, or even stay overnight. There are a few houses that take in paying guests. Oh, and the crypt is still there, but it's got a wrought iron gate across it to keep people out. I've never been inside. It's probably unsafe. I don't even know where the key is now.'

'Is it because of the nuns that the house is called Greyladies?'

'Yes. Their habits were of plain grey cloth, you see. The house you've inherited was the former guest house

at the abbey. The villagers still call it "the big house".'
He waited for this to sink in.

'It's a *big* house?'

'Yes.'

'As big as yours?'

'Much bigger.'

She looked at him uncertainly, unable to believe she could own any house, let alone a big one.

'It's been the home of the Latimers ever since the abbey was closed. The first owner was called Anne Latimer and she used to be the abbess, but she chose to marry a cousin in order to preserve what was left. They had eight children. The descendants of those children have inherited the house ever since. I might add that the legacy of kindness and sanctuary the nuns offered people in dire need has also lingered. And it's partly for that quality of kindness and compassion that an owner chooses her heir.'

'But how would Agnes Latimer know I'm suitable?' Harriet asked, puzzled. 'She's never met me.'

'The Latimer women seem to know instinctively, don't ask me how. They say the ghost of Anne Latimer helps them with their choice. Miss Agnes was convinced that the lady still walks round the house.' He shook his head. 'She would not see reason about that. But I don't believe in ghosts, and as for this craze for spiritualism and contacting the dead, well, it's just plain ridiculous.'

Harriet had occasionally seen ghosts too. Her father

said she was just imagining things, but her mother had admitted having similar experiences. She'd told Harriet to keep quiet about it, though, because it annoyed her father, and anyway, most people wouldn't believe her.

'I believe in ghosts,' Joseph said. 'I've even seen one at our town house – more than once. But I didn't tell anyone, because no one else saw them.'

They both turned back to Mr Lloyd, waiting for him to continue.

'It's the tradition for the new Lady to go into the house on her own the first time she takes up her new position.'

'Oh.'

'You needn't be afraid to do that. It's a very peaceful old place. Now, look out of the window and you'll see the roof.'

Steep grey gables were visible from the main road but nothing else, because the house was surrounded by trees. The roof was enough to show that the house was even bigger than Harriet had expected.

She turned to Mr Lloyd, mouth open in shock. 'Surely that isn't . . . It can't be Greyladies?'

'It is.'

'All of it?'

'Yes, indeed.'

'But it's a *huge* house!'

'Not as country mansions go. It's considered quite a small one by neighbouring landowners.'

'It seems enormous to me.' She shot a frightened

213

glance at Joseph for reassurance, but he was looking as amazed as she was feeling.

The carriage turned off the main road onto a narrow country road with hedgerows still crowded with plants, many with seed heads waving gently in the breeze. The village houses began almost immediately on the right, but the carriage turned left along an even narrower lane, which seemed to lead only to Greyladies.

The wrought iron gates stood open and beyond them, down a short, tree-lined drive, was a rambling stone house. A massive oak tree stood sentinel just inside the gate, so big it must have been there for hundreds of years.

The carriage stopped in its shade.

'Take a few moments to study your inheritance, Harriet.'

'What a beautiful house,' Joseph said softly.

Harriet still felt it couldn't be hers. 'Didn't Agnes Latimer have any other relatives?'

'A nephew, Damian, who used to visit her every month. He was annoyed about the will, though she'd told him he wouldn't inherit. He went up to Scotland for the shooting and hasn't come back yet.'

'Was that because he loved the house?'

Mr Lloyd shook his head. 'No. I believe he was more interested in the money. Though he did his duty and kept an eye on Miss Agnes when she grew old and infirm.' He pulled the string and the carriage set off again, drawing to a halt outside the front door of Greyladies.

Mr Lloyd opened his briefcase and gave her a big old key. 'As I said before, it's the custom for the new owner to go into the house on her own. Don't be afraid.'

The coachman opened the carriage door and let down the step. She got out, feeling as if she was in a dream, and began to move slowly towards the house.

'And Harriet—'

She turned at the foot of the three shallow, worn stone steps that led to the front door.

'Take all the time you need once you're inside. Mr Dalton and I will enjoy a quiet chat about how exactly I can help him while we wait for you.'

She nodded, took a deep breath and moved on.

Miss Bowers turned round as a lad from one of the farms near Challingford came rushing into the village shop, shouting, 'I just seen a carriage turn into Greyladies. It's that lawyer fellow again and there was someone with him. I bet he's brung the new owner.'

He rushed out again and went to stand on a bench so that he could see across to Greyladies more clearly. 'It's pulling up at the house now. Come and see.'

Another lad clambered up beside him.

The women looked at one another, shaking their heads at what he'd assumed, but they all followed the lads out of the shop, not wanting to miss anything.

'He might be right. We knew Miss Agnes would find another female Latimer to carry on the tradition,' Mrs Pocock, the shopkeeper, said. 'Didn't I say so?'

'Well, I think it's about time a man owned the house,' the nearest lad said stubbornly. 'A man would do something useful with it instead of keeping it like a stupid museum full of dusty old rubbish.'

Miss Bowers gave the group of younger folk a stern look. 'The furniture and other things at Greyladies are priceless, part of our English history. Don't you remember how I took you to see them from school?'

The lads rolled their eyes at one another. They hadn't been impressed, but hadn't dared misbehave, not with Miss Bowers in charge. She had been the village schoolteacher for many years until her recent retirement, and she knew more than anyone about the history of the old house.

Everyone knew that Miss Bowers was now fulfilling her lifelong ambition to write a book about Greyladies and the Latimers. Agnes Latimer had let her read the old family diaries, an honour and a fascination, she told people, and she was hoping the new owner would be equally generous.

'You'll be able to ask the new Lady about seeing the rest of the diaries,' Mr Pocock said.

'Yes. I shall look forward to meeting her.'

'Because she ent got nothing better to do than muck around with books,' one lad muttered to the other.

Miss Bowers let out an exasperated sigh at his lack

of grammar. Tom Craik was one of her educational failures, like his father before him. Good farmers, the Craiks, poor with books and writing. 'Stop gossiping, Tom, and get your mother's shopping done. She's probably waiting for it and that poor pony of yours is getting restless. You always were a chatterbox, even when you were a little boy.'

He threw her a resentful look but did as she'd ordered and went back into the shop to hand over the list of items his mother wanted. His friends waited for him outside, clearly eager to continue their chat before returning to their own errands and duties.

She smiled at the way they were looking at her with exactly the same sulky but wary expressions they'd worn when scolded as children in her classroom. Though she'd loved teaching, she was glad a small legacy had allowed her to retire while she still had some life and energy left. She wanted to do other things than teach before she met her Maker, but most of all, she wanted to finish her history of the Latimer family.

She found the continuity of old traditions here in the heart of Wiltshire rather comforting in this hectic new world, where speed and money seemed to be more important than people's lives.

Railways had been taking people to every corner of the country since she was a girl. She was used to that, though *she* had no desire to dash around England like a madwoman. And at least the trains were kept away from people using the roads.

She wasn't at all sure about these new-fangled motor cars, like the one Damian Latimer drove. Now that the Red Flag Act didn't apply to them, and no one had to walk in front of each vehicle carrying a flag to warn passers-by of the danger, motor cars were whizzing along at speeds of up to 14 miles an hour, knocking down and killing people not used to them. She had read of several such accidents in the *Swindon Advertiser*, her favourite daily newspaper.

As for telephones, she didn't know what to think about them. All she knew was, there wasn't one in the village and people seemed to manage perfectly well without.

Every now and then she wondered what would happen next, what marvels she'd see before she died. Some said men would build flying machines that took people quickly from one place to another, but she didn't believe that. How could heavier-than-air machines possibly stay up in the sky?

Greyladies wouldn't change, though. She felt quite sure of that. It had been there since the sixteenth century, and would still be there in the twenty-first, as her history of it would show.

She went home and was guilty of going up to her attic and leaning out of the dormer window to see what was happening at the big house. But all she could see was a carriage standing outside and a gentleman pacing up and down near it. It looked like the family lawyer, whom she'd met a few times, but she couldn't see him well enough to be certain.

Sadly, her eyesight wasn't very good these days and her new spectacles only made things close at hand clearer, so that she could read more easily and see across a room. But she did hope the question of an heir had been resolved. Oh, she did. She was longing to get back to her research.

Harriet walked slowly up the worn stone steps to the front door. When it opened of its own accord, she expected to see a servant of some sort standing there, but there was no one.

She didn't feel frightened, though she still felt like a visitor, not the owner.

As she stepped into the hall she heard a bell tolling somewhere, not a loud bell like the ones in churches, but one that sounded smaller, with a very melodious tone.

Three times the bell rang out, there was a pause, then it rang three more times.

She was just about to carry on exploring when it began to ring again, so she waited. But after three more peals there was only silence.

Three times three, she thought and wondered where she got the phrase from.

Presumably this was to welcome the new owner, but who had been ringing the bell, and why? Was there someone in the kitchen?

In front of her she saw shafts of coloured light

reflected into the hall through the stained glass window above the front door. She walked through the light, holding out her hands and enjoying the sight of the bright patterns of jewel colours flowing across her skin.

When she reached the shadows beyond, she twisted round to look up at the window, and saw a scene of beauty, with a garden of flowers in the foreground, and a small building and one grey-clad figure in the distance.

'How lovely!' she said aloud, then glanced round guiltily. Her voice had sounded much louder than usual, though she'd spoken quietly. There must be an echo in here.

She moved to the foot of the stairs at the rear of a spacious hall that was bigger than the whole ground floor of the house where she'd grown up, calling out, 'Is anyone there?'

Her words echoed back to her. 'Anyone there . . . anyone there . . .'

Still no one came to see who had entered the house. She should have asked Mr Lloyd if there were any servants here still.

When she listened, she could hear a faint movement. It sounded like a full skirt brushing softly across the floor as its owner walked. Mrs Dalton had evening gowns with skirts that did that.

'Hello?' she called again, but received no answer, so moved to the foot of the stairs because that sound had definitely come from above her. But there was no one in sight, either on the stairs or the landing that ran round three sides of the hall.

She had such a strong urge to go up the beautiful wooden stairs that before she could even consider the wisdom of it, her right foot was on the bottom tread. As she climbed, a light began to shine from the landing at the top, faint at first, then growing brighter.

She looked round for a window, but it wasn't sunlight this time. She hesitated, then continued.

The light seemed to be gathering round a portrait hanging on the wall. It was large, showing a life-sized figure of a lady clad in old-fashioned clothes: a long grey skirt, with a grey bodice. The bodice had a square neckline filled in by white lace inserts, and the grey oversleeves spread out over white under-sleeves, edged in lace.

The lady's hair was parted in the middle and she had a stiffened half-moon-shaped headdress, from the back of which finer grey material hung down past her shoulders. She was holding up the folds of her skirt with one slender, elegant hand and a pointed shoe peeped from beneath the heavy folds which reached the floor.

It was the lady's face which drew Harriet's eyes again and again as she studied the portrait. Such a wise face, not old but not young either, and beautiful in a gentle way. No, it wasn't her face that was beautiful, Harriet corrected herself mentally – it was the lady's expression. She looked out at the world in a kindly way, as if she loved everyone and wanted to help them.

The faint noise sounded again, coming from Harriet's right, and she turned to see the shimmering outline of a woman's figure a few feet away from her, transparent against the oak panelling. As she stared, the figure came into sharper focus and she recognised the lady from the portrait.

A ghost! But smiling directly at her, it seemed.

Harriet didn't feel afraid and couldn't help smiling back.

The figure blew her a kiss, then began to fade.

'Don't go!'

As the outline wavered, the ghost lady raised one hand in farewell.

Harriet couldn't move for a moment. Had she been imagining this? No. She shook her head. The figure had been so real, she couldn't doubt the spirit existed.

It felt as if the lady from the picture had been welcoming her to the house, it really did.

She looked at the picture and saw a small metal plaque at the bottom, saying simply, 'Anne Latimer'.

Harriet looked down into the big entrance hall from the landing which ran around three sides of it. Everything was dusty. It needed love and care. She could love it. She could. And who knew better than she did how to care for the interior of a house?

She walked along the landing, first one way, then the next, peering into the two bedrooms that opened off each longer side, then turning into a corridor which led off at a right angle near the top of the stairs. She found herself in a short wing with two other bedrooms.

So many rooms!

Stairs led both up and down from the rear of this wing, probably servants' stairs, going to the attic or kitchen. But she didn't go up them because the two men were waiting for her outside and it would be bad manners to keep them waiting any longer.

'I'll do my best to look after you,' she whispered to the house as she walked slowly down the stairs.

Chapter Twelve

Harriet went to the front door and called, 'Would you like to join me inside?'

'We'd love to,' Joseph said at once, then grimaced as he got down from the carriage onto the uneven gravel. 'Could someone please bring the wheelchair into the house for me? I can't push it along myself on such loose surfaces.'

'I'll do that.' Mr Lloyd dragged it across and Joseph followed more slowly.

Harriet watched him, seeing the shame in his face at needing to ask for help and wishing she could do something to help him realise what a wonderful man he was.

The coachman came round the corner of the house. 'I've found some water, Mr Lloyd. All right if I take the horses round the back now and see to them? I brought some feed for them.'

'Yes, of course.'

Frank stood near the carriage. 'Do you want me

to push you round the house, Mr Dalton, or shall I go and help with the horses?'

'I'll be happy to assist your master, if he needs it,' Mr Lloyd said. 'You help with the horses. Oh, and watch out for the cart bringing your luggage. They've been told to take it round to the back.'

Joseph moved towards the house, seeing Harriet waiting for him on the top step, smiling. *She* never seemed to notice how he walked.

He smiled back involuntarily. 'Who'd have thought it, you being left such a big house?' he said as he reached her side. 'Isn't it exciting? How did you feel, going inside? What's it like?'

'I felt welcome. I've only explored upstairs so far, though. I wanted to see the portrait at the top of the stairs.' She turned and gestured towards it, and was it her imagination or did it brighten as Joseph turned towards it?

Mr Lloyd had lifted the wheelchair up the steps and now he helped Joseph sit in it, looking beyond her as if expecting to see someone else. 'I saw the front door open for you, Harriet. There aren't supposed to be any servants here but someone must have done that.'

'No. It just . . . opened of its own accord.'

He looked puzzled. 'But I locked it myself last time I was here.'

'Perhaps someone else has a key?' Joseph suggested.

Harriet took a deep breath and risked the lawyer's scorn. 'When I went up to the landing, I saw the Lady.

Her ghost, anyway. I think she was welcoming me to the house.'

Joseph frowned at her. 'The Lady?'

'The owner of this house is always called "the Lady",' Mr Lloyd said.

Harriet nodded eagerly. 'There's a portrait of her at the top of the stairs and she . . . materialised next to it. I wasn't imagining it. I really did see her.' She looked uncertainly at Mr Lloyd. 'I know you don't believe in ghosts, but I did see her.'

'I believe you,' Joseph said.

'Well, I don't believe in ghosts when I'm elsewhere,' Mr Lloyd admitted, 'but when I'm here they seem all too real. And the Lady always comes to welcome a new owner – if that owner is the one who was meant. It's a good sign.'

'I heard a bell too. Three times three.'

He nodded. 'Yes. That's what they say is the proof that the right person has taken over. Three times three, as the saying goes.'

'I wish I'd seen your ghost,' Joseph said wistfully.

'Perhaps you will one day. I've not been into the rooms on this floor, so let's look at them together now. Shall we start with this one?'

Mr Lloyd fell back to let them go first.

'What a lovely room!' Joseph exclaimed involuntarily as they went through the door on the right.

'They call this the sitting room,' Mr Lloyd said.

The room was timeless and comfortable in appearance, not smart and fussy like his mother's rooms. Two big armchairs took pride of place at either side of the fireplace and a large sofa stood between them. Another smaller armchair was set to one side of the square bay window.

'Let's look out of the window,' Harriet said and began to push him, knowing it was harder for him to move the chair about on carpet.

Joseph let her take him wherever she wanted, feeling very happy for her. His father would throw a fit of rage when he found out his former maid had been left a large house. Joseph wished he could be there to see it. No, he didn't. He didn't want to be anywhere but with Harriet.

He and the lawyer would have to find some way to protect her, though. He couldn't bear the thought of anyone hurting her. He glanced down at his body. He couldn't do much physically, but perhaps he could use his brain to help her. Or hire somebody strong. He'd mention it to Frank.

He watched Harriet sit down at a small desk set invitingly at one side of the bay window. 'What a lovely place to read or write letters! That view must be beautiful in the summer when everything's in bloom. It's very pretty still.'

A path curved through the flowerbeds to an open wooden gate with a stone arch above it. Through it some ruins could be seen.

Joseph managed to roll his chair forward to her side. 'I wonder if I could get down that path. I'd love to explore the ruins. Wouldn't you?'

'I'll push you, or Frank will. I want to explore every corner of this house and the grounds. Oh, Joseph, isn't it wonderful? Who would have thought it could be mine?'

'I'm so glad for you.'

'I'll try my best to look after it, to be worthy of the trust placed in me.'

Her voice seemed to echo and something made him add, 'And I'll help you in every way I can.'

She came to stand in front of him. 'Does that mean you'll stay here?'

'If you're sure you want me to.'

'Of course I do. You're my only friend, and you know so much more about the world than I do. I shall need your help.'

He laughed then, a laugh tinged with bitterness. He had never wished more fervently that he'd been born normal than since he'd met Harriet.

She smiled back at him serenely. 'We'll learn about Greyladies and the world around it together. It'll be a joy.'

'A joy,' he thought. *She* was the real joy in his life. Every day he was more sure of that.

'Let's go round the rest of the ground floor.' Harriet didn't wait for his answer, but pushed the wheelchair out into the hall where Mr Lloyd was now sitting, smiling at their eagerness. He waved them on.

Behind the sitting room was a dining room with a massive table. It had a very ugly ornament in the centre that made them grimace. 'That has to be put away,' Harriet said. 'It's horrible. It'd put me off my food.'

On the other side of the entrance was a library with two of its walls lined by shelves of books, all higgledy-piggledy as if they'd been read many times and replaced rather carelessly.

'Look at all the books!' they chorused, then laughed at themselves.

'Plenty to read here.' He looked longingly at the shelves, dying to check the titles, but she wasn't having that. She wanted to see all the rooms on this floor.

There was a small sitting room behind the library, then two doors at the rear of the hall. Harriet left him and peeped through the door on the right. 'It's just the kitchen. I can look at that later. Let's try the other door.'

Unfortunately it was locked.

Mr Lloyd came to join them. 'How do you like your house, Harriet?'

'I love it. Do you have a key to this door, Mr Lloyd? I can't bear to be locked out of part of my own home.' Oh, how wonderful it was to say the words 'my own home'!

'Yes, I do have a key. But this door only leads into

the oldest part of the house, the original guest house of the abbey. It's not used now and it's kept locked because we're not sure it's safe, especially upstairs. You should only go a little way inside and not upstairs until it's been checked out.'

When he pulled a heavy old key out of his briefcase, she held out her hand. 'Please let me open it.'

'There you are. You can lead the way in and I'll push Mr Dalton.'

'I can roll my wheelchair myself if the floor continues to be wood, as long as it doesn't have any rugs.'

Harriet was relieved when Joseph held out one hand to keep the lawyer back. He seemed to know instinctively that she wanted to go in on her own at first. She turned the heavy key in the lock and moved forward.

The room was about twenty foot long and twelve foot wide, with big oak beams meeting at points in the centre. There was an old-fashioned table, narrow but long, its wood dark with age and polish. She stopped when she thought she heard faint sounds of people eating and drinking, chatting, and a tinkling sort of music. She shook her head to clear it and the sounds vanished.

Joseph rolled across to join her. 'This must have been a medieval hall originally.' He looked up to the narrow balcony overhanging the far end. 'Perhaps that was a minstrel's gallery.' He frowned.

'What's the matter?'

He turned back to her. 'I could have sworn I heard music, a happy tune with a jigging, three-beat rhythm.'

'I heard it too!'

He glanced back at Mr Lloyd. 'Shhh. Don't say anything. He'll think we've lost our wits.'

'Maybe we have.'

'No. I think we're both finding ourselves.'

Mr Lloyd came to join them. 'This part is hardly usable, my dear Miss Latimer. It's a very primitive type of construction. It's surprising it's lasted so long.'

'I like it.' There were two closed doors along the left side. Harriet went to open them. 'Empty rooms,' she said in disappointment. 'No furniture at all.'

'I don't think any of the old part of the house is properly furnished, apart from bits and pieces. That table has benches to go with it. They're stacked somewhere.' The lawyer looked round in disapproval. 'I've never been upstairs, I must admit, and I don't intend to risk it. Nor should you.'

Harriet was going up there as soon as she could, she decided. Whatever Mr Lloyd, or Joseph, said. But she would do it later. Now wasn't the time to argue.

'Shall we go back into the main house, Miss Latimer? Even that is now in need of a thorough cleaning, because it's several weeks since Miss Agnes died. I can arrange for the cleaning, if you wish, and of course, you must stay with us until it's done.'

Harriet had been expecting to stay here tonight and she was going to do it, too, she decided. 'Thank you, but I'd rather move in straight away. After all, our luggage is on its way. We shall need to find bedrooms for myself, Joseph and his manservant. And see if we can buy some food in the village.'

The lawyer looked at her. 'But you'll need servants, and the place needs cleaning . I hadn't realised it was quite so run down. You mustn't even consider it. When the cart arrives with your luggage, perhaps you could leave some of it here, and just take back what you'll need for a few nights.'

Harriet felt stubborn. 'I'm sorry to disagree, Mr Lloyd, but I want to move in tonight. After all, we've already agreed that we don't wish to attract attention to ourselves. Where better to hide than at Greyladies?'

'It'd increase the risk greatly for me to move back to the hotel,' Joseph agreed. 'People do notice the wheelchair, you know.'

'But it won't look good if you move in here with two men, Miss Latimer. People will talk.'

'Oh. I hadn't thought of that. And I don't want to get a bad reputation, but oh, I do want to stay here. So very much.'

Even the lawyer's stern expression softened at her words.

'Are there any families in the village who might supply maids, even temporarily?' Joseph asked. 'In the country, my mother often uses locals to help out at busy times and they're usually glad of the money. One of them could stay and chaperone Harriet.'

The lawyer was silent for a few moments, then snapped his fingers. 'I know! We could ask Miss Bowers to stay with you. I'm sure she would. She loves Greyladies.'

'Who's Miss Bowers?'

'She used to be the schoolmistress till she retired and there isn't anyone more respected in the entire village. If anyone will know how best to manage things, it'll be her.'

'Shall we send Frank with a note for her?'

'I could walk over to the village by the garden path. It'd only take a few minutes. I can call on her and ask her help. Do you mind waiting here, Miss Latimer, Mr Dalton?'

Joseph laughed. 'Mind waiting in a house filled with books? I should think not.'

'I love it here,' Harriet said. She decided she'd do a bit more exploring while the lawyer was gone.

She walked to the front door with him, then turned to Joseph. 'I'm going to look upstairs at the back.'

'Mr Lloyd said it wasn't safe.'

'I'll watch where I'm placing my feet, I promise you.'

The words were out before he could stop them. 'I wish I could come upstairs with you. I'm too tired to try it today, I'm afraid.'

She went to clasp his hand. 'I'll just have a quick look round. You go into the library and wait for me there.'

'You'll be careful?'

'Of course I will.'

Chapter Thirteen

Reginald Lloyd walked briskly into the village, turning left just before he reached the shop. Miss Bowers' neat cottage stood in a terrace of similar dwellings, each with a small garden in front. No one had such a pretty garden as hers, whatever the time of year. He stopped briefly to admire it.

As he raised his hand to knock on the door, it opened and she stood there, head on one side. She always reminded him of a sparrow waiting to pick up some tasty morsel. Only in her case, it was information not worms which she enjoyed gathering.

'What can I do for you, Mr Lloyd?'

He could see curtains twitching in the next cottage. 'I wonder if we could discuss this in private?'

'Of course. Do come in.'

He sat on the sofa, refused a cup of tea and explained exactly why he was there.

'You need a chaperone,' she summed up.

'Yes. Or rather, Harriet does.'

'What is she like?'

'The Latimer line has bred true in her, unlike . . .' He didn't say it, but she finished it for him.

'Unlike her nephew, who doesn't even look like a Latimer with that crinkly blond hair. He always reminds me of a ram my uncle used to keep. Magnificent animal, but chancy tempered.'

She fell silent, staring into space, so he said nothing to disturb her.

'I'd be happy to come and act as a chaperone, but she'll need a maid or two as well, and a gardener-cum-general helper. It's a big house and she must present herself as a lady from the start, not be scrubbing her own floors.'

'Yes. I agree absolutely. She'll find that strange, though. Do you know anyone suitable?'

She smiled, a cheeky smile, incongruous but charming on such a wrinkled face. 'Of course I do. Shall I come over to the house now, or shall I collect Miss Latimer's new staff first?'

'Collect the new staff, if you please, and . . . you couldn't order some groceries as well, could you? Miss Latimer is eager to move in at once.'

'She's met the ghost? She's been accepted as the Lady.'

'You know I don't believe in ghosts. But she does seem to think she saw one and she did go straight upstairs to the portrait without being told. How long will you need to sort things out?'

Another of her thoughtful silences, then, 'I've changed my mind. I think it'll be best if I come to meet Miss Latimer and we decide on servants together, not to mention food. I don't want to seem as if I'm taking over.'

He found himself saying meekly, 'Whatever you think best,' and waited for her to put on her hat and coat.

He was usually in charge of a situation, but as he'd discovered before, with Miss Bowers you often found yourself doing what she wanted, whether you agreed with it or not.

Harriet went back into the old part of the house, standing in the middle of the long room and turning slowly on the spot. She stretched out her arms, feeling as welcome here as she had in the newer part of the house. When she went to examine the side rooms more carefully, she found closets in the walls, filled with all sorts of small household items, some needing repair, some so old-fashioned they were no longer used.

At the rear of the long room was an area behind a wooden screen, with a pump standing in the corner over an old-fashioned slopstone. She tried the pump and clear water gushed out. When she collected some in her hand and drank it, she thought she'd never tasted anything quite as fresh and delicious.

She nearly missed the dark, narrow staircase in one corner because it had been boxed in. Opening the wooden door, she tried the stair treads, moving slowly from one to the other. She was at the top before she knew it.

This area of the old house was long and narrow, running along the side of the old hall, and the rooms leading off it were tiny. Servants rooms, she decided with a smile. She knew about those. Some had bedsteads, but there were no mattresses or bedding to be found.

Again, she almost missed the stairs leading up to an attic at the rear and she hesitated about whether to go up there. Why not? She could stand at the top and look round, didn't need to risk putting her foot through a rotten board.

The attic was dim, with a window at only one end and a very low roof, too low for her to stand up in parts. Like the attics at Dalton House, it was heaped with stuff: old furniture, wooden chests, the debris of centuries. Rich people had so many possessions they could afford to throw things away that could have been repaired.

The afternoon was drawing in, so she didn't try to explore the attic's contents. Joseph would be waiting for her. She felt guilty at having left him on his own for so long.

As she went down the stairs to the ground floor, she again experienced the illusion that people were in the hall, eating together, chatting, with someone playing a musical instrument. How strange! But it was a happy sound, like a group of friends.

She wished she had a group of friends.

She immediately scolded herself. She'd been given more than she'd wished for even in her wildest dreams, *and* she still had her dear friend Joseph with her. She had nothing to complain about.

I'll try to be worthy of it, she vowed again.

As she rejoined Joseph, she heard voices outside and ran to the window. 'It's Mr Lloyd and that must be Miss Bowers.'

The lawyer came into the house and stood back in the doorway to let an older lady come into the sitting room before him. She couldn't have been more than five foot tall, but she had a presence that instantly made itself felt.

'This is Harriet Latimer. Harriet, this is Miss Bowers, who has kindly agreed to come and help you settle in. I can't think of anyone more fitted to do that.'

The schoolteacher came forward, holding out her hand like a man and keeping Harriet's hand clasped in hers. 'My dear, you're a true Latimer. There are portraits of some of the ladies who've lived here and they could be your sisters. I am *so* glad Mr Lloyd has brought you here. Miss Agnes was quite sure you'd fit in.'

'I hope so.'

'You and I need to have a chat, but first, won't you introduce me to your friend?'

'This is Joseph – Joseph Dalton. He's helped me greatly over the past few years.'

Miss Bowers studied him carefully, then nodded as if he'd passed some test. 'I'm pleased to meet you and shall look forward to getting to know you. Now, Harriet, we can't settle in until we organise a few things, so we'd better make a start. I'm sure the gentlemen won't be interested so we'll leave them to chat on their own for a while.'

She led the way out and Harriet followed.

Mr Lloyd chuckled. 'She's an amazing woman, Miss Bowers. I'll be leaving you in good hands.' He pulled his pocket watch out and studied it. 'I shall have to set off for home soon because I don't want to travel after dark, so I'd better see that your luggage has been unloaded. Or have you changed your mind about coming back to Swindon?'

Joseph laughed. 'I don't think anything would persuade Harriet to leave Greyladies. She's come home.'

His words echoed in the quiet room. Strange that. Their voices hadn't echoed before.

Chapter Fourteen

At ten o'clock, after a nice lie-in, Winifred and her son got up and began to eat their breakfast. She heard the mail drop through the letter box and went into the hall to pick it up. She frowned as she studied the top envelope, which was addressed to her. It was plain but expensive-looking, with the address embossed on the back: Dalton House, Welworth, Hampshire.

Norris reached for the marmalade jar and began slathering some on his toast. 'Who's that from?'

'I've told you before, spread that marmalade more thinly. I'm not made of money.'

He waited. 'The letter, Ma. Who's it from?'

'It must be those people Harriet's working for.' She turned it in her hand, wondering why she felt so reluctant to open it, then got angry with herself and deliberately tore through the fancy embossing.

'Goodness me, it's from Mr Dalton, not his wife.' After a moment, she exclaimed, '*What?*' then reread it carefully.

By this time her son's attention was fully on her and his toast was lying unheeded on his plate. 'Is something wrong? What's happened?'

'Harriet's upped and run away, the ungrateful bitch. I find her a job, not just any job, mind, but a good one, and this is how she repays me.'

'The money will stop now.'

'So Mr Toffee-Nose Dalton says. But he wants to know where she might have gone, says she hasn't worked her notice and must be brought back to complete her obligations.'

She let out a huff of amusement. 'He can use all the long words he wants, but how the hell would I know where she's gone? And why should I care if she works out her notice for him or not if I'm not getting paid?'

'Can I see it?' He stretched out his hand.

She passed it to him.

Norris frowned as he read it. 'You didn't mention the lawyer's letter. Why would a lawyer be writing to Harriet?'

Shrugging, his mother poured herself a cup of tea.

'Dalton gives the name of the lawyer, see: Harrington and Lloyd, Swindon. We should find out what they want with her.'

'I'm not going off on a wild goose chase to Swindon. It's probably nothing.'

He was drumming his fingers on the table. 'Lawyers don't usually write letters for no reason. Think about that, Ma. Why do lawyers usually write to people?'

'To try to get money off you when you're in debt,' she said promptly.

'Or . . . ?'

Their eyes met and suddenly she was as interested as her son. 'Or they write to tell you a relative's died and left you something. She couldn't have run away from the Daltons without money, could she, because I take all her wages? She must have got hold of some money.'

'Did Harriet have any rich relatives, Ma? You always said Benson's folk were as poor as church mice.'

'They are. But *her* relatives, those of his la-di-da wife, might have had some money, I suppose. James told me there weren't any rich ones, but you never know. Sometimes an old person dies and leaves more than people expect.'

'If Harriet's been left anything,' Norris said slowly, 'then it should come under your control. You're her guardian till she's twenty-one, after all.'

'*If* she's been left anything,' Winifred said sarcastically. 'It's a big word, *if* is.'

'Might be worth poking around, though, to find out for sure. We're doing all right these days, you an' me, but I've only just started making my way. You can never have too much money, and *she* would only waste it. Tell you what: I'll go down to the library later and see if they have a town directory for Swindon.'

'Even if they do have one, it'll be out of date.'

'Worth a try, isn't it? Legal firms often pass from

father to son, so it probably won't matter if it's not the latest directory. If I can find an address, we'll write to them. I bet they'll know where she is. We'll claim to be *soooo* worried about *poor* little Harriet.' He chuckled as he crammed the last of the toast in his mouth, then pushed his chair back and stood up. After wiping his hands on the dish cloth, he went to don his outdoor clothes.

'Where are you going? It's not time for you to start work yet.'

'Got to see a fellow.'

She stared down the hallway, watching him pull his bowler hat right down and button up his overcoat. He'd fallen in with some rough types. And though he was making money, it wasn't in the way she'd wanted for him. Or for herself.

He opened the front door and she heard him curse at the sight of the rain slanting down. He turned up his collar, slammed the door shut behind him and left at a run.

Winifred shut the hall door and went to sit near the stove. It was going to rain most of the day, she reckoned, with those lowering skies. She wasn't going out today, not without a very good reason.

She couldn't stop thinking about that letter, though. She'd done well out of Harriet and didn't want the money to stop, though it was bound to one day, of course. It had mounted up, that money had. Every quarter she got a postal order from the Daltons' man of business, and took great pleasure in paying it into her savings bank account. What with that and James's insurance money, her life had become easier than she could ever remember.

She earned enough for her daily needs by helping Norris with the accounts for his various little businesses he'd set up. Debt-collecting for others round men's paydays, lending out small sums of money himself, nudging those who'd borrowed to pay him the interest weekly, even if they couldn't pay the loan back. Stupid fools they were to borrow like that. She'd never got into debt and she was never going to.

Norris had grown into a big, strong man and people were scared of him, but he had been careful not to get on the wrong side of the law. 'One day I'll have enough money to be respected in this town,' he always said. 'So though this isn't *nice* work, I'm doing it honestly.'

She found doing accounts easy, had always been good at figures, while Norris hated paperwork of any sort. He was like his father in that, but not in other ways, thank goodness. She'd been young when she married Philip Harding, too young to realise how lazy he was, or how violent.

Harriet's father had been a better husband. She missed James sometimes still. It could get lonely of an evening. He'd been pleasant to live with, had never hit her, not even once, and had brought home money regularly. He'd also been good in bed, very good. She missed that.

But she wasn't getting married again. She didn't intend to give up her savings to any man. Not even her son. It was her security, that money was.

Miss Bowers led the way into the library at Greyladies. 'This is my favourite place in the whole house. Miss Agnes used to allow me to borrow her books. Such a joy, reading! She knew I'd take care of them.'

She waited and when Harriet didn't play hostess, she went on, 'Shall we sit in the bay window, dear? It's so light and airy there.'

Harriet did as she was told, feeling rather shy with this confident old lady.

'My first question is: do you *want* to have a chaperone?'

'Mr Boyd says I need one if Joseph's going to be staying here, which I'd like him to do. He's such a good friend, you see, and he has nowhere else to go because he's only just left home. Would *you* mind coming to live here with me?'

'Mind? I'd be delighted. It's lonely living on your own, and besides, I'm writing a history of Greyladies and the Latimers, and all the diaries and other old papers are here in the house. Miss Agnes wouldn't allow me to take *them* away. She said they belonged here.' She waited as the young woman studied her.

Harriet smiled at her, suddenly looking happier. 'I'd really like you to be my chaperone, Miss Bowers, and to help me. I was a maid before, so I don't know how

246

to be mistress of a big house like this.' She gestured round her. 'And to tell you the truth, I still can't believe I *own* it.'

'You'll soon learn what to do. You seem an intelligent young woman. I can always tell the clever ones. It shows in the eyes.' She paused, head on one side. 'All right. I'll take you on.'

As the younger woman beamed at her, Miss Bowers said thoughtfully, 'The first thing you'll need is to get some help in the house, which means hiring a few servants. The place has been empty for a while.'

Harriet's smile faded. 'A *few* servants? I thought just one maid for the rough work and . . . and perhaps we'd send the washing out.'

'One maid won't be enough in a house this size, as you'll realise if you think about it. Don't worry, dear. I'm sure you'll have more than enough money to pay them and I'll not need paying. I'll only cost you my keep.'

'Oh.'

'People need to earn a living, you know, so you'll be helping them by giving them jobs. One of the housemaids is still in the village, living with her family and doing occasional days helping out here and there. Flora, she's called, and I know she'd love to come back here. It was her home for twenty years and she was the senior housemaid for half that. The under housemaid found herself a job in London as soon as the house was closed down and off she went, but Flora wanted to stay near her parents, who're getting on a bit.'

She waited but Harriet was still looking shocked at the idea of employing several servants. 'There are one or two families in the village with daughters of the right age, and they'd be glad to find them work here, close to home.'

'You think I should hire *two* maids?' Harriet said faintly.

'And a cook, also a scrubbing woman, a visiting laundry woman, plus a lad to help in the garden and with the odd jobs. That's the least you can get away with.'

'Oh, my goodness!'

'If you don't need fancy cooking, Livvy Hessing was widowed a couple of months ago, and not only does she need the money, she's lost with nothing to do, because she never had any children. She's a good plain cook, but she couldn't put on a fancy dinner party, mind.'

Harriet laughed. 'I wouldn't know how to hold a dinner party, fancy or not, even if I knew any people to invite to one.'

'You will one day.'

Miss Bowers heard her own voice echoing and could see that Harriet had heard it, too. 'There it goes again.'

'What?'

'The echo. It happens when someone in the house foretells what will happen. Haven't you heard the echo yet?'

'Yes. But I thought it was my imagination. Do *you* believe in such things? Mr Lloyd doesn't.'

'Oh, yes, I definitely do. Especially at Greyladies. Strange things happen here sometimes, and even then not everyone sees them. *You* must have the family gift if you've been chosen as the Lady, so you'll see and hear them, but you mustn't be afraid. The spirits who visit this house are good ones.' She let that sink in for a moment or two, understanding that the poor girl had a lot to take in.

But Harriet surprised her. 'I've already heard the echo and seen the Lady – if you mean the lady in the portrait at the top of the stairs, that is. It says Anne Latimer on the frame.'

'She was the first Mistress of Greyladies. She always comes to welcome a new Lady. Now, we must get back to practicalities. We can manage without a full-time gardener for the time being, but in a few weeks, we'll need one to start planting the vegetable garden. We need to hire the four indoor servants straight away and—'

Harriet's voice came out all squeaky. 'Do we really need *four*?'

'At least. It's a big house. The owner doesn't scrub her own floors or wash her own dishes, you know.'

Harriet let out her breath in a big whoosh. 'It's a good thing I'll have you to help me, Miss Bowers.'

'I think I was meant to help you, dear. I know the house better than anyone else, because Agnes and I were very friendly, and during her final year or two she showed me many of its secrets.' She patted her young companion on the shoulder. 'It'll work out all right, you'll see.'

She glanced towards the window. 'Now, let's send Mr Lloyd home while it's still daylight and start settling in. If you will choose which bedrooms people should have – and you can put me anywhere, I'm not fussy – I'll nip into the village to see Flora and Livvy, and order some food. Those two men must be getting hungry now. Men eat so much more than women.'

She moved towards the door, then stopped to add, 'After you've chosen the bedrooms, you could start making up the beds, if you don't mind. There's plenty of linen up in the attics, first cupboard on the left at the top of the stairs. If the sheets don't feel damp, don't bother to air them, because there are far too many other things to do before we can seek our beds tonight.'

She watched with approval as Harriet visibly pulled herself together.

'I'd better say goodbye to Mr Lloyd, then, and tell Joseph you'll be coming to live here as my chaperone, so it's all right for you to stay. I wonder where to put him. He doesn't find it easy to go up and down the stairs.'

'Is he badly crippled by his infirmity? I haven't seen him get out of the wheelchair.'

'He can walk, but not easily, and stairs are painful for him.'

'He has a kind face, not bad-looking, either, and he seems intelligent, so it's only his body that's not working properly. I don't know how we can find him a bedroom on the ground floor, though.'

'I've got an idea,' Harriet said. 'There are two empty rooms in the old part of the house, just off the big hall. They didn't seem damp or anything. He can sleep in one of those and his man Frank can have the other.'

'What a good idea. They're quite big rooms, too, and it'll be much more acceptable to the people round here if he lives in a separate part of the house from you.' She smiled mischievously at Harriet. 'The villagers will find out every detail of what you do at Greyladies, you know. Better be prepared for that.'

'I suppose so.'

'Being the Lady is a big responsibility and you won't be able to hide away and live quietly, because you'll be wanting to use your money to help others. The Ladies always do.'

'I'd like to do that, help others, I mean.'

'You'll have enough money to do a lot of good. Helping people used to give your Cousin Agnes a great deal of pleasure.' She looked at the clock and clicked her tongue in annoyance. 'I'd better go and see Flora and Livvy. You say goodbye to your lawyer, then sort out those bedrooms.'

Mr Lloyd was just coming back into the house as they went into the hall. 'Ah, there you are, my dear Miss

Latimer. I have to leave now, but I'll come back in a day or two to sort out the paperwork with you. You'll have to come into Swindon one day as well.'

She looked puzzled.

'You need to have access to the bank account to pay your bills. We'll arrange to meet the bank manager and hand things over to you.' He pulled out a purse he'd brought and pressed it into her hand. 'Here are fifty pounds to start you off.'

She stared at the money in amazement. 'But . . . I don't need that much.'

He laughed. 'You don't have to spend it unnecessarily, but you ought to be prepared.'

'I've never had even a savings bank account before. My stepmother took nearly all my wages.'

'It's not difficult to manage the accounts. Miss Bowers will show you how.'

Harriet looked very young, standing at the top of the front steps to wave him goodbye. He hoped he could keep her safe. She had no family to do that, so what she really needed was a husband, a strong man who would be kind to her and keep her stepmother at bay.

But before she could find a suitable husband, she had to learn to live as a lady should.

Well, at least he'd left her in good hands for now. He had a lot of respect for Miss Bowers. She would guide the new Lady better than anyone else could.

* * *

When Norris came home that evening, he twirled his mother round the living room.

'Stop that, you fool! What's wrong with you?'

'There's nothing wrong with me. In fact, everything looks very promising. I consulted a lawyer today. If Harriet has inherited anything, the money will be in our charge while she's a minor. And it'll stay with us after that, if I have any say in the matter.'

'You don't know that she's inherited anything,' Winifred said sourly.

He tapped his nose. 'I can feel it. Money. It makes my nose itch.'

'I hope you're right.'

'Well, we'll soon find out. I'm going over to Swindon on Friday to see this lawyer chappie.'

'I thought you were going to write to him.'

'I want to see his face when I tell him you'll be in charge of the inheritance. Exchanging words on paper doesn't show you whether a man's lying or not.'

'I still think you're wasting your time and money. Harriet won't have inherited anything worthwhile.'

'We'll see.' He tapped his nose again.

When the schoolteacher had left to go into the village, Harriet suggested to Joseph that he take one of the bedrooms in the old part of the house.

'Good idea. Let's choose it now.'

The rooms were spacious but empty, the floors and window sills dusty. There was no furniture, though there were cupboards filled with junk.

'I suppose that can be cleared out later,' she said. 'I need to find some paper and start making a list of jobs to do. Anyway, if you've decided on this room, I'll go and find Frank to help me move some beds down.'

He caught hold of her hand. 'Thank you, Harriet.'

'What for?'

'Letting me stay here.'

'You're my only friend.'

'And you're mine.'

They stood staring foolishly at one another for a few seconds, then she flushed and pulled her hand away. 'I'll go and find Frank.'

He'd been exploring the old stables and was just coming back to find his master. 'I don't think those stables and outhouses have been cleared out for years, miss.'

'Never mind those. Miss Bowers is going to move into Greyladies and Mr Dalton will be staying here in the old house, so I need you to help me with the beds.'

He scowled. 'Making beds is women's work.'

'We all need to help where needed,' Joseph said quietly from behind them.

'Anyway, I don't need you to make up the beds,' Harriet said. 'I want you to pull some beds to pieces from the new part of the house and bring them down, so that you and Mr Dalton can use these two rooms. *I* can put the sheets on the beds, if that's too hard for you.'

Joseph frowned at his manservant. 'Nonsense. Frank can help with that as well. Maybe I'll try to help him. It can't be all that hard to hold one end of a sheet.'

Somehow Joseph's quiet words seemed more effective than an outright scolding.

Frank shuffled his feet. 'Sorry, sir. Miss. I wasn't thinking.'

Harriet nodded acceptance of his apology. 'I can help you carry the pieces of bed frame down, if you need help. I'm stronger than I look. Let's go upstairs now and see if we can find some single beds. Will you be all right, Joseph?'

'Yes, of course. You don't mind if I explore the old part, do you?'

'Not at all.'

With so many bedrooms in the new part of the house, they soon found some suitable beds and while Frank went off to look for tools in the outbuildings, so that he could unbolt the frames, Harriet went up to find the linen room that Miss Bowers had told her about.

She still had to choose rooms for herself and Miss Bowers. She quickly sorted out some sheets and pillowcases for Joseph and Frank and took them down to the old house.

Then she went back to the new house, where she found two particularly lovely bedrooms, one at each end of three- sided landing, both looking out over the front gardens. It was easy to tell which one had belonged to her cousin Agnes, because it was still full of the old lady's possessions, while the drawers and cupboards in the similar front-facing room at the other end of the three-sided landing were empty.

Yet it was Agnes's room which attracted Harriet. She found herself speaking aloud, as if her cousin could hear her. 'Would you mind if I use this room?'

It was probably silly, just her imagination, but she felt a sense of warm approval.

From the bangs and thumps, Frank was busy dismantling and erecting the bed frames.

When she went to check on his progress, she found he'd set up the two beds already and had started to make them up, with Joseph's inexpert help. She paused in the doorway to watch them, two young men of about the same age. They were laughing hysterically over the mess they were making of such a simple job. She didn't think she'd ever seen Joseph having fun before, so crept away and left them to it.

Feeling thirsty now, she went into the kitchen, but was hesitant to tackle the task of lighting the big, old-fashioned cooking range. She didn't want to dirty her clothes because she hadn't many decent ones, and if this range was anything like the one at Dalton House, it'd have its own peculiarities. Better wait for the new cook to do that.

She began to check what was in the cupboards instead.

A few minutes later Frank peered in. 'We've made

up Mr Dalton's bed.' He grinned. 'It doesn't look as good as when my mum makes a bed, but it'll do. Mr Dalton said I should sleep in the room next to his. Is that all right with you, Miss Latimer?'

'That's fine. I'll leave you to make up your own bed.'

He saw the open door of the unlit stove and came to join her. 'Want me to light that thing for you first? Talk about old-fashioned. I could do with a cup of tea and something to eat, if you don't mind me saying so, and I daresay Mr Dalton will want one too.'

'You light it, I'll make the tea.'

There were slow, dragging footsteps and she turned to see Joseph walking slowly along behind his chair.

'I thought I'd move round a little . . . if you don't mind, Harriet?'

'Of course I don't mind. Why should I?'

There were footsteps outside the kitchen door and Miss Bowers came in, carrying a bag and a basket. She was followed by two women who were similarly laden. 'Oh, good. You're making some tea! I'm parched.'

She gestured to her companions. 'I offered Flora and Livvy jobs, as you wished, and they're happy to start straight away. This is your new mistress, Miss Latimer.'

Harriet smiled at the two women, both many years older than her. She was determined to make their working lives as happy as she could. 'I'm so pleased you can start now. There's such a lot to do here.'

Livvy moved forward. 'I can finish making the tea, miss, if you like. Mr Pocock from the shop is sending up some food to put us on till we can give him a proper list, an' he's sending word to Farmer Brunson that we'll need milk regular and Mrs Brunson sells eggs, so I said to send a couple of dozen . . . *if* that's all right. Miss Bowers said it would be. But me and her brought her milk and bits and pieces of food from home, so we can use them now. No use letting good food go to waste, is there?'

'Certainly not. I don't even know where things are here yet, but I'm sure you will, Flora, so perhaps you can help Livvy to settle in. Oh, and this is Frank, Mr Dalton's manservant.'

The two women looked him over curiously, then turned back to their new mistress.

'You leave this to us, miss,' Livvy said. 'I'll soon get used to things. It's a fine big kitchen.'

Flora beamed at Harriet. 'It's good to be back. It's a nice place to work at, Greyladies is, such a happy house.'

Miss Bowers beckoned to Harriet to follow her into the hall. 'Best to leave them to get on with making us some tea. It's their job, after all. Livvy had a little cry when I spoke to her, she was so happy to find a job, and Flora hasn't stopped smiling since I told her you needed her back.'

'I'm glad.'

Miss Bowers picked up her small suitcase. 'I'll go

home and pack the rest of my clothes tomorrow and get someone to bring my trunk up to the house. Which bedroom have you chosen for me?'

They went upstairs and she approved the choice, to Harriet's relief.

As they walked along the landing, Flora called out from the hall below, 'Tea's ready, miss. Do you want it bringing up?'

'No, we'll come down, thank you. Could you send Frank to fetch Mr Dalton from the old part of the house, please?'

Harriet knew better than to take her tea in the kitchen, even though that would have been quicker. It'd make the maids uncomfortable to have her there. Miss Bowers suggested they use the small morning room for their meals as Miss Agnes had done.

Frank was soon back, pushing Joseph's wheelchair. 'Shall I see to the oil lamps after I've had a cuppa, miss?'

'Yes, please.' Suddenly Harriet felt extremely weary and she saw that Joseph was looking pale and tired. She sat down and let her head fall back against her chair.

'We'll have a restful evening. You don't need to sort everything out at once, as long as we've got somewhere to sleep,' Miss Bowers said.

'Thank you for letting me use the old part of the house, Harriet.' Joseph smiled at her. 'It feels very welcoming, if that doesn't sound silly.'

'It doesn't sound at all silly.' Harriet felt the same about the whole house.

'We'll unpack our clothes after we've drunk our tea,' Miss Bowers decided.

There was a tap on the door and Flora peered in. 'Frank says you've not eaten anything since breakfast, Mr Dalton, so I've brought Miss Bowers' tin of biscuits. We can buy another tin from Mr Pocock till Livvy can make some of her own.'

'Good idea.' Miss Bowers handed round the biscuits and insisted they both eat two or three, to keep up their strength.

By eight o'clock that evening, they'd had a scratch meal.

Afterwards, Joseph gave up trying to stay awake and went off to bed. Harriet was wondering if it would be impolite to retire early too. 'Perhaps . . . an early night?'

Miss Bowers had watched her try to hide another yawn and laughed. 'You sound so hesitant. Don't be, my dear. You can do anything you like in your own house, stay in bed all day, dance the night away, whatever you want.'

It would take some time for her to get used to that freedom, Harriet thought. 'I will go to bed, then. I'm exhausted.'

The bedroom was quiet, with more shadows than light. Harriet set her oil lamp down on the small bedside table and sat on the bed for a few moments, looking round, thinking what a lovely room it was.

Then she got her nightdress out and snuggled down under the covers, where she found that one of the maids had put an earthenware hot-water bottle. Such a luxury to have that done for her!

She'd expected to have trouble sleeping in a strange house, but could feel herself slipping into sleep straight away.

Her last thought was that she'd come home. She really had.

Chapter Fifteen

William Dalton grew angry all over again when he didn't receive a reply from the stepmother of the maid who'd run away. The woman should have written back immediately when she received a letter from one of her betters.

He decided to summon the lawyer and find out what was going on. When his wife looked in to see what he was doing, he complained to her about the manners and morals of the lower classes.

Sophie waited till he eventually ran out of steam, then ventured to ask, 'I presume it's about Harriet again. Is she really worth all this fuss?'

'No, she isn't. It's the principle of the thing that matters. It's the duty of our class to set standards. And since that stepmother of hers didn't reply, I'm damned well going to insist the maid do the right thing. Which means contacting the lawyer and asking what's going on. What a lawyer could be writing to a *maid* about, I cannot think.'

He sent off a peremptory note to summon Mr Lloyd, while his wife took refuge in her bedroom, to sit worrying about how short-tempered William had become since the troubles with Selwyn. She no longer enjoyed his company and wouldn't have Joseph to talk to from now on, either.

To her surprise, she was missing her youngest son more than she'd expected to – his gentle wit, his interest in the wider world he read about in newspapers, his kindness. It worried her that she didn't know where he was, worried her greatly.

For the first time it occurred to her that Joseph had left at the same time as Harriet. Surely they hadn't gone off together? Surely even someone as unworldly as him wouldn't have seduced one of his mother's maids?

No, Harriet had been a virtuous girl, not the sort to behave immorally. You could always tell. Sophie frowned. You *could* tell, couldn't you?

She couldn't help remembering how much time the two of them had spent together over the past few years. They'd seemed so comfortable together.

No, what was she thinking of? They couldn't possibly have gone off together. Joseph wouldn't do that to her.

She wasn't going to mention the possibility to William. He'd go mad at the thought of his son being involved with a maid. If he hadn't gone mad already.

He'd been in a strange mood ever since he'd had

to publicly refute Selwyn's debts and stop living in the London house. And who wouldn't be upset about that? She was, too.

Reginald wasn't able to go back to Greyladies to see Harriet on the Friday, as planned, because one of his rich clients suddenly dropped dead on the Thursday. That meant Reginald had to help the fluttery spinster daughter deal with the situation. Her father's death at the age of eighty-two wasn't unexpected, but she was acting as if it was the end of the world.

Knowing what his daughter was like, the old man had left a will and full instructions for his funeral, but even so, Miss Chapman was panicking and couldn't be left to deal with undertakers and other arrangements alone. Besides, Reginald had promised her father he'd help her when the time came, and he prided himself on keeping his word.

There was just time to catch the last post, so he wrote to Harriet, explaining the situation and assuring her that he'd be with her on Monday, without fail.

After all, she'd be busy settling in and she had enough money to manage on for quite a while, and she had Miss Bowers to help her. So there was no great rush. He smiled, remembering her shocked expression when he gave her the money. He didn't think she'd waste it.

He wondered for a moment what she would do

with herself at Greyladies once she'd settled in. She had a very different background from the other lady owners.

Friday started badly. Mr Lloyd's clerk sent word that he was too ill to come to work, which left him and his partner to the mercies of the junior clerk and a new office boy not yet sure of his duties.

That may have been why a man was shown into Reginald's room without any warning. 'Gentleman to see you, Mr Lloyd.'

Before Reginald could say anything, the office boy had left a man standing in front of the desk, not even giving his name.

'Do I know you, sir?'

'No. Name's Harding.'

He held out his hand, but Reginald stayed where he was on the other side of the desk. This was clearly no gentleman, and in fact, his visitor looked a rather rough type.

The man scowled and let the hand fall. 'I think you know my stepsister Harriet Benson, though. You wrote to her recently.'

Reginald's heart sank. Of all the times to be confronted with this, when he had Miss Chapman waiting for him. 'How can I help you, Mr Harding?'

'You do know Harriet, don't you? After all, you wrote her a letter.'

'I cannot discuss a client's business with anyone else.'

'But she *is* your client?'

'May I ask what business that is of yours?'

'I'm here on behalf of my mother who is her guardian. Harriet is only nineteen. She's a minor. So she's not the one you should be conducting business with.'

Reginald breathed deeply and slowly, trying not to let his worry show. Unless he mistook matters, this young man was a sharp customer and poor Harriet was, as she had feared, about to become the target of her step-relatives' attentions. They'd been taking her wages and now, no doubt, wanted to take over her inheritance.

How the hell had they found out so quickly? And what had they found out? He didn't ask the man to sit and remained standing himself, hoping to get this over as soon as possible.

'First off, we want to know what she's been left.'

'As I've already told you, Mr Harding, I cannot discuss a client's business with anyone else.'

'Not even with her guardian? If necessary, we'll get the local magistrate involved. He'll soon insist you deal with us.'

'If what you say is correct, and your mother is indeed Miss Latimer's guardian, then it's her I need to deal with, not you. She hasn't come with you today and, actually, you could be an imposter, for all I know.'

'How would I know about this if I was an imposter? My mother sent me, asked me to find out what's going on. She's a busy woman.'

'Then perhaps she could write and make an appointment to see me when she isn't busy.'

'And *perhaps* you're trying to avoid telling us the truth. If you're dipping your fingers into the pot, we'll find out, you know.'

'If you make any more remarks like that, I shall sue you for slander.'

Reginald let the silence continue for a couple of minutes, with Mr Harding's heavy breathing and the faint sounds of passers-by in the street the only things interrupting it.

'I think you'd better leave now, Mr Harding. Tell your mother to write to me and arrange a meeting, if she claims to be Miss Latimer's guardian. And she will need to bring proof of that, of course.'

'Miss Latimer? Harriet's a Benson, not a Latimer. That was her mother's name.'

Reginald could have kicked himself for making this mistake.

'It *is* something to do with her mother's family, then.'

'As I said, I'm busy.' Reginald went towards the door and cried out in shock as his visitor grabbed his arm and swung him round, slamming him against the wall.

'I'll bring my mother to see you on Monday morning. Ten o'clock sharp. See that you're in, Mr Bloody Lloyd.'

Reginald was afraid because the brute was so much

bigger than him, and much younger too, but he wasn't going to give in to violence. 'I'm sorry but I have an appointment at that time.'

'Then change it, or we'll go straight to the nearest magistrate and get a paper saying you have to tell us about Harriet and hand over her business to us. I've already spoken to my own lawyer and that's his advice. Get you to hand things over to Harriet's guardian. We don't *want* to make a fuss, but we will if we have to.'

He slammed Reginald into the wall again, smiled and walked slowly out.

Reginald staggered across to his desk on legs suddenly gone wobbly and plumped down on the chair, his heart thumping with the shock of this assault. Unfortunately, he wouldn't be able to prove that Harding had laid hands on him, but he'd take care never to be alone with the fellow again.

It took quite a while and two cups of strong tea before he felt capable of giving the junior clerk and office boy the dressing-down they deserved for letting in his unwelcome visitor. As he'd suspected, Harding had simply pushed his way in.

He couldn't avoid the visit to Miss Chapman, but he made his apologies for only being able to spend an hour with her, then went home to have lunch with his wife and tell her about the incident.

She was indignant on his behalf and anxious about Harriet, to whom she'd taken a great fancy.

'You can't let a man like that get hold of her and her money, Reggie, you just can't.'

'There's not much I can do to prevent it if that fellow's mother is her legal guardian.'

'Well, I'm sure you can think of something. You can be very cunning when you need to.'

'Sometimes, my dear, you can't win a case, even when natural justice is on your side. Sometimes the law is an ass and uses its might to kick reason out of the way.'

When he went back to the office in the afternoon, he found another unpleasant surprise, a peremptory letter from Mr Dalton, summoning him to visit Dalton House in Welworth, Hampshire, for an urgent consultation about the runaway maid, Harriet Benson.

The note was rather confusing and it took a while for Reginald to figure out that Mr Dalton wanted to drag Harriet back to work out her notice *and* he seemed to be intending to manage her inheritance for her, if that was needed, even though he didn't know what it was.

Had the man run mad?

Reginald wrote a quick reply to say that he was too busy to visit Mr Dalton and was sure there was no need for Miss Benson to work out her notice, especially as he gathered that Mr Dalton had not been able to pay her the wages she was owed. Let that suffice instead of her giving notice. He remembered to use Harriet's official surname this time, but reminded himself that they needed to change it legally as soon as possible.

No wonder the poor young woman had run away, if she had men like this harassing her. The trouble was, she had no one but a cripple and her lawyer to defend her from the two bullies who were pursuing her.

Harding was the more to be feared physically, but Dalton was a gentleman and might have other methods of getting his own way against a mere maid.

Reginald wasn't sure what he could legally do to help Harriet. At the last resort, he'd have to suggest she run away again and hide till she was twenty-one.

He didn't think a magistrate would look kindly on that.

But he didn't think Harding would give up easily, so she might not be safe physically if the fellow pursued her.

Harriet woke with a start as someone knocked on her bedroom door. For a few seconds she wondered where she was, then remembered and lay back, smiling. 'Come in.'

Flora brought in a cup of tea.

'Oh, how lovely! Thank you so much. Did you sort out a bedroom for yourself and sleep all right?'

'I slept like a baby, miss. I'm back in my own room in the attics instead of sharing with my niece, who can't lie still for more than a minute. Begging your pardon if I'm being too familiar.'

'Oh, no. You're not.' Understanding how much servants saw, whether they admitted it or not, Harriet decided on honesty from the start. 'You must be aware that I was a maid myself until a few days ago. I still can't believe I've inherited all this.' She waved one hand to indicate the house.

Flora's rather severe face softened. 'It must have been a shock, though a pleasant one. Didn't you have any idea at all, miss?'

'No. I'd never even heard of Greyladies or Miss Agnes. So I'd be grateful for any help you can give me, never mind that I'm the mistress here. Just tell me if you see me doing something wrong. I'm terrified of upsetting the people in the village or the local gentry till I know my way around and what to do.'

'We'll get you through the first few days, don't you worry, and I'm sure you'll soon feel at home. My mother can remember Miss Agnes coming here and *she* didn't know much about Greyladies then, either. The house always passes to the one most able to care for it. Though how the ladies know who that is, no one can tell.'

'I'm glad I'm not the first to be surprised by the inheritance.'

'Well, for a start, you'd better drink your tea before it goes cold, miss, and I'll see if Mr Dalton is awake. I daresay he'll be glad of a cup of tea, too.'

At the door she paused for a moment and said thoughtfully, 'It's nice to have someone staying in the old part of the house. It fair gives me the creeps when I have to go in there on my own. You can hear people talking and laughing, even though there's no one there. Not that they've ever hurt me, but them as don't believe in ghosts haven't lived here, is what I say.'

There was no help for it. Reginald had to see Harriet and let her know about this latest development, then discuss what to do.

He hired an enterprising young man who owned a motor car to drive him to Greyladies, making an early start at eight o'clock on Saturday.

The journey was much quicker in a motor car, thank goodness, and he asked Stanley to wait for him at the rear of the house. 'I'm sure the servants will provide you with some refreshments. I'll not be staying long.'

'Very well, Mr Lloyd.'

Flora answered the front door.

'Nice to see you working here again,' Reginald told her.

'Nice to be back, sir. You'll be wanting Miss Latimer. Would you like to come through into the sitting room then I'll go and find her?'

Harriet came hurrying in to greet him soon afterwards. 'Is something wrong, Mr Lloyd? You said you weren't coming again till at least Monday.'

'I fear we do have a problem.'

'Oh dear. Look, before you tell me, let me ask Flora to prepare a tea tray and then I'll see if Joseph and Miss Bowers can join us. If you don't mind, that is?'

'I think it's a good idea. They'll need to be prepared for trouble as well, I'm afraid.'

She stared at him for a moment, wide-eyed, then hurried away.

As he watched her, he frowned. She needed better clothes, and as quickly as possible. And she should get used to ringing for her maids, not running errands herself. Which reminded him: she needed to hire another housemaid and find a lad to do the odd jobs. Especially now. The more people she had around her, the safer she would be.

When Harriet came back, Miss Bowers was with her. A few moments later, Joseph joined them in his wheelchair.

'Shall we wait until Flora has brought some tea, so that we can talk without interruptions?' Reginald suggested.

Harriet was looking so worried, Miss Bowers reached out to pat her hand.

The maid wasn't long with the tea and when they'd each been given a cup, Reginald swallowed a mouthful or two, then allowed himself two biscuits because he was hungry.

However, he refused a refill and put his cup down,

waiting till they'd done the same. 'I had a visit from your stepbrother yesterday, Miss Latimer.'

Her face went deathly pale and she put one hand up to her mouth in an age-old gesture of fear. 'What did Norris want?'

'To know why I'd written to you. He said if it was a matter of an inheritance then it was for your stepmother to deal with, because she's your guardian. How he found out about the letter, I don't know.'

'My father, I should think,' Joseph said. 'He'll have sent them notice that you've left his service and he won't be paying them your wages.'

'But even so, how did they find out that I'd received a legacy?'

'Easy enough to guess. Legacies are often the reason why lawyers contact people unexpectedly, after all,' Miss Bowers said.

'My stepmother made herself my guardian!' Harriet said bitterly. 'It wasn't because she cared about me, or because anyone asked her to, but so that she could take my wages.'

'She wasn't formally cited as your guardian in your father's will?'

'He didn't leave a will. He wasn't even fifty when he died and he didn't seem at all infirm, so everyone was shocked by his death.'

'I see. Hmm.'

'Does that mean she isn't really my guardian?'

He considered this, then said slowly, 'It certainly

complicates the issue. But she'd be the natural person for the courts to appoint, if she took this matter to law. Even a magistrate probably wouldn't quibble with her claim to be your guardian.'

'Oh, dear.'

'And I must confess that I let slip your new name, even though we haven't made it official yet. I'm hoping your stepbrother won't find out where you are, but if he does, he may turn up here without consulting me. He seems a very *forceful* young man.'

'He's a bully.'

'Yes. I can believe that. He slammed me against the wall as he threatened me, but unfortunately we were alone, so it's his word against mine about that assault.'

Reginald gave her a moment to take this in, then went on, 'I'm trying to delay things until I can think of a way to help you, but I must admit, a solution doesn't come readily to mind, not in law. I've refused to deal with him, since he isn't your guardian, and that's delayed matters a little. But he said he'd be bringing his mother to see me on Monday, and I'd better be there. I fear he may bring a legal representative, too. He said he'd already consulted his lawyer.'

'Norris has a lawyer? *Norris?*'

'So he said.'

'He doesn't usually have two pennies to rub together, and he's always been a scruffy brute. Why would he need a lawyer, or even know one?'

'He was well dressed when he came to see me, didn't look to be short of money.'

'Then he's changed a lot since I knew him. I . . . don't like the thought of that. What's he been doing to make money?' She thought for a moment, then said firmly, 'If he and his mother try to take over Greyladies, I'll have to run away again till I turn twenty-one. I'm not living with him again, not for anything on earth.'

'We'll try to find a way round this, even if it means paying them off. They might accept that.'

She shook her head. 'You won't be able to. Why would they accept part of my money when they could have access to it all?'

'Why indeed?' He turned to Joseph. 'What do you think, Mr Dalton?'

'I don't know what to think. Except that I don't want Harriet falling into their hands.'

The warm look he gave her as he said this made Miss Bowers stiffen and exchange quick glances with the lawyer.

'I can't do much more till I know exactly what they want,' Reginald said. 'But I'd suggest you be on your guard from now on. Don't leave the front door unlocked, and tell Flora not to let strangers inside by the front or back doors. In fact, you'd better warn the servants about Harding and his mother.'

Harriet felt numb with fear. Just when she'd been feeling safe and happy, *they* had reappeared in her life.

'Would you like to stay to lunch, Mr Lloyd?' Miss Bowers asked.

She should have made that offer, Harriet realised in shame.

'If you don't mind, I'll send for Stanley and his car, so that I can get home again. My wife and I have a family gathering planned for this afternoon. It's our younger daughter's birthday.' He stood up.

Harriet rang the bell and gave the order to Flora, then moved towards the door with him. There were sounds from the rear of the house of someone trying to crank up a car motor and after a couple of attempts, an engine started.

The car came chugging round from the back of the house and Mr Lloyd got in, waving one hand as he was driven away.

She didn't realise she was still standing outside the front door, staring into the distance, till Miss Bowers touched her arm. 'Come inside, dear.'

She did as asked, but could only stare numbly at her two friends and ask, 'What am I going to do?'

'I'm not sure, dear, but between us we shall think of something, I'm sure. In the meantime, I'm going to show you the secret hiding place in this room, then if your stepbrother turns up unexpectedly, you'll have somewhere to hide.'

'I can't hide in there till I'm twenty-one.'

'No. But you may need to hide for an hour or two.' She walked across the room to the fireplace.

'This is how it works.' She tugged at the carving on the overmantel and a section of the wooden panelling further along slid slowly sideways.

Joseph went to investigate the aperture at once. 'How exciting! I've read about secret panels, but I've never seen one. Dalton House didn't seem to have any.'

Behind the panelling was a small space about a yard deep and two yards wide, with a narrow bench along the back. It was just big enough for two people, if they didn't mind being squashed.

Harriet couldn't resist going inside and Joseph left his chair to follow her, tripping on his way in and catching hold of her hand to steady himself.

'Are you all right?'

He grinned. 'Nearly fell then. I do fall sometimes, but I don't seem to hurt myself much, beyond the odd bruise, so you mustn't worry.' He lowered his voice, 'Whatever I do, though, I'll never be strong enough to protect you from people like your stepbrother. I regret that.'

She returned his smile, and for a moment, forgot her worries in the pleasure of knowing he cared about her.

'This is just one of the secrets of Greyladies,' Miss Bowers said from the entrance to the hiding place. She could sense the invisible bond that joined them and wondered if they fully understood where their own feelings about each other were leading. She thought not. There was a naivety about them both. Well, not for her to wake Sleeping Beauty.

'You can close the door once you're in by lifting that lever at the side of the bench. And if you lift it again, the door opens.'

'I hadn't even noticed any difference in this panel,' Harriet said.

'It's been cleverly done. Why don't you try it out?'

'Could we?' Joseph asked.

Harriet didn't like the thought of being shut in such a small space. What if the door stuck and they were trapped in here? But Joseph's face was alight with eager interest, and she couldn't say no to him. 'You do it, Joseph. You're closer to the lever.'

He seemed to have no trouble lifting it.

'You must be stronger than you look.'

'My arms are. They sometimes have to help my legs.'

The door closed gradually and when they were sitting in darkness, she drew in a shuddering breath and reached for his hand. 'I don't like being shut in dark places.'

'You'll be fine. I'm here. Would you mind waiting a minute to see if there's any light coming in?'

'Not as long as you keep hold of my hand.'

As their eyes grew used to the dimness, they began to see shapes faintly.

His voice was quiet, but the sound of it comforted her. 'There's a draught coming from somewhere, so you'd be able to breathe easily, even if you get shut in here for a long time.'

'I'm glad to know that. But I don't think I want to come in here again, except in an emergency.'

His head was close to hers and he couldn't resist leaning forward and planting a gentle kiss on her cheek. 'Your skin is as soft as I'd imagined.'

'Oh, Joseph.' She wanted him to do more than kiss her cheek and when he began to move his head away, she surprised herself by leaning forward to give him a quick kiss. She'd intended to kiss his cheek, but he was moving his head and the kiss landed on his lips.

'Harriet.' He cupped her face in his hands and kissed her back, as gently as he did everything else, but still, the kiss stirred a warmth inside her and made her long to kiss him again.

But he pulled away, saying bitterly, 'Sometimes it's hard not to be a proper man. I shouldn't be doing this.'

'You're proper enough for me.'

Silence, then, 'You deserve better.'

'I don't need better than you. Only I thought . . . well, the differences between us are so great.'

He laughed, then. 'You're a rich woman, Harriet. The differences have turned round, and it's I who am unsuitable, because I lack the means to support a wife.'

'A wife! Me?'

'Did you think I'd consider any lesser relationship with you?'

'I didn't think you'd consider me at all in that way.'

She suddenly became aware that someone was banging on the entrance panel and calling out to ask if they were all right. 'Oh, bother!'

'We'd better open the door. And we'd better both think hard about . . . things. You really can do much better than me.' He pulled the lever.

She'd have refuted this hotly, but the door began to open just then and Miss Bowers peered in.

'Did you have difficulty opening the panel again?'

'We were letting our eyes grow accustomed to the darkness,' Joseph said quickly, seeing Harriet was still upset. 'We wanted to see if any light came in, and a little does, though from where, I can't work out. Sorry if we worried you, Miss Bowers.'

He gestured to Harriet to leave the hiding place first, and followed her, standing looking back inside it, then moving away towards his wheelchair.

'We should check the locks on doors and windows and tell the servants to be careful who they let in from now on,' he said.

'And we need to hire another maid and a lad,' Miss Bowers added. 'We'll ask Flora if she knows anyone. She's a very sensible woman.'

'Let's talk to them straight away,' Harriet suggested. 'And you'd better come with us too, Joseph, because you'll want to warn Frank as well.'

She couldn't help feeling bitter that Norris and her stepmother had even marred her joy in her new home.

* * *

The two maids and Frank listened quietly, then Livvy said, 'We won't let any strangers in if we can help it, miss, you can be sure of that. But if your stepbrother is a big man, there's only Frank to deal with him, and he's not what you'd call a fighting man, is he?'

Frank scowled at her.

'The blacksmith's youngest!' Miss Bowers said suddenly.

They all looked at her in puzzlement.

'Do you mean Mickey? He's a blockhead, that one,' Flora said scornfully. 'His father won't let him near the forge.'

'That's because he's clumsy. *I* think he needs to wear spectacles, but he won't even try them. He's all right when it comes to simple jobs, but if he needs to deal with something like hot iron, he's a danger to himself. Still, he's a big, strong lad and they'd be glad to find him a bit of regular work. I'll go and see Mr Deems straight away. I've always got on well with him.'

'You need a wardrobe and other things moving down to your bedroom, Mr Dalton. With Mickey to help Frank, that'll be easy.'

'My niece would be glad of a job as maid,' Flora said hesitantly. 'They won't let her work away from home in a town, but they'd let her live in here at Greyladies, I'm sure.'

Miss Bowers looked at her in surprise. 'Phyllis? Is she that old already? My goodness, they do grow up quickly. Yes, she'd be good. I always found her a sensible child. Shall I pop in and see her mother?'

'Tell her I sent you.' Flora smiled ruefully. 'As long as I don't have to share a bed with her ever again.' She glanced at Harriet. 'Is that all right, miss? You don't look happy. Should we have left it to you? Only you don't know anyone round here.'

'Oh, sorry. It's not that. I just can't believe I'm hiring so many servants.' Harriet flushed.

'That's all right, then, miss,' Livvy said. 'We do understand. I'd feel just the same if I was in your place. But at least you've had a good education, so you'll fit in well enough with the local gentry once the dust has settled. I heard you talking to Mr Dalton about some book you'd both read. Wonderful, it was, to hear you. I couldn't even understand some of the words you both used, and you remembered more than he did.'

She sighed. 'I never can remember things if I've only read about them. If you show me, and I can get my hands on it, I'll remember every detail, but if you ask me to find something out from a book, I'm lost. Them letters all seem jumbled up, somehow.'

'Maybe you need glasses as well,' Harriet suggested. 'We'll send you both into Swindon to get tested when things settle down, then I'll buy you a cookery book, one full of new recipes.'

'Well, I must say, I might enjoy being able to read a cookery book,' Livvy allowed. 'Even if I had to wear glasses to do it.'

Miss Bowers beamed at them as if they were pupils

of hers. 'There we are, then. Now, I'll go into the village this afternoon and pack the rest of my clothes while I'm there. If Mickey's father agrees to him working here, he can bring my things back, and he can fetch yours too tomorrow, Flora and Livvy. We'll take it in turns to go back and pack up, shall we?'

It would all be so simple and pleasant, Harriet thought, if she didn't have the threat of her stepbrother hanging over her. She didn't know when she'd met a nicer bunch of people than her new servants and Miss Bowers.

And Joseph. Oh, it was wonderful to be with him. And if he meant what he said . . . Her heart nearly skipped a beat at the thought of marrying him.

Chapter Sixteen

On Monday morning Norris and his mother took an early train to Swindon. She grumbled intermittently as the train rattled along, seeming to have no belief in the chance of them finding that Harriet had inherited anything of value, let alone the money he craved.

'She couldn't have, Norris. Her mother had nothing except a few mouldy old books.'

Later, she said, 'Son, I'm sure it was all stories that mother of hers made up.'

And later still, 'Them Latimers didn't come to James's funeral, did they, so why would they leave Harriet anything?'

Her son made soothing noises each time and let her talk. He felt sure there would be something for them. He was developing a nose for money.

Outside the lawyer's office she stopped to ask, 'Is my hat on straight?'

'Yes. But Lloyd won't care if it's crooked.'

'I'll care.'

'Well, it's straight, though why you want to wear such a huge thing, I don't know. It was ridiculous, going out and buying that specially to come here.'

'It's fashionable, what *ladies* are all wearing. It makes me feel I can face them.' She patted the hat self-consciously.

'Come on, then, Lady Winifred.' He offered his arm and led the way in, saying in a low voice, 'Move slowly and try to look confident.'

This time an elderly clerk was stationed in the outer office. 'May I help you . . . sir, madam?'

'I've got an appointment with Mr Lloyd,' Norris said.

'Your name, please?'

'Harding.'

'Ah, yes. Mr Lloyd said he was expecting you.'

The clerk's words might be polite, but his expression was that of a person who can smell something rotten. 'If you'll take a seat, I'll tell Mr Lloyd you're here.'

Norris debated pushing his way into the office, as he had last time, just to show he wasn't going to be condescended to, but decided against it. He'd give things a try the legal way first, using polite words and acting slowly. But he wasn't going to be patient for long.

He glanced up at the clock. He wasn't going to let them keep him waiting for long, either.

There was the sound of footsteps and a burly man came out of the inner corridor. He looked towards

Norris and his mother. 'Mrs Benson? Mr Harding?'

Norris stood up. 'Yes.'

'Mr Lloyd will see you now. This way, please.'

Norris held out his arm to his mother, but the gesture was spoilt by the corridor being too narrow for them to walk side by side, so he gestured to her to go first, wishing she didn't look so nervous and wasn't wearing such a silly hat.

The man led them into the office and Mr Lloyd stood up, staying behind the desk.

I rattled him last time, Norris thought gleefully. 'This is my mother, Mrs Benson, Harriet's guardian. Mother, this is Mr Lloyd.'

He gave them a tiny nod, but didn't come out from behind the desk to offer his hand. 'Please take a seat.'

The man who'd escorted them in pulled out a chair for the lady, but left Norris to fend for himself. When they were both seated, the fellow went to stand to one side of the desk, arms folded, scowling at them.

Bodyguard, Norris decided. I could beat him easy, though.

The lawyer's tone was icy. 'Before we discuss anything, do you have proof that you're Harriet's guardian, Mrs Benson?'

Winifred scowled at him. 'I've got proof that I married her father, which made me her stepmother. What other proof do you need?'

'Proof that you were appointed her guardian.'

'First time I've heard you need proof to look after your own children.'

'That's the point. She's not your child. May I see your marriage certificate?'

She fumbled in her bag and produced the brand-new envelope they'd bought to put the certificate in, leaning forward to slap it down on the desk. 'Be careful how you handle that. It means a lot to me.'

Norris hid a smile. His ma was angry at the way Lloyd was looking down his nose at her and had lost her nervousness. Good.

Reginald made a big play of studying the marriage lines and showing them to the bodyguard. 'I'll just write down the details.'

He seemed to take a long time to do that, Norris thought.

The lawyer eventually gave the marriage certificate back to Mrs Benson. 'Do you have a copy of your husband's will?'

'He didn't leave one.'

'Then some proof that you inherited his estate.'

'I don't have any proof, I just did. He was my husband, so everything came to me. No one else to inherit, was there? Anyway, that's all water under the bridge now. What's that got to do with Harriet?'

'You weren't actually appointed her guardian, so I'll need to consult my client about your claim, and also ask advice from other lawyers.'

'Her wages were sent to me by Mr Dalton, weren't

they? That's proof *he* accepted me as her guardian, if anything is.'

'Not if someone else ought to be her guardian. In fact, if that were the case, you might not be entitled to the wages and might have to return them.'

'*What?* I'll not—'

Norris put a hand on his mother's arm to stop her saying anything else. He was getting fed up of this. He leant forward, but to his annoyance, that caused the big fellow to take a step forward and scowl at him.

He leant back again. It would do their case no good to make trouble today, that was sure. They had to tread softly, use the law to get what they wanted. 'Go on,' he told the lawyer. 'What happens then?'

'As I said, I shall have to consult Miss . . . er, Benson. When I saw her a while ago, she said she didn't need a guardian, and let's face it, she's nineteen now and can support herself, so I see no need, either.' He stood up. 'Perhaps you could come back next week?'

'We'll be back tomorrow,' Norris said.

'Then you'll be disappointed. I have other clients I need to look after and your stepsister doesn't live in Swindon. Monday of next week would be better.'

'Friday. That's the latest I'll accept.'

'It'll have to be Saturday. I have a court case on Friday.'

'Very well. But don't try to postpone it. We'll be here on Saturday.'

Norris let the snooty sod of a lawyer have them

shown out by the big fellow and didn't speak till they were standing outside. 'We're going to have to see a magistrate in the end, Ma. He's playing for time. Since we're here now, we'll ask around and make sure we know where to find one if we get no satisfaction next time.'

'You're letting him delay things.'

'I'm letting people see we've been reasonable.'

She snorted in disgust.

He offered his arm again and they began walking. 'You did well in there, Ma.'

She sniffed. 'It'd take more than a stuffed shirt like him to frighten me. Come on. Let's find somewhere we can get a meal and a pot of tea. I'm famished and this hat's given me a headache.'

The following day, Norris went back to the public library and asked to see the Swindon directory again.

He scowled as he sat down. If there was one thing he hated, it was books. Smelly, dusty ones like this especially.

But he felt even more sure there was money to be had from Harriet, or else why would that lawyer be delaying things? So he went through the directory carefully, searching for the word Latimer. He didn't find it.

The librarian looked down his nose at Norris as he complained you could never find something when you wanted it. 'You could try one of the directories for the county of Wiltshire. If this family you're looking for isn't living in Swindon, their name won't be in the Swindon directory, will it?'

Another damned book to go through. But the librarian was right and this time Norris found what he was looking for.

Latimer. Family name for the owners of Greyladies in the village of Challerton. The family has owned the house since the sixteenth century. Inheritance is down the female line. Not a large residence, but of some interest architecturally, because it contains . . .

The rest of the entry was double Dutch to Norris, but he copied down the names Challerton and Greyladies, and sat back smiling. He knew where she was now. Where else would she have gone but to her mother's family? It sounded as if they were worth a lot, too.

Maybe he should go to this Challerton and have a look around on the quiet. Yes, that's what he'd do.

He went up to the counter and handed in the book. 'Thanks. That was very helpful. Now I wonder if you can help me find out where a village called Challerton is on the map?'

The man's scorn softened a little. Everyone liked to feel superior, Norris thought, even a scrawny old muffin-face like this one.

They pored over a map and found Challerton, a

tiny place by the size of the dot and the name which you had to squint at to read. That wasn't good if he wanted to find out about Harriet. In small villages everyone knew everyone else's business and they might mention seeing him.

'I've been to Challerton,' the librarian said. 'Years ago, it was. I'd forgotten till I saw it on the map. My cousin and I were out hiking and it was a hot day, so we called in for a bottle of lemonade at the village shop and went to look at the ruins of the abbey. Not much left to see, so we didn't stay long. There's a big house, Greyladies – is that the one you're looking for? Yes, well, it's a private home, so you can't go and look round it, so you're wasting your time.'

'It's a big house, then?'

'Oh, yes. And old.'

'Greyladies is a strange name for a house.'

'Used to belong to the abbey and the nuns wore grey habits, the shopkeeper told us.'

'Habits? How can you wear habits?'

The librarian sighed. 'That's the name for nuns' clothing. You've seen nuns?'

'Ah. Long, black frocks and sort of hoods over their hair.'

'That's it. Their clothes are called habits. Only these nuns wore grey ones, not black.'

'How did you get to Challerton?'

'We walked, of course. That's what hikers do.'

'I see. Well, thank you. You've been very helpful.'

He wasn't bloody walking, Norris thought as he left the library. He'd go to Swindon on Wednesday and find a way to get to this Challerton place. He could pretend he was there to look at the abbey and ask a few questions.

If it was that big, Harriet couldn't have inherited the house, but she might have got a cottage in the grounds. There were all sorts of possibilities if you had rich relatives. Perhaps they would pay him and Ma to leave her with them.

It'd be good if she'd inherited some money or valuables. In that case, he'd force her to come back home with him and Winifred. He'd have to work out the best way to make money out of this situation. You couldn't take someone's money out of the bank. You had to persuade them to give it to you. There were ways. There were always ways, if you weren't too timid.

He'd tell his mother he was going to check out the place where Harriet was living, but he'd not tell her anything else, because she was a proper old gossip.

He smiled again. It was shaping up to be a very interesting week. He'd have to find someone to do his other jobs.

On Monday morning, Miss Bowers watched Harriet worrying herself sick about her lawyer's meeting with Winifred and Norris. The poor girl couldn't settle to anything, so in the end, Miss Bowers took her out for a brisk walk round the village, introducing her to the people there.

She was pleased to see that the new owner made a good impression. Harriet had an innate friendliness and personal charm, which were in contrast to Miss Agnes's dignity. Not that Miss Agnes had been disliked. She hadn't. But she'd always kept her distance.

Unless Miss Bowers much mistook the matter, the new owner would quickly endear herself to people with her shyness, frankness and sheer niceness.

Where she could, Miss Bowers spread the word that Harriet had some relatives trying to take advantage of her and asked people to watch out for strangers asking questions about the new owner of Greyladies. She made a particular point of asking Mr Pocock to pass that information on to his customers at the shop.

'Do you really think so?' When she nodded, he said in tones of disgust, 'I can't abide thieves and cheats. And she seems a really nice lass.'

'She is.'

Joseph challenged Harriet to a chess game in the evening, but he won so easily, they soon abandoned the attempt to play.

He understood why she was so distracted. When Miss Bowers was out of the room, he took her hand. 'It'll be all right, I promise you.'

'Will it? You don't know Norris. I wouldn't put

anything past him, including murder.' She raised his hand to rub her cheek against it and gave him a smile that curled through him like molten honey.

He couldn't believe she cared for him. Was it really possible that he might find happiness with her?

So he had to kiss her again. And she kissed him back.

He wasn't going to let anything happen to her. And whatever his father or mother said, if she'd have him, he was going to marry her.

He could imagine nothing better than having her as his wife.

Tuesday was fine, the sun shining brightly, though a cool breeze reminded people that winter wasn't long past. A letter arrived from Mr Lloyd by the afternoon post, written in haste, telling Harriet about the meeting with Norris and his mother.

> *I'm afraid I can't come over to Challerton this week unless it's an emergency. I have a funeral to attend on Wednesday and I've arranged a meeting with a local magistrate on Thursday to discuss our options. He's going to consider the specific facts of your case and will discuss it with a couple of fellow magistrates after that.*
>
> *If you can think of anything that will disprove your stepmother's claim to be your guardian, please let me know.*

She didn't like the sound of that.

Before Harriet could spend the rest of the afternoon moping about this, a man rode up on horseback, a bald gentleman with a ruddy face. He dismounted with more agility than his plumpness suggested and stood looking round as if expecting something.

Miss Bowers, who had gone to peep out of the window, darted across the room and set the bell pealing for Flora, explaining, 'It's Mr Greenlow. He'll expect someone to take his horse round the back. Let's hope Mickey's as good with horses as his father said.'

She turned to Harriet. 'Mr Greenlow is the local magistrate. You need him on your side. He's a good man.'

Flora reappeared in the doorway almost immediately. 'I've sent Mickey round to take the horse. I'll get Cook to make some tea once I've answered the front door, shall I?'

'We'll answer it. Mr Greenlow is an old friend of mine.' Miss Bowers took Harriet to the front door and called out, 'Good afternoon, Mr Greenlow.'

Mickey came panting round the corner of the house, stopped dead when he saw Mr Greenlow, then moved forward at Miss Bowers' urgent beckoning signal.

'That fool's not going to try to shoe it, is he?' the visitor demanded.

'No. He'll just give it a drink and see that it's comfortable.'

Mickey took the reins and walked off beside the horse, murmuring to it.

'Let me introduce you to Miss Latimer, the new owner. Harriet, Mr Greenlow is one of your new neighbours.'

He turned back to Harriet. 'Sorry. I'm being rude and ignoring you.' He bounded up the steps. 'Pleased to meet you, my dear young lady, very pleased.' He pumped her hand vigorously then studied her openly. 'You have a look of the Latimers.'

'So Miss Bowers tells me. And of course there are the portraits. I can see the resemblance in them myself, my hair colour for one thing.'

He laughed. 'Gloomy old things, aren't they, those paintings? Probably need a good clean.'

'Please come into the sitting room and let me introduce you to Joseph Dalton, my good friend.'

'Joseph's staying in the old part of the house till he can find himself a home of his own,' Miss Bowers put in quickly. 'We're very happy to have the old place occupied.'

Mr Greenlow frowned at this. 'They said you had a young fellow staying, but no one's set eyes on him in the village.'

She lowered her voice. 'Mr Dalton has a problem walking. Don't be surprised by the wheelchair.'

'Oh. I see.' His face lost its suspicious look.

When they went into the sitting room, they found Joseph standing up next to his wheelchair. After the introductions were made, he moved it across the room and sat down.

'Have a fall, did you?' Mr Greenlow trumpeted.

'No, sir. I was born with a bad hip.'

'Shame, eh. But you look healthy enough otherwise.' He turned back to Harriet. 'Now, tell me about yourself, my dear. You'll excuse an old man's curiosity, I'm sure.'

She wasn't sure what to tell him, feeling rather shy of this loudly confident old gentleman, but as he began to draw her out, she quickly realised that for all his gruffness and blunt way of speaking, he was of a kindly disposition.

With the help of his questions, she managed to summarise her life, and in doing so soon came to realise that he was a clever man beneath that bluff exterior. No wonder he was a well-respected magistrate.

'It's always good to know about your neighbours. I used to breed horses and do a bit of farming, but I leave that to my son now. Four sons we have, nice lads, too. Well, they're not lads now, got children of their own, but I still call them my lads.'

'How lovely to have a family. I don't have anyone now.'

He heaved himself to his feet. 'I can't stay long today, but my wife wanted me to invite you and Miss Bowers to take tea with us. Tomorrow afternoon, perhaps? If you'd care to join us, Mr Dalton, I can send the carriage.'

Behind their visitor's back, Miss Bowers nodded vigorously at Joseph, so he accepted the invitation.

When Mr Greenlow had left, Miss Bowers said thoughtfully, 'I'm glad he came today. Since he's the local magistrate, I wanted you to meet him as soon as possible, just in case we need his help.'

'He's very . . . blunt spoken,' Harriet said.

'Yes. But he's kind-hearted and he'd help anyone in trouble, and often does. Never be afraid to ask his help.'

'I'm praying we won't need it. Surely Mr Lloyd will find a way to prove that Winifred isn't my guardian.'

'I don't think that'll be easy, dear. You are under twenty-one, after all, and this is a big inheritance for someone so young. Still, Mr Lloyd seems to be on your side, at least.'

But what if he couldn't do anything about the situation? Harriet wondered. She'd have to run away and stay hidden for two years.

She'd have to leave Joseph.

When Miss Bowers had gone off to find her embroidery, he said quietly, 'If you'll take my advice, Harriet, you'll work out an escape plan now and even pack a few things. Just in case. You have money and I'm sure if you set your mind to it, you could stay hidden till you're twenty-one. I'm certain Mr Lloyd would prevent them from getting hold of this place in the meantime.'

'But I've only just come here. I don't want to leave.

And I don't want to leave you.' She could have wept at the mere thought of having to flee again, be on her own again.

'I know. And I don't want you to go. But we have to face facts. Don't tell Miss Bowers what you're planning yet. Don't even tell me the details.' He sighed and looked down at himself. 'I'd come with you, but I'd only slow you down, and anyway, they'd easily trace someone in a wheelchair.'

Miss Bowers rejoined them just then. 'We need to go and see the village dressmaker, my dear, and then go shopping in Swindon for materials. In your position, you need some better clothes.'

Harriet looked down at herself. 'I don't want to spend a lot of money yet . . . in case I need it for . . . something.'

Miss Bowers' expression said she could guess what her companion meant, but she didn't mention the possibility that Harriet might have to flee. 'Remember the hiding place, if your stepbrother turns up unexpectedly. And before you do anything . . . um, rash, remember Mr Greenlow may be able to help. We're going to tea there tomorrow, so you'll know where he lives.'

'I'll remember.'

She had a fair idea why Miss Bowers wasn't discussing things openly: so that she could swear on oath that she had known nothing about Harriet's plans and didn't know where she was.

Running away seemed the most likely outcome to all this. But oh, Harriet didn't want to do that! She already loved living at Greyladies, waking up each morning in a spacious sunny bedroom. She had so many plans for improving the old place.

And Joseph was right. He couldn't come with her. He'd be too easy to trace.

Life could be so unfair.

Chapter Seventeen

On Wednesday afternoon, the Greenlows' carriage arrived to collect them, with a groom sitting by the coachman to help with Joseph's wheelchair.

Their neighbours lived in a pleasant gentleman's residence, about half a mile away on the other side of the village, not large enough to be called a manor, but still larger than most. The stables at the back had clearly been extended, and there were a couple of horses being exercised in the next field.

The carriage drew up at the front door and they got out. The groom took Joseph's chair off the back and pushed him across the paved area to the front door, following Harriet and Miss Bowers.

Their host and hostess had come out to greet them, but tactfully, they took the ladies inside and left Joseph to get out of and back into the wheelchair once the groom had lifted it up the steps and into the hall.

'This way, sir.' The man pushed it into the room on the left.

Mrs Greenlow beamed at him so warmly, Joseph began to relax.

'I'm so glad you were able to come and visit us, Mr Dalton. We do enjoy having young people around and it's always good to know one's neighbours, don't you think?'

They chatted for a while, then tea was served, after which Miss Bowers said abruptly, 'I think Harriet should discuss what to do about her situation with you, Mr Greenlow, since you're the local magistrate. Would you mind? Her lawyer isn't at all sure what will be decided.'

'Shall I leave you alone?' Mrs Greenlow asked.

'No need. I think the details of my life are becoming known to everyone in the village.' Harriet already felt at ease with this friendly couple.

'I've already shared what you told me with my wife,' her host said. 'I didn't think you'd mind. We've been discussing it and I have a few more questions.'

'Of course not. It's kind of you to take an interest.'

When she'd finished answering the questions, Joseph winked at her and gave her a nod, as if to say she'd done it well. She smiled at him, then had to apologise and ask her host to repeat what he'd said.

After a few more shrewd questions, Mr Greenlow shook his head, his brow furrowed in thought. 'It's a difficult situation to judge. You'd be better if you had someone else to stand as guardian, apart from that woman. If it goes to court, they're likely to appoint your stepmother to the position. I would have done that myself if I hadn't met you and found out how well Miss Bowers thinks of you. She's the best judge of character I know.'

The former schoolteacher smiled ruefully. 'You can learn a lot about human beings from children, if you're observant.'

Harriet felt it was important to make sure they all understood one thing. 'I won't go back to live with my stepmother, whatever anyone says or does. Apart from the fact that I can't stand the woman, I wouldn't be safe living in the same house as Norris.' She didn't actually say she would run away, but she could see in their faces that they all knew what her only alternative might be.

When the carriage was brought round to take them home, Miss Bowers whispered to Harriet, 'You get into the carriage with Joseph. I just want to have a word with Mrs Greenlow, who is a good friend of mine.'

She might have to keep them waiting a few minutes, because she had something to discuss with Mr Greenlow – a possible solution for Harriet. But from what she'd seen, the two young people never had difficulty finding something to chat about, so she was sure they wouldn't mind how long it took.

After a while Mr Greenlow escorted Miss Bowers out and the two of them stood at the top of the steps leading into the house watching Harriet and Joseph laughing and chatting.

'You can see that those two are close friends,' she said softly. 'It does my heart good to see them. They've neither of them had a happy life so far.'

He waggled one finger at her. 'You're doing it again. Interfering in people's lives.'

She chuckled. 'I only do that when it's necessary. And I've never harmed anyone, have I?'

'No. But be careful you don't break the law with this one, my dear. Though I will agree, what you suggest might make a difference. Now, let's get you safely installed.' He went to the carriage door, gestured to the groom to move back and helped her into it himself, closing the door and stepping back.

Then he went to find out exactly what his wife thought of Miss Bowers' suggestion.

Norris arrived in Challerton in a very bad mood on the Wednesday. It'd cost him more than he'd expected to get here and taken longer, too. For the first time, he had begun to doubt what he was doing, but having started, he was damned well going to find out the facts before he gave up on it.

Even if nothing else worked out, he wanted to see what sort of a woman Harriet had grown into, and if she was still as appealing to him as she'd been at fifteen, when he'd first met her. He was going to finish what he'd started with her. He'd never forgotten the feel of her soft body under his, still thought about her lovely hair whenever he saw a red-haired woman in the street.

He intended to pose as a hiker when he got to the village, even though it was a bit early in the year for anyone to go on a walking tour. He'd agreed with the fellow who'd brought him to pick him up in a couple of hours, and to wait for him, if necessary, where the road from the village met the main road to Swindon.

The first thing he saw as he turned towards the village was a big house on the left. It looked very old. A lad was passing so he stopped him to ask, 'What's that place called?'

The lad gave him a suspicious stare and started to edge away.

Norris grabbed his shoulder. 'Tell me what it's called!'

'Greyladies.' He again tried to move away, but Norris dragged him back. 'I'll give you threepence if you tell me more about the place and who lives there.'

The lad brightened and stopped struggling. 'Latimers live there.'

'Ah. And which Latimers are living there at the moment?'

'Just one. Miss Latimer.'

'Old lady, is she?'

'No. The old one died. This one's younger. She's just inherited it.'

Norris was so astonished by the implications of this, given the size of the house, that he couldn't speak for a moment. Then he saw the lad looking at him hopefully and fished in his pocket for a threepenny bit, holding on to it as he asked, 'How old is the new one, exactly, and what does she look like?'

'She's got red hair – well, reddish, not ginger. I only seen her once, though, and not close. She's not as old as my mum.'

'That's good enough.' Norris tossed the coin in the air and watched the lad catch it and run off.

He stood by the gate for a few minutes, staring at the house. It was big. Surely *Harriet* couldn't have inherited a place like this? He'd have gone down the drive to look at it more closely, but he didn't want her to see him. And anyway, it didn't seem to be a very welcoming place.

But who else could the new owner be but Harriet, with that age and description?

He whistled softly. If what the lad said was true, Norris and his ma were going to live soft for the rest of their days.

The lad turned and ran back into the village, intent on spending his windfall on some sweets before his mother could take it off him.

Mr Pocock stared at him when he plonked the money down on the counter. 'Where did you get that from, Jimmy Taylor? Last I heard, your mother hadn't enough to feed you properly.'

A customer moved closer. 'Did you steal it?'

'No, I didn't. A man give it to me.'

'What for?'

'Tellin' him about Miss Latimer an' Greyladies.'

The shopkeeper and his customer exchanged startled glances, then the customer moved to stand between the lad and the door.

'Come into the back,' Mr Pocock said. 'I'll give you a liquorice stick if you do.'

Jimmy scowled at him, sensing a trick. 'Why?'

'I want to ask you some questions, too.' He reached into a jar and took out one of the twig-like sticks of liquorice root, much beloved by village children for chewing on.

Hardly had he got Jimmy in the back than the customer called out, 'There's a stranger coming down the street.'

Mr Pocock looked at the boy, thrust the liquorice root into his hand and said to his wife. 'See Jimmy stays here. And if you're quiet, Jimmy, I'll give you another stick after the man leaves.'

He went back into the shop, all smiles as he faced the stranger, even though he was suspicious of anyone asking about Miss Latimer, after what Miss Bowers had said.

He wasn't surprised when the man bought a bar of Fry's Cream chocolate and lingered to ask questions.

'I don't know anything about the new owner,' he lied. 'My wife says she's about thirty and ugly with it.'

'The sign says you do cups of tea.'

'Only in the summer. Not much call for it at this time of year.'

'I could murder a cup of tea.'

'Two shillings.'

'What?'

'I've not got help so it's a lot of trouble, takes me away from my work. Two shillings or nothing.'

Norris scowled but paid, sitting at the little table in one corner to drink the tea to the last drop.

When he stood up, he asked directions to the abbey, pretending he wanted to look round it. As if he cared about sodding ruins!

He slouched off, wondering who to believe. Usually children told you the truth, as long as you didn't frighten them.

He hadn't liked the looks of that shopkeeper, either. All smiles but slippery as an eel when it came to talking about the big house.

Was he reading more into the situation than he should? How could a girl like Harriet inherit a big old house like that? No, it wasn't really likely, much as he'd love it to be true. Things like that only happened in fairy tales.

A cold spot hit him on the face, followed by others. Damnation! It was coming on to rain. He pulled out his pocket watch and glared at it. Over an hour to go before the carter would be returning.

He looked round for somewhere to shelter and found a three-sided wooden hut near a gate leading into a bare field. It was the sort of place where farm labourers sheltered from the weather, he reckoned, and thank goodness for it.

Sighing, he sat down on the rough bench. Coming here hadn't helped as much as he'd expected. He wasn't really sure of the facts. The shopkeeper had laughed at what the boy had told him and why should the fellow want to deceive a stranger like him?

No, he must be imagining things because he *wanted* Harriet to have inherited money.

He heard a carriage coming along the lane and watched it pass by, envying those inside. Then he gasped as he saw that one of them was Harriet, sitting there being driven along like Lady Muck. He didn't see what the two other people looked like, just sat very still watching her as the carriage drove slowly past along the narrow, rutted lane. He stayed in the shadows at the back of the hut, not wanting to draw attention to himself.

When the vehicle had gone, he laughed, slapping his thighs and making crowing noises. It was her. It was *definitely* her.

Raising his eyes to the sky, he said out loud, 'Thank you for the rain. I'd have missed her otherwise.'

So the lad had told the truth and Harriet was the new owner of Greyladies.

Why had the shopkeeper lied, though? Perhaps he hadn't seen Harriet, only heard about her. Yes, that'd be it.

Norris punched one hand into the other, doing it again and again, laughing. Just wait till he saw that bloody lawyer. Just wait till he saw Harriet.

He was going to get hold of that big house – him, Norris Harding. He was going to be rich.

There was one obvious way to make sure of that, a way that would mean nobody could ever take it away from him: he'd have to marry her. And he wouldn't mind, either. Harriet had grown into a fine-looking young woman.

She might say no at first, but his mother was going to be her guardian, and since she'd be able to live with Harriet, so would he.

And if he planted a baby in her, she'd soon change her mind about marrying him. Women always did, because no one wanted to be landed with a bastard.

When William Dalton read the curt note from Harriet's lawyer saying he couldn't afford the time to visit Hampshire, he turned dark red with rage.

His wife, who was sitting at the breakfast table with him, asked, 'What's wrong, dear?'

'That lawyer chappie is refusing to visit me here.'

'Well, you're not one of his clients, after all.'

'But I'm *dealing with* one of his clients.'

'Harriet isn't here any longer, so you're not dealing with her. William, do be sensible. It's not worth all this fuss.'

'I may be forced by circumstances beyond my control to live out my days in poverty in the country, but I am a gentleman born and bred, and I will *not* let my standards slip.'

Not for the first time, she cursed their eldest son, who had brought all this on. Selwyn was still continuing to live beyond his means and she had no doubt that when the house passed to him, he'd have to sell it. And where would that leave her, if she outlived her husband?

'William . . .'

'Mmm?' He opened another letter.

'I've been thinking. About Selwyn.'

'Ungrateful pup. How I sired such a fool, I don't know.'

'Do you think you should still leave the house to him? I'm sure he'll only sell it because he'll be even deeper in debt by then.'

William stared at her as if she were a complete stranger, giving her a cold, unfriendly glance. Then he said slowly and distinctly, 'Selwyn's the eldest son. We Daltons *always* leave this house to the eldest son.'

'Even if that son has proven himself unworthy, with his gambling and spendthrift ways?' She waited then added, 'And if he inherits and has to sell, what will happen to me?'

He opened and shut his mouth, then grunted and got up, leaving the room without another word.

She hoped she'd given him something to think about, but to her dismay, later that day she saw another letter to Harriet's lawyer on the silver tray in the hall.

He hadn't turned his attention away from their former maid as she'd hoped, was still writing to her lawyer.

What did he hope to gain by it?

Joseph made his own way up the steps of Greyladies, even though it was a slow and ungainly business. At the top he turned to Harriet triumphantly. 'A year ago, I couldn't have done this. Moving about more is working.'

His face was alight at this small triumph and in that moment she loved him so much it took her breath away. 'The more you practise, the better you'll get, I'm sure, as long as you don't overreach yourself. Just take it steadily, Joseph dear.'

The word 'dear' hung between them, then he smiled.

'I will. Let's go into the sitting room. I love to watch the sun set over the abbey. If you get Mickey to cut back some of the bushes, we – I mean *you* would have a better view of the ruins.'

But when they went into the sitting room, it was her he was looking at, not the ruins, and so wistfully, she couldn't help moving towards him, hand outstretched. He wouldn't say it, so she must. 'Oh, Joseph, don't let anything stop you loving me, because I don't think I could live without you now.'

Neither of them saw Miss Bowers pause in the doorway, smile, and move away again on tiptoe.

'You can't want to marry someone like me.'

'I do.'

'And I love you. You're the most wonderful woman I've ever met, and if I were a proper man, I'd ask you to marry me this very minute.'

'You *are* a proper man.'

'We both know I'm not.' He shook his head, with an obstinate look on his face, a look she recognised from the years of knowing him. She couldn't think what to say to change his mind and anguish filled her at the thought that he'd throw away their happiness because of how he felt about himself.

No, she suddenly realised, it was because of how his family felt about him. *They* didn't value him as he deserved, so he felt unworthy. Only how could she persuade him that he was the man she loved and always would be?

In the dimness of the room, a light suddenly began to glow in one corner.

They both turned to stare, expecting to see Flora bringing in a lamp. But there was no sign of the maid, just a steadily increasing glow that formed into a figure.

Joseph reached out for Harriet's hand. 'Is that who I think it is?'

'Yes. It's the Lady,' Harriet whispered back. 'I saw her before, the first time I came here. She was standing at the top of the stairs then.'

The brightness drifted slowly towards them and the

transparent figure stretched out both hands, smiling at them as if offering a blessing. She pointed to her left hand, where a ring seemed to catch sparks of light, and then to Harriet's hand.

Then the figure began to fade. For a moment, the ring seemed to shine more brightly than the Lady, a gold wedding band.

Both stood watching as the figure began to dim and the light glowing around her dispersed. The gleaming ring vanishing last of all.

'We didn't imagine that, did we?' Joseph asked in hushed tones.

'No. She was really there. I think she came to give us her blessing.'

'Two people can't possibly imagine the same thing.' Joseph's voice was so soft it didn't carry beyond the two of them.

'People are usually frightened of ghosts, but I'm not frightened of her, not at all.'

'Neither am I.'

She looked sideways at him. 'Joseph, you know what she was encouraging us to do.'

'Yes. But—'

'Please don't say *but* in that tone!'

'You don't know how horrible my body is, Harriet,' he said desperately. 'And I don't know if I can love a woman as a husband should. You'll despise me, I know you will.'

'I could never despise you.' She bent to drag him up

315

from his wheelchair and after a moment's resistance, he let himself stand close to her.

As he stood there, he groaned. 'I shouldn't take advantage of you.' But before she could answer, he'd drawn her into his arms and was kissing her, gently, tenderly but with increasing passion.

When he pulled away, he gave a shaky laugh. 'I can't even get down on my knees to propose to you, but Harriet, my darling Harriet, will you marry me?'

'Of course I will.'

Someone sighed and they both jerked round, to see Miss Bowers looking at them from the doorway with a sentimental expression.

Giving them a beaming smile, she hurried across the room, to kiss first Harriet then Joseph on the cheek. 'I'm so sorry. I didn't mean to eavesdrop, but it was so lovely to hear your declaration that I couldn't move away. Let me be the first to congratulate you.'

'Then you approve?' Joseph asked.

'Of course I do. I guessed almost at once that you were in love with one another, but you were so young, so inexperienced, I didn't say anything until you did.'

'Did you see the Lady?' Harriet asked.

'What lady?'

'The ghost.'

'Oh, no. I never have done. Did you see her?'

'Yes. We both did. She seemed to be giving us her blessing.'

'Well, there you are, then. It was meant to be.'

She looked from one to the other. 'We must arrange a wedding immediately.'

'I'd need permission, surely? I'm under twenty-one,' Harriet said.

'We'll ask Mr Greenlow what the law says about that. I know a magistrate can give people permission if their parents refuse, as long as the request is reasonable. I remember it happening in the village once. So maybe he can give you permission, since you no longer have parents.' She wrinkled her brow in thought. 'Dear me! How you forget details as you grow older.'

She looked at Joseph. 'You're over twenty-one, aren't you?'

'Oh, yes.'

'That's one of you old enough, then. Look, I'll send Mickey over to the Greenlows immediately with a note that we need to see Mr Greenlow in his capacity as magistrate first thing in the morning, because something's come up and it's urgent. If anyone will know the law, he will. And once you're married, then it'll be your husband who is your guardian, my dear girl, so you'll be safe.' She beamed at them triumphantly.

Harriet frowned. 'I can't imagine anything I'd like more than to marry Joseph, but . . . it all seems too easy.'

'Don't say that.'

'We must try,' Joseph said. 'We may be able to find a way through all this. And if not, you can still run away. I'd wait for you.'

'Well, we have a little time,' Harriet agreed. 'Mr Lloyd hasn't told my stepmother where I am, and he won't unless he's forced to. Only . . . Norris can be very violent when crossed. He got into a lot of fights as he was growing up.'

'If he comes near here, we'll whisk you *both* away,' Miss Bowers said. 'I know any number of people on the farms near the village who'd give you shelter. We'll find a way through this somehow.'

Harriet smiled at her, then at Joseph, letting herself hope. They might meet difficulties, but surely they'd find a way through.

But the following morning, she woke up feeling apprehensive, her feeling of optimism stifled by a grey cloud of doubt and a sense that something was going to go wrong.

Mr Lloyd would be seeing Norris and his mother again tomorrow. And he'd written to say that nothing definite had come up to allow her to escape her stepmother's control.

What would he say when he found out she was going to marry Joseph? Would he approve?

Would marrying Joseph be enough to free her? Surely it would? It had to be.

If not, she'd run away till she was twenty-one.

When Norris got home, bubbling with excitement, his mother looked at him sharply. 'What did you find out?'

'Make me a cup of tea and I'll tell you. No, make it

a glass of port. We have something to celebrate.'

Her face brightened. 'She's inherited some money?'

'Better than that.'

She looked at him blankly. 'What can be better than that?'

He grinned and mimed sipping from a glass.

'Oh, you!' She went into the front room and poured them both a brimming glass of port, coming back to hand one to him. 'Well?'

'Harriet has inherited a huge old house called Greyladies. It'd have at least twenty rooms and it has big gardens round it.'

'You're having me on.'

'No. This is too important to joke about.' He raised his glass. 'To Harriet and her inheritance.'

She took an impatient sip. 'You're sure of this?'

'Well, the lawyer will have to confirm it, but everyone in the village is talking about it and . . .' He lifted the glass again, tormenting her.

She punched him in the arm to make him go on. 'What else do you know?'

'I saw her, riding in a carriage. And it turned into the drive of Greyladies.'

'Oh, my life! And I'm her guardian. We're rich.'

'Not yet, we're not.'

'What do you mean?'

'I mean, you don't think that lawyer will let us sell the house or take over everything permanently, do you?'

'If I'm her guardian I can do what I want.'

'Till she's twenty-one. That's only, what, two years? Less than. Her birthday's in May.'

She scowled. 'You can do a lot in two years. Sell all she's got.'

'You can't rob people of everything they own, not when they're rich. Someone is bound to kick up a fuss. No, we need to do something more permanent.'

She looked at him suspiciously. 'Such as?'

'I'll marry her. Then I'll have her *and* whatever she's inherited.'

'What about me? I'll have nothing.'

'You know I'll always look after you, Ma.'

'You'd better. Only your plan won't work because she won't marry you. You tried to force her and she'll never forgive you for that.'

'Well, if necessary I'll force her again, and when she's carrying my child, she'll have to marry me.'

'I wouldn't, if I were her.'

He scowled. 'Are you on my side or not?'

'I'm telling you how any woman would feel.'

'I'll find a way to persuade her, believe me.'

'*We* will find a way. That's why you need me. And then *we* will share the money. And unless you put that in writing, I'm not going on with this.'

'Ma, once I've married her, you'll be set up for life.'

'I don't know anything about what you'll be like if you get your hands on a lot of money. No, I'm making sure from the start. I'll find a piece of paper and we'll write down an agreement. Then I'll get my friends to witness it, two copies. And I'll lodge one in the bank, for security.'

There was dead silence, then he shrugged. 'All right. There'll be more than enough to share.'

And his mother wouldn't live more than another ten years, twenty at most, after which it'd all come back to him. He smiled. 'You're a cunning devil, Ma.'

'You won't soft-soap me, Norris. I know you too well. We'll put it in writing.'

Chapter Eighteen

Mr Greenlow rode across to see Joseph and Harriet on the Thursday morning, setting off as soon as he got the letter announcing their engagement.

'Congratulations, my dear young people,' he boomed at them as soon as he entered the house.

Joseph had to ask, 'You feel it's the right thing to do, sir? Marrying Harriet, I mean. It's what I want – more than anything – but am I being selfish?' He looked down at himself.

'Not at all, lad.' He gave the wheelchair a dismissive wave. 'That doesn't matter; it's what's in here that counts.' He clapped his hand to his chest.

Joseph smiled at Harriet, feeling that he'd got permission to love her from a man whose judgement he valued and who could do something to help them get married. 'So how do we set about it, given that Harriet is under age and needs permission to marry? I think we need to act as quickly as possible, don't you?'

'Sounds like it, if that stepmother is as greedy as

Harriet says. I can give her permission to marry, but I'd better call in a colleague so that it's not a single decision. Much safer to have two opinions on that – harder for anyone to overturn.'

'How quickly can you organise it?'

'I'll ask Murborough to come and see me. It'll have to be on Saturday because he's presiding over a court sitting today. He's a very reasonable fellow and lives only a couple of miles away from me. I assume you'll come to a hearing at my house if I send you word? I'll send my carriage to bring you, of course.'

Harriet put her hand on Joseph's shoulder. 'We'll come immediately. We'll do whatever it takes. And thank you so much for your kindness.'

Mr Greenlow shrugged and made a few huffing noises, clearly not at ease being praised. 'Once we have officially given you permission, you can get a special licence and be married a day later. But you'll have to go into Swindon for that, Joseph. I'm happy to lend you my carriage again.' He looked across at the clock. 'Now, I'll have to go, I'm afraid. I've got someone coming to see me.'

As he stood up, he cocked one eyebrow at Miss Bowers. 'You knew this would happen, didn't you?'

She smiled back serenely. 'I guessed. I can always tell when people are in love.'

Joseph went with him to the door, not bothering about his wheelchair, because he felt quite at ease with this visitor.

When they were alone, Miss Bowers turned to Harriet with some concern. 'You keep frowning. You are sure of what you're doing, aren't you?'

'Marrying Joseph? Oh, yes. I'm quite sure of that. I don't know why I didn't realise earlier how much I loved him. It's just . . . I still feel something could so easily go wrong.'

'Don't say that. It'll bring bad luck.'

Harriet shrugged. 'I'm trying to believe things will go smoothly. Please don't mention my worries to Joseph. He looks so happy.'

Miss Bowers smiled. 'So do you when you're with him.'

Five minutes before Harding and his mother were due to arrive on the Saturday, the post was delivered to Mr Lloyd. When he saw a letter from Harriet, he called the junior back. 'Send Perkins in to me.'

The clerk was there within seconds.

'Perkins, I've received a letter from Miss Latimer. Don't send Harding and his mother in to me till I've read it and seen what news it brings. I may have to think what to do if there's another crisis at Greyladies. Is your nephew here?'

'Yes, sir. He's waiting in the inner corridor.'

'Fine, strong fellow, your nephew. Tell him to stand outside my office. I'll send him along to fetch them when I'm ready.' If it was cowardly to have what could only be described as a bodyguard present, Reginald didn't care. He was not a big man, while Harding was burly . . . and brutal. There was no other word for the expression on that young man's face.

Reginald slit the letter open and read it quickly. 'Ah!' Then he read it again more slowly, nodding a couple of times. 'That's the answer, especially with Greenlow on their side. He's a jolly good fellow, Greenlow is.'

But they needed time to arrange everything, so he had to persuade Harding to wait before he did anything else. Not only did Harriet and Joseph need time to gain the magistrate's permission to marry, but they needed to do the deed *before* they faced her so-called guardian.

Thank goodness Harding didn't know where she was. That should give the young couple plenty of time if they started organising things straight away.

Unless Harding got a magistrate to insist he give them the information about where Harriet was. Reginald sighed. You could only bend the law so far.

So he'd better be conciliatory with them. Difficult that. He didn't know when he'd disliked someone as much as Harding.

On the Saturday morning, Norris once again escorted his mother into Swindon. She was wearing the silly hat and he didn't care, because he was feeling happy. As an afterthought, he'd asked his friend, Pat, to come along with them, just in case he needed someone to back him up in a difficult situation.

'Don't forget, Ma,' he said as the train approached Swindon. 'Don't make any threats. And above all, don't let on that I've been to Challerton already and know exactly where to find her. And Pat, you stay outside. Only come in if I call you.'

'As long as you pay me, I'll stand outside all day,' Pat said with a grin.

Winifred scowled at her son. 'Why do we have to pretend you don't know where she is?'

'Because we don't want him to warn her that we're on to her. This'll all fall to pieces if she runs away and manages to stay hidden till she's twenty-one. No money for us then. She might even marry someone else.'

Winifred sighed. 'I was looking forward to telling that uppity sod we know what's happened and making him dance to our tune,' she grumbled.

'We can tell him we know she's inherited a house. That'll upset him nicely. But we'll pretend to be patient and agree to wait until he arranges a meeting.'

Norris didn't feel patient, though. The glimpse of Harriet in the carriage had set him off again, wanting her, needing to show her who was master. She'd had that effect on him even when she was younger, and she was much prettier now. Ripe for the plucking.

His mother looked at him, head on one side. 'I don't envy her. You get that look to you sometimes when you talk about her.'

'What look is that?'

'The same one your father used to get when he

was feeling like some bed play. I don't envy that girl if you're as active as he was in bed. It's exhausting. If he'd lived, you'd probably have had half a dozen brothers and sisters.'

Behind them, Pat chuckled. 'You don't know the half of it with your son, missus. He's a terror with the women.'

Norris smiled. 'And a man has rights over his wife.'

'Yes. So I found out,' his mother said. 'It's why I'm not marrying again.'

As they approached the lawyer's rooms, Norris stopped. 'You wait for us here, Pat. When we come out, you follow us till we're out of sight of their windows. Make sure they've not set anyone on to follow us.'

Pat obligingly stayed where he was.

Norris pointed his forefinger at his mother. 'Remember what I said!'

'You're in a bossy mood today. And why you had to bring that fellow Pat along, I don't know.'

'I don't want anything to go wrong. You'd be no good in a fight.'

'You said you could do it without violence.'

'I can. But I'm taking no chances from now on.'

The elderly clerk greeted them with the same sour expression. 'Mr Lloyd won't be a minute. Please take a seat.'

'He isn't going to be long, is he?' Norris waited for his mother to sit, then took the chair beside hers.

'I shouldn't think so. He's expecting you.'

The same burly man came along to collect them a few minutes later. Norris waved his mother to go first and sauntered into the lawyer's office behind her.

Mr Lloyd stood up and gestured to the two chairs. 'Please sit down.'

They did that and waited, but he didn't speak, just continued to stare thoughtfully at them.

Norris wasn't putting up with that. 'Well? What did Harriet say?'

'She was upset. Wants me to ask you to agree terms.'

'Terms?' Winifred asked.

'She thought you might accept a regular payment to leave her where she is, living with friends. She'd be able to pay double her former wages.'

Norris wasn't in the mood for playing around. 'That seems a very low payment, considering she's just inherited a big house.'

The lawyer's mouth fell open and his voice came out rough with shock. 'How did you find out about that?'

'I've got friends too, more than she has, probably. And I don't see why we should put up with such a small payment or even pay rent ourselves when there's a big house available. No, we'll move in with her.'

'I'll . . . um, consult her. Perhaps she could offer you more money?'

'And perhaps we *prefer* moving in with her to

money,' Norris threw back at him. 'We'll be able to look after her properly then. She's only got us in the world, you know.'

'You can call it consulting. I call it making her face facts,' Winifred snapped. 'I'm not spending good money coming to and from Swindon, just so that you can charge us for all these meetings.'

'It's Miss Latimer who's paying me.'

'Miss Benson.'

'It's a condition of the inheritance that she takes the name Latimer, and her husband too if she ever marries.'

'That's a strange thing to ask,' Winifred said.

'It's always been that way with the family. The house passes down the female line, but the name stays the same.' He didn't say the word Greyladies, didn't want them to go there.

'Tell her we want to see *her* here next time, and then we want to go and see the house.' Norris could have laughed at the sour expression on the lawyer's face but he kept himself under control. He had to play this very carefully. There was a big prize at stake, but Harriet had to be caught first. Literally.

He didn't care if he had to change his name to get the house, but it'd go to his son after that, not a daughter.

'We'll give her till Monday,' Winifred said. 'Tell her to be here then.'

'I'm not sure we can arrange matters so quickly,

not over a weekend. Make it Tuesday, at least, to allow time for the post.'

She looked at her son and at his nod, said, 'Tuesday, then. But no later. And no playing tricks. She's to be here.'

Norris stood up, nudging his mother to move. He wasn't sure she could keep quiet for much longer. Lloyd was talking to them carefully and slowly, as if they were stupid. There were spots of red in her cheeks and her eyes betrayed her anger. He wished he dare let her off the reins. He'd love to watch her give that idiot what for.

'We'll be here at the same time on Tuesday, then. If Harriet isn't waiting for us, we'll go straight to the nearest magistrate and get a piece of paper that says she has to do as we say and *you* have to tell us where she is. We've been patient – very patient indeed – giving her time to get used to the idea. Tell her that. But we're starting to run out of patience now.'

When they were out in the street, his mother would have spoken, but he started walking more quickly, saying, 'Shh. Not till we're away from there. And let's make sure they haven't set anyone on to follow us.'

Pat fell in behind them, whistling cheerfully. After a while, he caught up with them. 'There's no one following you. Go all right with that lawyer, did it?'

'It went very well indeed. Are you free for more work like this?'

'Of course. Didn't even have to do anything today, did I? Easy money.'

'Has your brother still got that motor car?'

'Yeah. You'd think it was a baby, the way he polishes it and talks to it.'

'I'll have to think about the best way to do this, and when I do, I'll need you both. I'll pay well.'

'We're both very fond of money.'

On Sunday morning, a motor car pulled off the road at Challerton and turned into the drive of Greyladies.

Harriet was in the hall, on her way to see Livvy in the kitchen, when Joseph yelled from the sitting room, 'Come here quickly, Harriet!'

She went running in, thinking to find him fallen or in some other trouble. Instead, he was standing up next to the fireplace and the secret panel was sliding slowly open.

'Peep out of the window. Is that your stepbrother?'

'Yes. And his mother. Oh, my goodness! He's brought the O'Sullivans with him as well. They're a rough pair. How did he know I was here? What am I going to do?'

'Get into the hiding place quickly so that the panel has time to close before he comes into the house. I'll tell him you're out. You may have to stay there for some hours. Will you be all right?'

'Yes. It's you I'll be worrying about.'

'Don't. Who'd suspect a poor cripple of being able

to do anything? I'll sit in my chair and pretend I can't walk. Put on a bit of a stupid act, too. They always think people in wheelchairs are stupid.' He pushed her inside. 'Close it now.'

He stood back. 'And remember how much I love you,' he called softly as the panel slid into place.

Then he moved across to his wheelchair, picking up his book and holding it on his lap as if interrupted in his reading. On a sudden thought he rolled his chair to a place from which he could see out into the hall.

When a car drew up at the house, with three rough-looking men in it and a blowsy female with a ridiculous hat, Miss Bowers went towards the sitting room to ask if they knew the visitors.

She heard what Joseph told Harriet, so rushed back into the kitchen to warn the servants. She told Flora to answer the door as usual, but to be ready to fetch help from the village if there was trouble.

The two younger women stared at her in shock.

'The man who's turned up is Miss Latimer's stepbrother and he's hurt the mistress before. And he's brought two rough-looking men with him.'

Phyllis let out a whimper.

'Pull yourself together, girl,' Miss Bowers snapped. 'If you act normal, they won't hurt you.'

She turned back to Flora. 'If you have to run for help, don't let them see you. Livvy, you must pretend to know nothing.'

She hurried across to the servants' stairs. 'I'll go up by the back stairs and come down by the front ones, so they won't know you've seen me.'

The knocker sounded.

As Flora answered the door, Livvy kept watch from the doorway at the rear of the hall. She'd run for help herself, if Flora couldn't get back. When she saw the stranger shove Flora roughly out of the way, she knew they were in for trouble.

But Flora was able to hurry back into the kitchen. 'They're up to no good. I'm going for help.' She looked over her shoulder anxiously and made straight for the back door.

As Livvy shut the back door behind her, she turned to Phyllis. 'You heard Miss Bowers. Pretend we know nothing about what's going on at the front.'

'What if he hits us?'

'He won't if we don't seem to know anything. You mustn't show any interest in what they're doing. Go and make a start on the dishes.'

She hoped the servants would be left alone. You could never tell with violent men, though.

When the door knocker sounded, Joseph saw Flora cross the hall.

'Yes, sir?' she began, then cried out in shock.

Joseph saw her stagger backwards as if pushed hard. That didn't bode well.

Harding strode into the house. He didn't even

notice Flora hurrying back into the kitchen, because he'd stopped to stare round possessively, as if he owned the place. How could he possibly feel like that?

Then Joseph realised what this meant. There was only one way that fellow could hope to own this place. He must be intending to marry Harriet! Well, over my dead body, Joseph vowed.

He turned his wheelchair slightly so that it'd not look as if he was watching the newcomer and called out, 'Is that you, Harriet?'

When Harding appeared in the doorway, he pretended to be surprised, hoped he was doing a good job of acting. 'Who are you?'

'Where is she?'

'Who?'

'Don't play the fool. Harriet of course.'

'I don't know. I thought that was her coming in. Who *are* you?'

'I'm her stepbrother.' His gaze flicked scornfully over Joseph.

More footsteps sounded in the hall and an older woman, with a face lined and soured by a hard life, followed Harding into the room. She also stared at the man in the wheelchair.

Where were the other two men who'd been in the car? Joseph wondered.

'This is my mother, Mrs Benson. She's Harriet's guardian.' Harding said. 'Who are you and what are you doing here?'

'I'm Joseph Dalton.' He held out his hand, letting it drop when the intruder made no attempt to shake it. 'Harriet has kindly allowed me and my manservant to rent the older part of the house until I can find a place of my own.'

'Dalton?' the old lady said sharply. 'That's the name of the folk she used to work for.'

'She used to work for my parents, yes.'

'Then why aren't you still living back with them?'

'I don't think that's any of your business.'

A meaty hand lifted him up by his jacket and held him half off the wheelchair. He didn't struggle, or protest, or plead. He merely waited, and after giving him a shake, Harding let him drop.

'Answer my mother when she asks a question, Dalton.'

Joseph pretended to have difficulty easing himself back into position. 'I won't answer questions that are none of her business. And if you hurt me in any way, I'll have you charged with assault.'

He looked towards the door as Miss Bowers came down the last few stairs. 'And I shall have a witness to prove it.'

They swung round quickly.

Miss Bowers crossed the hall and came into the room. She moved to stand beside Joseph. 'Who are these people?'

'Harriet's stepbrother and stepmother.'

Harding kicked the wheelchair so that it rolled

back. 'Keep your mouth shut, you, unless I tell you to speak.'

'Shame on you, whoever you are, to bully a cripple like that!' Miss Bowers said loudly. 'What are you doing in our house?'

Harding's scowl grew blacker. 'How the hell many folk has Harriet got living here? Who are you, old woman?'

'I'm her companion, Miss Bowers, and I'm helping her settle in.'

'Well, you can pack your bags and get out after we've seen Harriet, because *I'll* be doing that from now on,' Winifred said sharply. She began to walk across the room, touching the ornaments on the mantelpiece, then fingering the upholstery on an easy chair, after which she squinted up at the nearest painting.

Every movement said she felt she had a right to do this. What a grasping pair they were! Joseph thought.

'I'll ask you again, Dalton: *where – is – Harriet?*' Harding said loudly.

'I think she may have been going into the village to visit a friend.' He frowned as if trying to remember.

'No, she went to church, then she was going on to see her friend Mary,' Miss Bowers said. 'She did tell you, but you weren't listening, Joseph. You must try not to let your mind stray, dear.'

She winked at him as she spoke, keeping her face turned away from the intruders, then she turned and glanced at the clock. 'Harriet won't be back for a while yet. The people in the village have really taken to her and are welcoming her into their homes.'

Norris looked at her suspiciously and she returned his stare with a bland look that betrayed nothing.

'Then we'll have to wait for her to return,' he said. 'We're in no hurry. After all, we've come to live here, haven't we? I'll just tell our driver to go round the back and keep an eye on the servants. Pat can come and sit in the hall in case either of you tries to cause trouble.' His smirk at Joseph said he didn't think this was possible with a cripple.

'I'll go and tell the servants to make you all a cup of tea, then,' Miss Bowers said.

'Oh, no, you won't. You'll stay here. You and that idiot.' He jerked his head towards Joseph. 'We want you where we can keep an eye on you. I'll go. Ma, yell for me if they try to leave this room.'

Miss Bowers gave a loud sniff and sat down in a chair near the window. 'In that case, I shall read my book. I certainly don't enjoy conversing with people like *you*.'

Norris paused at the door to add, 'And don't let them talk to one another, either, Ma.'

From where Joseph was sitting, he could also look through the side of the bay window. He saw Harding go outside at the front of the house and speak to the driver. When the fellow came back in, one of the men followed him.

But neither of them came into the sitting room.

Joseph was still able to see part of the hall. Harding gestured to a chair and then, as the other man sat down, moved towards the back of the house. Presumably he was going to inspect the servants' area and see who was there.

Joseph picked up his book and pretended to read, but all his attention was on Mrs Benson, who had sat down near the door. She was alternately staring at them and studying the room. Once she left her chair to pick up a china figurine and examine it, a gloating expression on her face. Then she went back to her seat, fidgeting.

That big flowery hat looked ridiculous on such a lined and harsh face. But there was nothing ridiculous about the power emanating from her son. A man to be wary of, Norris Harding.

There were no sounds coming from the kitchen, so Joseph kept wondering what was going on there, hoping the servants were all right.

But most of all, he was worried about Harriet. He knew she hadn't liked being shut up in the hiding place, even with him beside her.

How would she be coping alone in the dimness?

Norris stood in the doorway of the kitchen. An older woman was cooking something and a girl stood in what looked like a scullery, washing dishes. They hadn't noticed him, so he watched them for a moment or two longer.

They didn't look as if they were anxious about anything, were just getting on with their work. Good. They'd not cause him any trouble, if he was careful not to upset them.

It was the biggest kitchen Norris had ever seen. Even the scullery to one side was bigger than Ma's kitchen at home. There was a row of pans on the kitchen wall – why did anyone need so many? – neat piles of crockery and dishes on the dresser, a knife cleaner, a mincer, and other gadgets he didn't recognise standing on a long bench to one side, and a huge kitchen range radiating warmth.

How many rooms did this place have? And were they all full of furniture and other objects? He smiled happily. They'd all be his soon.

He couldn't wait to explore the house properly, though he had to admit that the hall and stairs gave him the creeps, he couldn't work out why. Almost as if they were haunted, if you believed in ghosts, which he didn't. It was just an old house where your footsteps echoed, was bound to feel strange. Ghosts had been invented to frighten children and fools. And he was neither.

He couldn't go and look round the place yet, though. He had to be ready to capture Harriet when she returned from the village.

About time the two servants noticed him. He cleared his throat.

The older woman turned and exclaimed in shock,

pressing one hand to her chest. 'Oh, my goodness! You gave me a right old turn. Who are you?'

'Miss Latimer's stepbrother.' She might call herself Latimer now, but she would be calling herself Mrs Harding before the month was over, he was determined about that. Even if she was officially a Latimer, people would still address her by *his* name. He'd insist on that.

The cook frowned at him. 'Miss Latimer didn't say she was expecting anyone. Did she know you were coming?'

'My mother wanted to surprise her. Where is she?'

'Gone into the village.'

'When will she be back?'

Livvy let out a snort of laughter. 'The mistress doesn't tell us servants things like that.'

Harriet must have upset her, from her tone. Well, she'd been a servant herself not so long ago so they'd be jealous of her good fortune.

Norris leant against the door frame and smiled at them. Best to win them round. 'My mother and I have come a long way, so we'll be wanting a cup of tea and something to eat in a little while, then some dinner later.' He'd heard the car chug round to the back and shortly afterwards there was a knock on the back door.

'That's our driver. He'll want something to eat and drink, as well, if it's not too much trouble. And there's another friend here too.'

She nodded. 'Four of you, then, two in the sitting room and two in the kitchen. Don't worry about your men. We know how to treat visiting servants. I'll bring the tea through when you ring for it . . . sir.'

Something was nudging at his mind, but it wasn't until he was in the hall again that he realised what it was and hurried back into the kitchen. 'Where's the other maid, the one who answered the front door to us?'

'Flora? She went up to finish the bedrooms. Did you want her? I can call her down if you like.'

He hesitated, but he couldn't believe the servants were trying to deceive him. They hadn't even cared what he was doing here once he'd told them he was Harriet's stepbrother. 'No, I just wondered where she was.'

He mustn't start seeing problems where there were none. Servants were a spineless lot and spent their lives doing as they were told.

He'd enjoy ordering them around. By hell, he would be set up for life here!

That same morning William Dalton shook his wife awake. 'I couldn't sleep, kept thinking what to do. I've decided to go over to Swindon to see that lawyer chappie. I'll insist he tells me where the girl is and why he was writing to her.'

Sophie jerked bolt upright in bed, her long, night-time plait of greying hair falling over one shoulder. 'William, this has to stop. I *forbid* you to do anything else about Harriet Benson.'

He goggled at her. 'Forbid me? You can't forbid me to do anything. I'm still the head of this household, thank you very much. I only woke you out of politeness, to tell you where I'm going.'

She threw back the covers. 'If you insist on making a fool of yourself, I'm coming with you. Someone has to have their wits about them, and you've obviously lost yours.'

'I'm not waiting for you. I intend to catch the early train.'

She was ready in record time, surprising her maid and cook, as well as her husband.

When the train pulled away from the tiny Welworth station, she leant back and groaned. 'I've not been out and about so early for years.'

'Nor have I.'

'I must look a mess.'

He smiled, the first hint that his anger might be abating a little, she thought. 'You look pretty with your hair looser like that.'

'Pretty. Ha! I'm past five and sixty.'

'You'll always be pretty to me.'

She sighed and took his hand. 'William, I'm begging you. Please reconsider. Don't do it.'

'My mind's made up. Don't spoil the journey by arguing, Sophie.'

She didn't know what to say or do to bring him to his senses. But she understood what was driving him.

He'd lost status because of his eldest son, had even lost the ability to use his London house, which was now rented out to rich Americans. That was why he was making such a point of proving he was still master at Dalton House. But he'd chosen a foolish, petty way to do it.

Anger was a poor master.

A minute later he said, 'It's nice to get out for a change. We haven't done much going out since we gave up living in London.'

Chapter Nineteen

From inside the hiding place, Harriet could hear every word spoken in the sitting room, though she had to listen very carefully to Miss Bowers' soft voice.

The scornful way her stepbrother talked to Joseph, as if her friend was a halfwit, made her want to rush out and yell at him that Joseph was a better man than Norris would ever be. But she knew only too well how strong Norris was. He'd grab her the minute he saw her, then she'd be helpless.

And surely he'd not hurt Joseph in any way that could get him arrested for assault? How brave of Joseph to stand up to him!

As the slow minutes crawled past, the darkness made the hiding place feel even smaller and increasingly airless. Even when her eyes grew accustomed to the faint light, it felt as if the walls were pressing in on her. There were no other shapes, just the box of walls and the narrow bench she was sitting on.

She'd never been comfortable in dark, enclosed

spaces, but she mustn't give in to her fears. She tried breathing slowly and steadily. That helped a little.

Then the people outside fell silent and she felt worse, as if she was cut off completely from everything she knew, as if she was buried alive.

Worries clamoured in her brain like live things. What was Norris doing to her friends now? Was Joseph all right? Why had they stopped speaking?

She couldn't help wondering if she should give in and let her stepmother take over the house until she turned twenty-one. If she did, surely they would let Joseph go? She wasn't even sure of that, or of her own safety. Accidents could happen. A human life was such a fragile thing. Norris might attack her again. No, *would* attack her, she was sure. She shuddered at that memory.

And once they got their foot in the door, her two step-relatives would try to steal all she had. She knew them. Greedy, even with the food they ate, gobbling it down, clearing their plates, looking round for more. No, she had to stay hidden here until . . . until what?

Until they went to bed, if necessary.

If she could bear it.

Perhaps they'd come to stay? She tried to remember whether there had been any luggage piled on the back rack of their car, but couldn't. She'd only caught a quick glimpse of the vehicle before she hid.

The silence in the sitting room continued. On and

on. No sounds except for her own breathing puncturing the darkness.

She began to feel panic creeping through her. She couldn't breathe. She'd used up all the air.

At the very moment when she was feeling utterly desperate to get out, a faint light began to glow in the corner. She couldn't work out what it was, then realised with a feeling of shuddering relief where she'd seen light like that before. The Lady had come to join her.

Gradually the figure became clearer, transparent and glowing slightly. The Lady was smaller than life size this time but so real Harriet couldn't doubt it was really happening. The Lady was looking at her lovingly, as her mother used to. That made her feel better, safer.

Was she imagining this? Harriet didn't think so. She hoped not. She didn't reach out to touch the apparition, though she'd only need to raise a hand to do that. It would seem disrespectful.

Others had seen the Lady over the years. Miss Bowers said she always looked just the same as in the painting, wearing the grey habit and semicircular headdress with a soft fall of material hanging down her back. It was the sort of garments ladies wore in Tudor times. Harriet had seen drawings of old clothing in schoolbooks.

The figure smiled again, nodding slightly as if in encouragement.

Harriet found herself smiling back and letting out

her fears in a long sigh. She wasn't alone any more. It wasn't even dark now. She could manage to hold on for a while longer, till she had a chance to escape and go for help.

She distracted herself by considering who she'd go to, coming to the conclusion that Mr Pocock would be the best person because Mr Greenlow's house was too far away to be sure of getting there before anyone pursuing could catch her. The shopkeeper was a man in his prime, a leader in the village.

Norris and Winifred were *not* going to steal her inheritance, if she could help it.

Taking the short cut through the shrubbery, Flora hurried towards the village, moving as quietly as she could, bending when she had to pass behind the lower bushes. Twice she stopped behind a tree to glance round and listen carefully, but didn't hear or see anyone on the way.

She sobbed in relief when she reached the lane and saw Farmer Brunson riding towards the village on his old chestnut gelding. *He* would know what to do. 'Stop! Mr Brunson, stop! There's trouble at Greyladies.'

He reined in his horse as she ran across to him, looking shocked as she gasped out her plea for help with intruders. 'Miss Bowers said to be quick. She said the man who came to the door is a nasty sort and there are two other men with him. They look rough. What are we going to do?'

'I'm too old to fight anyone, so we'll have to get some younger men to help.'

'Miss Bowers said to send word to Mr Greenlow, too.'

'Good idea! Look, I can see to that. You go and tell Mr Pocock. Tell him to find three or four other men, strong ones, and he must take care how he goes into the house. Maybe by a back window. We don't want your intruders threatening to hurt the ladies or that lad in the wheelchair, do we?'

She watched the farmer ride off in the direction of Mr Greenlow's house, then got angry with herself for wasting time and ran headlong up the village street. She nearly fell through the door of the shop, shouting, 'There's trouble at Greyladies. Miss Bowers sent me for help.'

She began to cry, couldn't stop herself. She was terrified of the intruders hurting people.

Mr Pocock came out from behind the counter and put his arm round her. 'Calm down, Flora lass. Take a deep breath and tell me what's wrong.'

Even before she'd finished her tale, he was untying his long apron, tossing it aside and telling his wife to look after the shop.

'What are you going to do, Sam?' Mrs Pocock called out as he moved towards the door. 'Don't go there on your own.'

'I'm not. I'm going to find Ben and Chas, Steve Hollis as well, and anyone else who's around. Once I have enough men to outnumber the three of them, we'll all go to Greyladies to help Miss Latimer. That family's helped people in this village time after time, and now *they* need *our* help.'

Flora hesitated, not knowing what to do.

Mrs Pocock beckoned to her. 'Leave it to my Sam. You've played your part now. Call me if anyone comes in the shop. I'm going into the back to make us both a strong cup of tea. That'll give us heart. You leave the fighting to the men.'

But Flora couldn't leave it. Greyladies was her home, had been since she was a young maid of twelve. She had to help get rid of that horrible man.

'I'm going to see if I can help,' she called out.

'Flora, no!' The doorbell was still jangling as Mrs Pocock burst into the shop, and when she went to the open door she could see Flora running down the street, heading towards Greyladies.

Her neighbours came out to see what was the matter, and before she knew it, Mrs Pocock was gathering together a group of women, armed with rolling pins and frying pans, all determined to make sure their menfolk were all right.

You couldn't be too careful with villains, especially when there wasn't a village policeman.

Farmer Brunson rode over to Mr Greenlow's house and dismounted more quickly than he had for years. Throwing his reins to a gardener and yelling, 'Hold him!' he ran past a motor car which must belong to a visitor and hammered on the front door. He didn't wait for anyone to open it, but went inside, yelling for his old friend.

Mr Greenlow popped his head out of the library. 'We're in here, John. What the devil's the matter?'

'There's trouble at Greyladies.' He saw that Mr Greenlow was entertaining a fellow magistrate. 'Sorry to disturb you, Mr Murborough, but this is an emergency.'

As soon as Farmer Brunson told them Miss Bowers had sent for help, the two men paid more attention.

'If *she* thinks there's danger, then we'd better get over there. Never met a more level-headed woman in my life. We'd better send for Miss Latimer's lawyer, too. We need to get this matter settled once and for all. Don't you agree, Murborough?'

'I most certainly do. If it's the stepmother you were telling me about who's bringing rough men to Challerton to bully people, the woman is no fit guardian. Though the girl must have someone to keep an eye on her till she turns twenty-one. That old house is a big responsibility.'

'Of course, she's under twenty-one.'

'We can deal with that together. Sometimes two magistrates are better than one.'

'Do you want me to ride into Swindon to fetch the lawyer?' Brunson asked, impatient of these technicalities.

Mr Greenlow looked smug. 'No need. We had the

telephone fitted only last week. I wasn't sure whether we'd use it much, but my wife was eager to have one. She's used it several times already, and here we are with an emergency, so *I* need it too. It's just the thing for a modern man. I'm sure Miss Latimer's lawyer will have a phone. Bound to.'

He went into the hall, where a table ebonised in 1901 in respect for the old Queen's death, sat in an alcove with the brand-new telephone sitting in its centre on a lace-edged mat. A chair was to hand for anyone using the device.

Never having seen anyone use a telephone before, Farmer Brunson walked over to watch his friend sit down and unhook the earpiece from a stand shaped like a silver candlestick which had a little trumpet shape pointing upwards. Mr Greenlow leant forward to speak into that.

When he got through to the operator, he asked to be put through to Harrington and Lloyd, lawyers of Swindon. And just like that, he was talking to someone several miles away.

Whatever would people think of next?

When he'd finished speaking, Mr Greenlow hung up the earpiece again. 'Mr Lloyd was out, but the clerk promised to find him and send him over to Greyladies immediately. He said he'd met Mr Harding and the fellow's a rough customer, so the ladies were right to be worried.'

He patted the earpiece as if it were one of his dogs,

setting it swinging gently to and fro in its holder. 'Got to move with the times.'

He didn't even try to hide his pride in his newest acquisition and Mr Brunson guessed his friend would soon be buying a motor car. How did you begin to choose something like that? he wondered. Then he realised the others were moving out to the motor car and went to reclaim his horse.

He'd follow them at a decent pace. He wanted to find out what was going on at Greyladies.

Half an hour passed. Their intruder was getting jittery, pacing up and down, scowling and muttering to himself. Miss Bowers and Joseph dared do nothing but exchange glances occasionally.

'Harriet's taking a long time,' Norris said at last. 'Hey, you, idiot fellow! Where is she?'

Joseph gave him a bewildered look. 'I told you, I wasn't sure where she was going. I'm not her keeper. I just rent the back part of Greyladies from her.'

'I'd guess she's at Mary Clarke's house by now,' Miss Bowers said calmly. 'It's at the far side of the village from here. We can't expect her home for another hour, at least.'

'Then we'll have to send one of the maids to fetch her. The one who answered the door will do.'

Miss Bowers held her breath, wondering what to say to hide Flora's absence. She looked at the fob watch pinned to her lapel and said calmly, 'Flora will have left by now. It's her half day. She goes home to see her parents, who are elderly and she—'

Norris cut her short. 'What do I care about your bloody maid and her parents? Very well. We'll wait a bit longer for Harriet. Ma and I are here to stay, after all.'

The Daltons arrived at the lawyer's rooms just as Perkins was putting down the telephone after speaking to Mr Greenlow.

'My name is Dalton. I need to see Mr Lloyd urgently.'

'I'm afraid you can't see him now, sir. There's an emergency and I have to find him.' The clerk tried to push past, but William was bigger than he was and refused to move from the doorway.

Then suddenly Perkins stopped trying to pass. 'Dalton, did you say? Are you related to a Mr Joseph Dalton?'

'Yes. He's our son.'

'Then you should know that he's also in danger, so will you kindly stop holding me up. I have to find Mr Lloyd and send him to Greyladies – that's where your son is.'

'Why is he in danger? And what is Greyladies?'

'It's Miss Latimer's house. I thought you'd have known that, since your son's living there.'

'I'm not acquainted with any Latimers. Are you, Sophie? No, I thought not.'

'You'll know the young lady who owns it as

Benson, sir. But she's changing her name to Latimer as a condition of the inheritance.'

'My former maid has inherited a house? And Joseph is living with her?' Mrs Dalton asked, her heart sinking in dismay.

'Yes. *Will* you let me pass, sir? They could be in danger with that young brute.' He snapped his fingers as if he'd just had an idea, called for the junior clerk and sent him running to find the young man with the motor car to take Mr Lloyd out of town on an urgent errand. Only then did he move towards the door again, to go after his employer.

To his relief, Mr Dalton stepped aside.

But as he opened the door, his employer arrived back.

By the time Perkins had explained the situation and the Daltons had introduced themselves, the driver had arrived with the car.

'I'm afraid I can't discuss this now,' Reginald told the Daltons. 'I've got to go and help Harriet. And your son.'

'If our son's in danger, we're coming with you,' Mr Dalton said. 'Are you game for a motor car ride, my dear? Or do you wish to find a hotel and wait for me there?'

'Of course I'm coming with you. No one's going to hurt my Joseph.'

Within minutes the three of them were crammed into the small car and it was chugging out of Swindon at a rate far faster than any horse could manage.

Mrs Dalton held on to her hat and prayed her son would be safe, and that they wouldn't have an accident in this smelly contraption that rattled and jolted along at a terrifying speed.

Mr Dalton was made of sterner stuff. He ignored their rate of travel and addressed the lawyer. 'Now perhaps you'd explain about this Greyladies place and this fellow who's causing trouble.'

Norris watched the damned clock hand tick slowly round the face of a big clock with curly gold bits round the edges. Tiring of that, he went to stare out of the window, then moved back to fling himself into a chair. Like his mother, he began to assess the contents of the room, which calmed him for a while.

After an hour had passed, however, he'd had enough and was beginning to wonder if they were trying to fool him to let her get away.

He glared at Miss Bowers. 'You were wrong in your estimate. Harriet hasn't come back. And I've had enough waiting around. We'll send the other maid to fetch Harriet back. You can write her a note. I'll tell you what to say.'

'I'm afraid I'm not prepared to do that.'

If a mouse had come into the room singing and dancing, this refusal could not have surprised Norris more. He gaped at her for a minute, then yelled, 'Are you defying me, woman?'

'If by that you mean, am I refusing to do something

which might hurt Harriet, then yes, I am, young man.'
She waited, as calm as ever, hands clasped in her lap. Just
so had she outfaced two generations of naughty children.

Norris could feel the rage that had been building
up roaring through his veins, as it had done sometimes
when he was younger. It was a long time since he'd
allowed himself to become this angry, though. He
jumped to his feet, clenched fists raised and took a step
towards her.

Before he could do anything, Winifred stood up
too, shouting, 'Norris!'

He ignored her, but she went across and shook
his arm. 'You're losing control of your temper, son,'
she whispered. 'Don't. You might do something you
regret. Remember, you have to stay respectable. If you
get charged with assault, you'll get nothing.'

He took a deep breath and closed his eyes for a
minute, letting his fists fall.

Winifred spoke more loudly. 'We can wait all day if
necessary, son. Harriet's got nowhere else to go, after
all. And if she tries to run away, she'll be easy to find
with that red hair.'

When he opened his eyes again, he nodded to his
mother, grateful for her intervention, then glared at
Miss Bowers in a way that said he still intended to
make her sorry for defying him.

Her calm expression didn't change as she raised her
book again and began to read.

Norris took two strides across the room.

His mother gasped.

He contented himself with knocking the book flying from the old hag's hands, then went back to look out of the window. Once he was master here, he'd only let people visit who paid him proper respect, he decided.

His thoughts were interrupted by his mother. 'We never did get anything to eat and we've been here hours. Shall I ring for that maid and ask for some food? I don't know about you, Norris, but I'm rather sharp set. We had our breakfast so early.'

'Yes, you do that.'

She rang the bell and when Livvy answered it, said simply, 'Bring us something to eat and a pot of tea.'

Livvy looked across at Miss Bowers. 'In the breakfast room, miss?'

'Where's that?' Norris asked.

'It's at the back of the hall. We eat all our meals there.' Miss Bowers looked at Norris, who stared for a moment then nodded permission.

Livvy bobbed her head. 'Very well, miss. I got something ready in case, just slices of that pork pie, with scones and cake. I'll take it through.'

Norris watched the way the old hag dealt with the maid. Polite as you please, acting as if they were two friends, not a lady and her servant.

He would give orders more smartly, and expect his servants to jump to it, yes and act far more respectfully to him. He tried it out. 'And hurry up with it.'

The maid shot him a dirty look. That settled *her*

fate. He'd sack her as soon as he was married and had got hold of the house.

Miss Bowers stood up. 'Shall I show you through to the breakfast room, Mrs Benson, Mr Harding? Joseph, are you joining us?'

'I'm not hungry. I'll stay here. But I'd be grateful if someone could pass me my book.'

Norris laughed. 'I'm not letting you out of my sight, so you're coming with us. But you don't need to eat if you don't want to. Why waste good food on a runt like you?'

'Someone will have to push me, then.'

Norris jerked his head towards Miss Bowers, who went to the back of Joseph's chair, pretending to help him sit in a more upright position before she moved it.

Harriet heard the discussion and the plans to have lunch in the morning room. She was hungry too. It felt wrong to be hungry when you were in danger, but her stomach had rumbled several times.

If they all left the sitting room, perhaps she could leave the hiding place and go for help? She could climb out of the window so that the man in the hall didn't see her.

She listened to them leave, then stood up, her hand reaching for the lever. Light blazed out between her and it, like a barrier, so she sat down again. But after a few minutes, she began to feel as if she was suffocating and no amount of reasoning made her feel better.

She had to leave the hiding place, just had to.

When she reached for the lever this time, no light came between her and it, so she took that as a sign she would be safe and pulled it.

Fresh air poured into the small space as soon as it began to open and she pressed closer to the gap, waiting for it to be wide enough to go through, looking out to check that she was alone in the room.

And she was, thank goodness.

A few seconds later, she was able to squeeze through the half-open door, sighing in relief.

'I thought so,' a voice said and Norris stepped out from the other side of the fireplace, grabbing her arm.

Her heart nearly stopped with the shock of it.

He smiled. 'There had to be a reason they were so keen to move me out of this room. And here you are. I've got you now, Harriet, haven't I? And I'm not letting you go again. You belong to me now, you and your big . . . beautiful . . . house.'

His voice took on a gloating tone. 'There's no one to help you. I've got my mother watching the cripple and that old hag. My friend Pat is sitting in the hall to stop anyone leaving, and my driver is watching your cook and housemaid. I've thought of everything.'

'I won't give you my house.'

He smiled. 'You will after we're married.'

'*Married?* I'd never marry you.'

'Oh, you will once your stomach starts swelling. You're not leaving this house again till you agree to wed me.'

She felt sick at what he was implying. And he was right about one thing: who was there to save her from him if he attacked her? As he'd said, a man in a wheelchair and a tiny older woman.

She tried to pull away from him, but he dragged her towards him and gave her a kiss, which made her feel sick. She couldn't get away from him, so stood rigidly still until he moved his head back.

Then she spat in his face, not surprised when he slapped her so hard he sent her flying across the room, sending the smaller pieces of furniture in her path tumbling about like skittles.

But at least it got her out of his arms.

And she didn't regret doing it, however hard he hit her. She'd do it again, every single time he touched her.

Chapter Twenty

Three men from the village, led by Sam Pocock, made their way quietly through the gardens at Greyladies, stopping when they heard footsteps behind them.

He nodded to the others, putting one finger to his lips to warn them to be quiet as he waited for whoever was following them to come into sight.

'Oh, it's you, Flora. Are you on your own?'

'Yes.'

'You'd be safer staying with my wife. Sounds like we have a violent fellow and some roughs at Greyladies.'

'I want to help. I can show you how to get right up to the laundry door without being seen. It's locked, except on washing days, but I know where the key is, so we can get inside without being seen from the kitchen.'

'Good idea.'

They followed her along the far wall of the stables, through a room where feed would be stored when there were horses. Now it was empty, the surfaces and floor dusty.

As they left it, Sam bumped into Mickey and the lad let out a yell.

Sam hastily clapped one hand to his mouth. 'Shut up, you fool. They'll hear you.' He removed his hand. 'Do you know what's going on?'

'There's three men pushed their way into the house. One of them's in the kitchen trying to flirt with Phyllis, but she don't like him. I been keeping an eye on them through the windows. They don't know I'm here.'

'How did you manage to stay free of them?'

'I was working in the garden when they arrived, weeding. They were all looking towards the house. The big fellow knocked on the door and when Flora answered, he shoved her back into the house hard. Visitors to Greyladies don't do things like that, so I crouched down behind a bush and stayed there. They didn't see me.'

'Well done. Go on. What happened next?'

'A bit later the big fellow come out an' told one of 'em to come in and sit in the hall. He told the one driving the car to go round the back and not let the cook and the maids leave the house. Got a loud voice he has, I heard it plain as anything. So I knew for certain they were up to no good. When the third fellow druv that car round to the stables, I followed him. An' he didn't see me, neither.'

'Why didn't you go to the village for help?'

'I seen Flora run along the side of the garden and I reckoned she was fetching help. I saw her white apron through the leaves, saw the bushes move as she passed. If that townie driving the car knew anything, he'd have noticed her too. But he didn't. I thought I'd best stay an' keep an eye on them.'

'Good lad. Follow us and don't make any noise. Don't do anything unless I tell you.'

Mickey nodded vigorously, but couldn't help adding, 'It's exciting, ent it?'

'No, it damned well isn't. They may be hurting Miss Latimer or Miss Bowers, and it's up to us to stop them. Now, keep quiet.'

He gestured to Flora and she took the lead again.

They got to the laundry and she opened the door, but Sam held up one hand. 'I want to see for myself what's going on before we go into the kitchen. I'm going to look in from outside. If I yell, never mind hiding, come running into the kitchen and help me.'

Five people nodded their heads. The three other men were determined, Flora was terrified and young Mickey's eyes were blazing with excitement.

Sam came back a couple of minutes later. 'The fellow's sitting there guzzling tea. Livvy's setting out food on plates. No sign of Phyllis.'

'Shall we go in and capture that fellow?'

'No. Not yet. The one in charge may threaten the

ladies if he hears us. I reckon we'd be best taking 'em by surprise.'

'I could go round the other side an' peep in the windows of the sitting room, see what they're doing,' Mickey volunteered.

Sam bit his lip. 'No, I'll do that. I need to know what's going on. I have a bad feeling about this.'

He came back a short time later, frowning. 'Mr Joseph and Miss Bowers are in the little room at the back. That fellow's got Miss Latimer in the front room, got hold of her arm, he has. Looks like he's hit her, because her face is all red on one side. I thought you said she'd hidden, Flora?'

'Miss Bowers said she had, but she must have tried to escape, thinking they'd all gone into the breakfast room.'

'Looks like he tricked her, then. We'll have to split up. We can—' He stopped, listening.

'That's another car,' Mickey said. 'Shall I go and have a look?'

He'd gone before Sam could stop him, coming back soon afterwards to say succinctly, 'Gentry. Two old men and an old lady, with a driver.'

'We'll have to wait and see what happens. If they've just come calling on Miss Latimer, they'll be sent away. Gentry won't be no good in a fight, anyway, 'specially if they're old.'

'Listen!' Mickey said suddenly. 'There's another car coming.'

'Your ears are better than mine,' Sam said, then a few seconds later he nodded. 'You're right. There is another car. Who the hell is it now?'

He grabbed Mickey by the scruff of his neck to stop him running to find out. 'I'll go.'

When the first car drew up, the two men got out.

Dalton pushed his wife back inside. 'You stay there, Sophie.'

'I'm not sitting out here if my son is in danger inside the house.'

Mr Lloyd looked back down the drive. 'Please do as we ask, Mrs Dalton. We don't know where the others are. They were just behind us. I think we'd better wait for them.'

'I saw a cart pull out in front of them,' Sophie said. 'It'll have slowed them down.'

Mr Lloyd looked round, frowning. 'No one's come to the door to check what we're doing here and they must have heard us coming. I don't like the looks of this.'

When a car turned into the drive, Norris cursed and shook Harriet hard, dragging her out into the hall out of sight. His mother joined them.

'Who are you expecting?' he asked.

'No one.'

'Then you can tell whoever it is to go.'

Winifred intervened. 'She can't answer the door

with a big bruise on her cheek like that. You're a fool hitting her, Norris.'

'She *spat* at me.'

His mother rolled her eyes. 'And what did you do to her first?'

'He tried to kiss me.' Harriet shuddered.

Winifred shook her head. 'Can't wait, can you, son? It'll be your undoing that impatience will. I'll answer the door. Take her to the others in the sitting room. Pat can come and help you keep an eye on them. You keep hold of Harriet and make sure she stays quiet. But control yourself, for goodness' sake.'

Miss Bowers and Joseph both gasped when they saw Harriet's bruised face, then glared at him.

He glared right back. 'You two had better stay quiet, or you'll get a thump that'll knock you senseless.' He jerked his head towards Joseph and asked Miss Bowers, 'Does the idiot understand that?'

'I'll make sure of it.' She spoke slowly and clearly, 'Joseph, dear, please keep quiet. If you don't, the nasty man will hit you.'

Joseph nodded and pretended to shrink back in his chair.

As the room became silent, Norris listened intently. 'They haven't knocked on the door yet. What are they doing out there?' Even as he spoke they all heard another car come along the drive and stop in front of the house.

Norris dragged Harriet across to where she could see out of the window. 'Stay back. I know Mr Lloyd, but who are them others?'

'Those two standing together are Joseph's parents. The other's Mr Greenlow, the local magistrate. I don't know the bald man.'

'Come over here, old woman. Do you recognise that one to the right?'

Miss Bowers moved forward to stand by his side. 'He's called Murborough. He and Mr Greenlow are our local magistrates.'

'Damnation. They're coming to the door.' His grasp tightened on Harriet's arm and he pulled her to him, squeezing her throat with one hand. 'All of you keep quiet or there'll be trouble. Understand?'

She nodded and the others stayed still.

They heard the door knocker go.

Winifred went to open it. 'Miss Latimer isn't well, so I'm afraid she can't have visitors.'

'Who are you?'

'Her stepmother, here to nurse the poor girl. Please give her time to recover and do come again.'

There were sounds that had Norris frowning, then he heard his mother say, 'No! Let go. I need to close the door. Pat! Come and help me!'

Pat looked at Norris, who nodded, still keeping his hand over Harriet's mouth.

But she took him by surprise, biting him hard and screaming for help before he could silence her again.

Joseph raised his voice, also calling for help, and Miss Bowers began yelling, too, moving away from Norris too quickly for him to thump her as she deserved.

Cursing, he threw Harriet down on the floor and ran towards the door. As he did, Joseph rolled his wheelchair forward and snatched an ornament from a nearby table, hurling it at him.

Growling with anger, Norris paused to kick over the wheelchair, but even when lying on the ground, Joseph managed to tug at the nearby rug, and though he couldn't drag Norris down, he did manage to throw him off balance and slow him down. By that time Harriet had scrambled to her feet and grabbed a poker, ready to join in the fray. But Norris had left the room and she hesitated.

'Well done, Joseph,' Miss Bowers said calmly. 'There's a lot of noise out there. Shall we arm ourselves and see what they're doing?' She went to pick up the fire tongs.

In the hall all was chaos, with the men from the village fighting with Norris and the two men he'd brought. All three of the intruders were big men and fighting dirty, trying to gouge eyes and kick their opponents where it hurt most.

Mr Dalton shoved his wife behind him, looked round for a weapon and found a walking stick in the hallstand. He began slashing at one of the men from behind.

Winifred added her bit to the confusion by seizing an umbrella and belabouring any opponent who came near her.

In the confusion Norris realised there were too many of them for him to win, damn it!

Bitter at the failure of his grand scheme, he figured the best he could do was escape. He feinted to one side, slipping past the two elderly magistrates, punching one of them as the old fool stepped forward, hand held up in a stop gesture.

No one seemed to have thought that one of them might run away, so Norris was able to run into the kitchen. Winifred went to bar the way to anyone following her son, giving a man who tried to pass her a hard shove, screeching like a banshee and delaying pursuit.

In the kitchen, Norris shoved Livvy aside when she tried to hit him with a saucepan. As he ran out into the back garden, he knew he'd lost his prize, but he didn't intend to lose his liberty as well. He'd enough money on him to hide out somewhere, then maybe he'd go to Australia or Canada, somewhere far away.

He wished he knew how to drive one of those motor cars. There were three of the damned things standing around. He'd be able to get a lot further in one of those.

Or they'd be able to pursue him more quickly.

He had to move fast and find somewhere to hide until nightfall.

* * *

When the two remaining intruders were overcome and tied up, Sam Pocock wiped a bloody lip and grinned at his friends. 'Got 'em, didn't we? Nasty buggers in a fight. And *she* was helping 'em.' He scowled at Winifred.

Harriet looked across at their prisoners. 'Where's Norris? There should be another man.'

Winifred chuckled. 'My Norris got away.' She began to laugh, a rusty sound with no mirth in it. 'He always was good at looking after himself, my son was.'

Mr Greenlow moved forward. 'Some of you go and look for this fellow. Who knows what he looks like?'

Sam stepped forward. 'Don't matter what he looks like. Any stranger in the village will stand out like a bear at a tea party. We'll find him for you, sir.'

'Good man. Good man.'

Sam and Chas set off at a run.

Now that things had quietened down, Mr Dalton moved towards his son. 'There you are, Joseph. We've come to take you home. You really shouldn't have run away like that, but I'm prepared to forgive and forget.'

His son leant back in his chair with a grim smile. 'There's nothing to forgive, Father, and I'm not coming home.'

'Don't be a fool.'

'You have no say in what I do with my life from now on.'

Mr Dalton spluttered and choked in shock at this. 'But what else can you do but come home?'

Joseph turned to Harriet, who was standing by the side of his wheelchair. He eased himself upright, standing proudly beside her. 'I'm going to marry Harriet and live at Greyladies.'

The smile she shared with him left his parents in no doubt about how the two of them felt about each other.

'But that fellow Harding may come back!' Dalton protested. 'You won't be safe here.'

'I doubt he'll be stupid enough to return,' Joseph said. 'And it makes no difference if he does. I'm not hiding myself away from now on. I'm going to marry the woman I love.'

'You can't marry a *servant*,' Dalton protested. 'Think of the family name. It'd be a disgrace.'

Sophie Dalton pushed past him. 'Don't be so stuffy, William. It's clear they love one another and I want to see my son happy.'

'But what about our *standards*? We're gentry. She's . . . just a maid.'

'You can take your standards and hang them on the washing line,' she retorted. 'And actually, if she owns this house, she's a very rich maid. But I don't think Joseph is marrying her for her money.' She cocked one eyebrow questioningly at her son.

He smiled. 'No. I'm marrying Harriet because I love her and for some reason she doesn't seem to mind what I'm like.'

'I love what you're like,' Harriet said at once. 'You're Joseph and that's more than enough for me.'

Mrs Dalton sniffed away a sentimental tear at hearing words she'd never expected in connection with her youngest son. 'Congratulations then, my dear Harriet. I'm sure you'll make my son happy and I hope you won't hold a grudge for what my husband just said about you. He'll come round eventually, I'm sure. I hope you'll let us both visit you.'

Harriet beamed at her. 'We'd be happy to have you here.'

'You need permission to marry. You're under twenty-one,' Dalton said. 'You'll have to wait anyway. That'll give you time to see whether this . . . this *thing* is going to last.'

'Don't interfere, Father!' Joseph said sharply.

Greenlow had been listening indulgently. Now he cleared his throat to gain their attention. 'My fellow magistrate and I held a sitting just before this happened, and we decided to give Harriet permission to marry.'

Joseph turned to his fiancée, a glowing smile on his face.

William opened his mouth and Sophie nudged him. 'Shut up. Have you ever seen your son look as happy?'

He sighed and subsided like a punctured football. 'No.'

She lowered her voice to add, 'And she has money.'

He sighed again and made no further protest.

Joseph wasn't even looking at them. 'Do you want a fancy wedding, Harriet, my love?'

'Goodness me, no.'

'Then I'll go into Swindon on Monday and get a special licence. We'll be married within a few days.'

'I'd be happy to help you with the details,' Mr Lloyd said at once. 'I'm only sorry Harding got away. If ever a man deserves to be imprisoned, that one does.' He stared at Winifred, sitting on a hard chair in the hall. 'As do you, ma'am.'

She shrugged. 'As long as my Norris gets away, it'll be worth it.'

When he got near the village, Norris cursed and slowed down. There was a bunch of women standing in the middle of the street. He hadn't even got a hat to tip as he passed them, so nodded his head politely and tried to hurry on. But they moved to block his way, damn them.

'I reckon this is one of them,' Mrs Pocock said. 'Look at that split lip. He must have been fighting.'

They surrounded him and when he lunged sideways, trying to get out of the circle, a plump young woman raised her arm and walloped him over the head with something very hard and painful.

He staggered, trying to keep running but failing as his legs gave way and everything blurred round him.

'I'll fetch my wheelbarrow,' one woman said. 'Good enough for my potatoes, good enough to wheel rubbish like him in.'

'We'll take him to Greyladies,' Mrs Pocock said. 'Well done, Lucy. You walk next to him and if he moves so much as a fingertip, hit him again . . . harder.'

Norris came to and found himself threatened by a large young woman brandishing a spade. He felt sick and dizzy, so lay back, trying to gather his strength for an escape the minute his head stopped spinning.

They went by way of the lane and the drive, and Lucy put one hand to her mouth and whistled loudly as they got near the house, then yelled, 'Come and see what we've found!'

People came running out and stood gaping as the women dumped Norris out of the wheelbarrow and stood in a semicircle round the figure sprawling across the gravel.

Norris groaned, trying desperately to pull himself together, but feeling too sick and dizzy to do more than lie there.

'You missed one, dear,' Mrs Pocock told her husband with a grin.

He grinned back at her. 'Well, we had to let you ladies have a bit of fun too, didn't we?'

Joseph chuckled, and even Mr Dalton was smiling.

'Won't you all come in?' Harriet asked. 'I'm sure Livvy can make some cups of tea.'

The blacksmith went down the steps and grabbed Norris by the front of his jacket, frogmarching him into the house and throwing him to the floor.

Everyone crowded round the sides of the hall to watch the show.

'Pity he hasn't tried to get away,' Lucy said regretfully. 'I'd like to hev hit him again.'

'Hit him anyway,' Mrs Pocock said.

Norris yelped and cowered back.

'No need to hit him. Just tie him up carefully,' Mr Greenlow ordered. 'You know, Murborough, we really do need a village constable here. You, fellow! You're under arrest for—'

As he paused to consider, Winifred edged round behind the other women, seeing her son watching her. She knew her son. Norris wasn't as woozy as he was pretending.

She got to the end of the line of people, standing near the door, and suddenly yelled, 'Run!' She shoved the woman next to her hard and lunged across to stop a man going after Norris.

But Joseph had seen what she was doing and had wheeled his chair quietly along the back of the row of standing people. As Norris rolled to one side and surged to his feet, Joseph moved the chair in front of him.

Cursing, Norris tried to get past the wheelchair, but by that time two men had grabbed the would-be fugitive.

Norris struggled and fought like a madman, but they subdued him and tied him up, while two of the women held Winifred, now sobbing.

'Well done, son!' Mr Dalton said in surprise.

But Joseph was back holding Harriet's hand.

Epilogue

A week later

Harriet stared at herself in the mirror. 'Do I look all right?'

Miss Bowers smiled. 'You look beautiful, my dear. As a bride should.'

Since Norris and his mother were now in jail, they'd delayed the wedding a few days to allow the village seamstress to make Harriet a new outfit. She'd chosen a skirt in one of the new fitted styles, in a subtle green wool, with a matching green three-quarter-length jacket, and a blouse in cream silk and lace, with the fashionable high collar.

Miss Bowers and Mrs Greenlow had taken her shopping to Swindon for a new hat, but after one or two, she'd refused to try on any more of the huge hats, which might be fashionable, but made her feel ridiculous and top-heavy.

Eventually they agreed on a neat felt with modest four-inch brims, worn at a slight tilt. It had a cream satin ribbon around the crown, with a spray of silk flowers to one side and a smaller spray under the brim at the raised side.

She still felt it was too much, but it *did* flatter her.

Since Joseph already had smart clothes, tailored to his needs, he had asked only for them to bring him a new shirt, which he wore with a black frock coat and trousers, top hat and a roll-collared waistcoat in beige. His grandfather's gold watch chain was draped across the front. It wouldn't now need to be sold and he could give the jewels he'd inherited to his wife – though he doubted Harriet cared about jewellery.

He spent the night before the wedding with the Greenlows and arranged to meet his bride at the Registry Office in Swindon.

He went there in his wheelchair, though it had to be carried up the stairs. But he insisted on getting out of it in the waiting room.

When Harriet appeared in the doorway, stopping to gaze round shyly, he got to his feet and simply held out his hand to her.

Her nervous expression vanished and she gave him a glowing smile.

'Y'know,' William Dalton whispered to his wife, 'I've never seen Joseph look as well.'

'He's happy. And well provided for. What more can anyone want for him?'

He nodded. 'I suppose so. And she doesn't look like a maid when she's properly dressed, does she?'

'Oh, you! She looks absolutely lovely.'

On the other side of the central space between the rows of wooden chairs, Harriet was watched by Miss Bowers, the Lloyds and the Greenlows. Doris Miller was sitting next to Miss Bowers, who had agreed to keep her company when Harriet assured her that the former housekeeper might have a sharp tongue but was nothing like her relatives.

The servants from Greyladies were sitting in a row at the back, because Harriet had insisted that they attend as well, and there were a few people from the village who'd not been invited but had come anyway, since Joseph had hired a motor charabanc to bring as many as wanted to attend.

They'd ordered a private room and special luncheon at a hotel in Swindon, then Joseph and Harriet would go back to Greyladies with their servants in the charabanc, and leave the motor cars to his parents and the Greenlows.

That evening Joseph limped into the bedroom wearing his dressing gown over a nightshirt, to find his bride sitting bolt upright in the bed looking scared.

'My dear, don't look so frightened. We needn't do anything if you don't want.'

Harriet gave a start and then relaxed a little, smiling at him. 'I was just remembering Norris attacking me.'

'You know I shan't do that. In fact . . .' he hesitated, then added, 'I've never done this before, so we shall have to find our way together.'

She relaxed even more, turned back the covers and patted the space beside her. 'I like the thought of that.'

He took her in his arms and they lay for a while, talking then kissing.

'Was that kiss better than your previous experiences?' he teased.

'I loved it.' She leant forward to pull him towards her and kiss him again.

When she nestled more closely against him, he said softly, 'With you, darling, I don't feel like a cripple.'

'I don't think of you as one. You're just . . . my Joseph.'

'And you're my Harriet. Aren't we lucky to have found one another?'

But she was eager for another kiss and after that they didn't talk for quite some time, as they discovered how wonderful it was to love one another.

On the landing outside their bedroom a lamp was burning low near the big portrait of Anne Latimer. Anyone passing by would have sworn she was smiling.

NEXT IN THE SERIES . . .

MISTRESS OF GREYLADIES

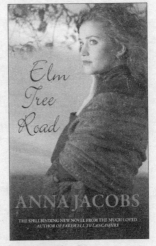

To discover more great books and to
place an order visit our website at
www.allisonandbusby.com

Don't forget to sign up to our free newsletter at
www. allisonandbusby.com/newsletter
for latest releases, events and exclusive offers

Allison & Busby Books
@AllisonandBusby

You can also call us on
020 7580 1080
for orders, queries
and reading recommendations